Spaghetti
Western

EM LYNLEY

a *Delectable* novel

Dreamspinner Press

Published by
DREAMSPINNER PRESS

5032 Capital Circle SW, Suite 2, PMB# 279, Tallahassee, FL 32305-7886 USA
http://www.dreamspinnerpress.com/

This is a work of fiction. Names, characters, places, and incidents either are the product of author imagination or are used fictitiously, and any resemblance to actual persons, living or dead, business establishments, events, or locales is entirely coincidental.

ISBN: 978-1-63216-134-5
Digital ISBN: 978-1-63216-135-2
Library of Congress Control Number: 2014944471
First Edition September 2014

Printed in the United States of America
ⓧ
This paper meets the requirements of
ANSI/NISO Z39.48-1992 (Permanence of Paper).

She stared down at him after she did her seat belt up. "What's wrong, honey?"

He looked into her face. The wrinkles around her eyes suddenly seemed like dry creek beds and her hair was more white than gray or brown these days. He was over thirty, so Aunt Lynn was well into her sixties. No wonder she was willing to hand off the most grueling of her responsibilities to someone else.

"How are you expectin' to pay this fancy-pants chef?" Colby switched gears mentally or he might have told her he was starting to worry about her. He went around and got in behind the wheel and started the engine.

"When that Mr. Wellington invests in the guest ranch, we'll have plenty of money to cover his salary. Don't you worry about that at all."

"The guest ranch is supposed to help cover the losses on the cattle side. It's not supposed to cost anything."

"You're starting to sound like Rachel. Did you get one of those MBA's while I wasn't lookin'?" She chuckled, as if she didn't take his concerns seriously.

Truth was money was always a problem. Whether it was the losses when several of the herd died from bad weather, or repairs on the fencing when a storm destroyed it, or battling the lawsuit from the Evil Anderson Empire over water and grazing rights Colby's grandfather supposedly sold them. Money was the one thing they absolutely had no extra floating around for unnecessaries like French chefs.

If it were up to Colby, they wouldn't have Mr. Wellington from Boston *and* New York City—if you believed everything his cousin Rachel said—coming in to discuss buying a share in the guest ranch and turning it into a World Class Establishment—Wellington practically spoke in capital letters, as Uncle Jake put it.

"When will the hordes descend?"

"The first guests show up in about two weeks' time. Next Sunday morning. The staff will all be there by Wednesday. Mr. Wellington will be arriving at the start of the second week. He wanted to see the place on his own first, before the guests arrive, but Rachel wouldn't have it. Needs to have the staff properly trained first."

"You keep him out of my hair, right? He doesn't need to be in the ranch side of business, does he?"

"Not in the ranch books or anything. But he's a keen horseman, so your uncle's expecting someone to take him around, show him the best views."

"I can't spare one of the hands just for him. Send a wrangler. They're supposed to be handling the guests."

"Maybe you're right. We've got Rita coming back this year. She's awful good with guests." She grinned and Colby got her meaning. A pretty face might make all the difference. Well, that wasn't how he would treat his staff, but at least Colby wouldn't have to spare a man to ride around with Mr. New York City. He'd probably show up in shiny new black boots and—

Then Colby remembered Riley's crazy urban cowboy get-up from the night before. How his initial confidence had melted away in the bar, then how it had returned when he'd been in bed with Colby. Adorable, naive, city-slicker Riley.

"What're you grinnin' at there, boy?"

"Nothing. Nothin' at all."

As Colby stopped at a red light, he glanced back in the direction of the Marriott and Club Rawhide, knowing he'd probably never see Riley again.

Readers love EM LYNLEY

Bound for Trouble

"There's mystery, the investigation, romance, excitement and hot smexy scenes in this fast-paced story, and I found it a very enjoyable read."

—The Blogger Girls

"This book kept me at the edge of my seat simply because I could not predict where the story was going at any given time. I loved that. At this point in my life, I've read 10's of thousands of romantic stories. Very few truly keep me guessing throughout about how the story was going to develop next and this one did."

—Smitten with Reading

"Once again, EM Lynley's written a winner."

—Chryselle's Bookeshelf

Out of the Gate

"I could not stop reading this book."

—Prism Book Alliance

"This is a great read! I found details about training and racing horses very interesting and striking me as very truthful."

—MM Good Book Reviews

"I found myself really enthralled with this story and I loved every second I spent reading it."

—Top 2 Bottom Reviews

By EM LYNLEY

Bound for Trouble
Disguises
Hostile Takeover
Out of the Gate

THE DELECTABLE SERIES
Brand New Flavor
Gingerbread Palace
An Intoxicating Crush
With Shira Anthony: Lighting the Way Home
Spaghetti Western

PRECIOUS GEMS SERIES
Rarer Than Rubies
Italian Ice
Jaded

Published by DREAMSPINNER PRESS
http://www.dreamspinnerpress.com

Recipe Index

If you climb in the saddle, be ready for the ride.

—Cowboy proverb

Chapter One

RILEY HAD been driving for four hours, and he couldn't wait to stop.

No, that wasn't entirely true. He was enjoying the drive through the most gorgeous landscapes he'd ever seen, but he was looking forward to his destination even more.

Plus, he had to pee, and he wasn't in the habit of doing his business on the side of the road, even if there had been a shoulder to pull out of traffic.

Or what passed for traffic out here in the middle of the most beautiful nowhere he'd ever been. He'd passed maybe ten cars in the past hour.

Let's see, that's one every six minutes or so. He could manage a pee in less time. He'd pull over as soon as there was any extra space. He really shouldn't have gotten the extra-large coffee at his last stop. But he'd been so damn tired. Between jet lag and excitement, he hadn't slept in a day or two. Instead of staying the night in Denver, Riley had headed off on his journey immediately.

He couldn't wait to get to Aspen and his first job out of culinary school.

But more than that, he couldn't wait to fall into Denny's waiting arms.

Just another hour or so and that dream would be a warm, wonderful reality.

They'd have the whole summer to explore the area, on their days off from the dream job at Antelope Inn in Aspen, where Denny had already started working while Riley finished his course at Le Cordon Bleu in Paris.

The pent-up excitement stimulated his bladder, pulling him back to reality in the tin can of a rental car (he'd never driven a Kia before. In fact, he'd never heard of a Kia before). Up ahead he spotted a good flat place where he could stop and take care of business, and there wasn't another car as far as the eye could see.

He pulled to a stop halfway off the road, got out, and inhaled the clean, crisp, completely invisible air. It smelled sweet and fresh, though thin, and it suddenly dawned on him he was the only person for miles and miles and miles.

Many people would find that idea irresistible, but not Riley Emerson. He was a city boy born and bred, and so much nothingness suddenly frightened him. He took care of his increasingly powerful need and got back in the car before all the empty spaces came crashing down on him.

He hadn't realized until this moment how much he'd come to love life in the big city: Paris, New York, even Boston where he'd grown up.

But Aspen, Colorado?

He really was in the wild, wild west.

FIFTEEN MILES, ten miles, three miles. The distance to Aspen dribbled away. Finally, Riley passed the "Welcome to Aspen" sign and felt his pulse rate double. He pulled into the first parking lot he saw and dug the Google Map printout from his messenger bag. He glanced at his cell phone sitting in the coffee cup holder.

Should he call Denny?

It was late morning, and Denny would be home catching up on sleep before heading into the restaurant to start prep for the evening service.

Riley shook his head. The whole point of coming a week early was to surprise Denny. Instead of stopping off in the Hamptons to see his family, Riley had flown straight to Denver from Paris. He hadn't missed much. A visit with his family inevitably deteriorated into his father questioning his decision to become a chef.

"Why don't you just invest in a restaurant if you want to be in the food industry?"

Dad's answer to every problem: buy it, sell it, or fire it and get a new one. He didn't understand passion for anything besides moving piles of money around on the Monopoly board that defined his life.

That wasn't what Riley wanted. He wanted to spend the foreseeable future in the kitchen of the best restaurant that would hire him. And the rest of the time in bed—or anywhere else—with Denny.

Mind made up, Riley glanced at the directions to the apartment Denny had rented for them, got his bearings, and headed for his exciting future.

With a minimum of error—Riley had a great sense of direction even in places he'd never visited—he found the apartment building and parked the rental in a guest spot.

Riley didn't have a key, but he knew Denny's habits well. A glance around the area outside the door and he knew exactly where the spare key was hidden. Riley found it in two inches of dirt near the ugliest plant. He wiped off the key, silently slid it into the door, and let himself in.

The place was deserted. Or at least the living room and kitchen were. What must be the bedroom door, located on the other side of the living room, was open about three inches. Riley grinned. This would be fun.

He hoped Denny was still sleeping. He'd slide into bed behind him and snuggle up and kiss his earlobes until Denny woke up.

A sound from the bedroom got Riley's attention. A soft moan, then another.

He smiled. Denny did have a thing for porn of the raunchiest and cheesiest variety. The soundtrack on this one was heavy on fake grunts and groans. Denny was going to be so glad to have Riley back in his bed.

Riley was halfway across the living room when the plan struck. He pulled his shirt off and slid out of his new jeans and boots. Next came the underwear. He was already half-hard from the anticipation of climbing into bed with Denny again. He finished the job with a couple of quick tugs and put his hand on the doorknob, trying not to laugh at the over-"acting" of the guys in the clip Denny was watching.

He flung the door open.

It wasn't a film. It was Denny with his cock up to the hilt in someone else's ass.

"What the fuck?" the someone else said.

Denny opened his eyes and stared at Riley.

"I don't do three-ways," Denny's new friend said.

"Oh, Riley. You're early." He barely slowed down what he was doing to the other guy.

No shit, Sherlock.

Riley's stomach plummeted through the floor and his face was on fire. He ran out of the room and was near the front door when he remembered he was buck naked. He grabbed his clothes and sped through the front door, covering himself with them until he was outside on the sidewalk.

Luckily no one else was around. He pulled his shorts on and kept moving to the car. He was sitting in the driver's seat with the door open, pulling on his pants, when Denny caught up with him. He had a towel wrapped around his waist and he was barefoot.

Riley tried to shut the door, but Denny held on.

"Hang on a minute, Rile."

Riley pulled harder on the door.

"I'm sorry you found out like this. I was going to tell you." He fought Riley for the door.

Riley let go, and Denny went flying back. Riley tried not to smile as Denny dropped the towel while trying to keep from falling over. He gave up and let out a laugh.

"I guess that makes it okay. As long as you were going to tell me." Riley exhaled slowly to calm himself. His stomach still hadn't caught up with him, and a heavy pit opened in his gut. "Just out of morbid curiosity, what would you have said?"

Denny held on to the towel with one hand and put the other on the top part of the door. This close, Riley could see tooth marks around one nipple. He could have lived without that. Denny shoved a hand through his thick, wavy hair. Once, Riley thought Denny was really hot with it pulled off his forehead in a certain way. Clearly he knew exactly how to achieve that look.

"Rile, I kinda fucked up. I know that."

"So you and this guy are more than fuck buddies?"

"No. Well, not at first…. It *was* just fucking, but then… I don't know. I really missed you, and I was lonely."

Denny had the good sense to look sorry, but Riley wasn't in a forgiving mood.

"And now what?" Riley didn't have to ask, and he really didn't want to know, but he could see the whole thing upset Denny too, and that's the only reason Riley pressed on.

"I don't know. We have fun together. And he's really different from you. But I do still love you."

"Are you asking me to forgive you and try to work things out?"

Denny chewed his bottom lip and shifted his weight. He made a sideways move with his head that was a cross between a nod and a shake.

"Yeah, I wasn't going to, even if you had asked. Or even pretended to ask." Riley yanked the door back from Denny's grasp and slammed it shut, then rolled the window down—it was such a beater it didn't even have electric windows. "I'm actually glad this happened, Denny. I hate to think we might have ended up together without me knowing what you're really like. Good luck."

Riley started the car and backed out of the spot. He noticed Denny's new boyfriend leaning in the door to the apartment, wearing a matching towel.

Riley had sent those towels from Paris. Under any other circumstances he might have decided to keep them, but he didn't want to even touch them now. He squealed out of the parking lot and managed to get half a block before the tears streamed so heavily he couldn't see anything. He pulled into the first available driveway and sat in the parking lot of a toy store and let it all out.

When the tidal wave of emotion subsided, Riley dried his face the best he could with his shirtsleeves, and when those were too wet to help, then the tail of his shirt. He still hadn't quite caught his breath, and he choked out a few more sobs before he managed to pull himself together.

Right, this is a good thing, he told himself a few times. At least he knew the truth about Denny. They'd only been together a little more than a year. They'd met in Paris, but Riley had been busy with the pastry course for much of that before Denny flew ahead to Aspen. That didn't make what Denny did okay, but the truth was Riley didn't know him that well. It wasn't a commentary on Riley's value as a boyfriend, but on Denny's.

Yeah, right. Riley didn't believe it either.

But he didn't owe Denny any more of his time sitting here in a parking lot. With no place to stay now, Riley had to find a hotel and decide what to do about his job at the Antelope Inn.

He got back onto the street and drove toward the edge of town. He'd passed a Motel 6 and a Red Roof Inn. Much more in his price range than the towering condos and exclusive-looking resorts he'd also driven past.

HE CHECKED into the Red Roof Inn, threw himself on the bed, and stared up at the ceiling.

He wasn't expected at the restaurant for another week. He could show up early and see if he could start working right away, then look for his own apartment or try and share with one of the other kitchen staff.

Did he really want to work at the same place as Denny? Maybe his new guy worked there too. That would be really awkward. Riley didn't want Denny back, but he didn't want to spend twelve hours a day in the same kitchen either. Restaurants were hotbeds of gossip. Chances were everyone in there would know what Denny had done to Riley, if they didn't already.

Nope. Riley would not subject himself to that.

He sat up and glanced at his watch. It was 7:00 p.m.

How had it gotten it so late? Then he remembered he hadn't reset it since arriving in the States. It was still on Paris time.

He grabbed his cell phone and pushed a speed dial.

"Riley!" his sister Estelle shouted, nearly breaking his eardrum. "You're back? I can't believe you got out of a visit home to New York. You are never going to hear the end of that from Mummy."

"I know." He frowned at "Mummy." Their mother had spent a year in London as a child and insisted her own children refer to her as "Mummy" in the British fashion. But never "Mum"; that was *common*. Once Riley understood the affectation, he always called her "Mom," no matter how she protested.

"So, are you in Aspen? Is it fabulous? I am so hoping you'll be there through ski season. I know it's terribly rustic compared to St. Moritz or Gstaad, but I can't wait to see it. I don't care what Daddy says." Dad was a ski snob, preferring to take the family to the Alps rather than the Rockies. Apparently anything European was infinitely superior to anything America, even mountains.

He let her finish rambling on about skiing for another minute without responding. When she stopped talking, he counted a few beats. "Yeah, I'm in Aspen."

"You don't sound excited. I thought you and Denny would be, you know, welcoming each other…."

"I got a special welcome from Denny… and his new boyfriend." He kept the emotion out of his voice, or so he thought.

"Oh shit, Riley!" She giggled. "Sorry, I wasn't laughing at you." She loved cussing since their parents and before that, the nannies, had always been the cuss police. "Do you want to talk about it?"

"Not particularly. But I do want your advice."

"How can I help you?"

"I don't know what to do about my job. Should I report in or try to find something else?"

"Oh God, there's no way you want to work around Denny all summer. You should come home. I'm sure the parents will take back everything they've said and pretend it never happened. I'd love to have you back for the summer. Oh, yes, please come home."

"Stell, that isn't one of the options I mentioned."

"Okay," she replied with a resigned sigh. "What are the options again?"

"One was to take the job. It's a great opportunity to work with a top chef, but I don't think I'll be able to keep my personal situation out of the kitchen." He paused. "I could try to get a job at another place here. Aspen's full of good restaurants. Or I could go to Denver or Boulder and look for a spot there." He shook his head. "I suppose the last option is to go to New York, where I know people."

"Do you know anyone at another place in Aspen? Why do you want to stay in Colorado?"

"I don't want to stay here, but it is beautiful. Really spectacular. I'm already here and it's easier to take a job here than to go home and start looking."

"That makes no sense, Riles."

"I'm not thinking clearly. Remember, my whole life just got turned upside down about an hour ago."

"You don't have to decide today. I think you should take a day or two before you make any big decision. Go take a drive in the mountains and enjoy yourself, and we can have this discussion again tomorrow. But I'm here if you want to talk about anything."

"I know." He was about to say good-bye when a thought popped into his head. "Stell, do you think I should forg—"

"If you're going to ask whether you should consider forgiving Denny and try to get back with him, then the answer is no."

"Just wanted to make sure." He smiled.

"If you get confused about that again, just call me and I'll set you straight. So to speak." She giggled. "Love you, Riles."

"You too. Thanks." He hung up, in a marginally better mood than when he'd called. She was right. He didn't need to decide that moment or even that day.

He lay back on the bed and looked up at the ceiling again, trying to decide if the tea-colored stain there reminded him more of a moose or an elephant.

It's Colorado. Has to be a moose.

AFTER A fitful night's sleep, Riley woke up with a headache. It hadn't helped that he'd walked down the block and bought twenty dollars' worth of cheap booze the night before and got microwave nachos at the convenience store on the way back.

He was a graduate of Le Cordon Bleu in fucking Paris, so why on earth would he eat crap like that? Clearly he was trying to kill himself. Microwave nachos were a definite cry for help.

Now, in the morning light, he could still taste the fake plastic-y cheese in the back of his throat, far worse than the bourbon he'd drunk. Maybe Le Cordon Bleu would take his certificate away now.

He boiled himself in the shower for the two minutes the hot water lasted, then tried to wash shampoo and soap off in the freezing water for the rest of his shower. There was only one towel in the bathroom, a hand towel that had a stain the same color as the blotch on the ceiling.

Drip dry it is. After a large latte—they did have decent coffee out here—Riley felt a little more human again. He'd bought a newspaper and started looking at help wanted ads. The few food service openings were for dishwashers or busboys. He called the first place and introduced himself, then asked about cooking positions.

"Can you wash dishes?" the woman asked.

"Yes, but…."

"I got cooks out the wazoo. I need a dishwasher."

"Okay, thanks." He hung up.

He tried two more restaurants with similar results before an idea struck him.

He scrolled through his cell phone and then dialed a number in New York.

"Golden. Good morning." A woman answered the phone in a voice so cheerful he could picture her smile.

"Hi. Can I speak to Josh Golden?"

"Sure. Who may I say is calling?"

"Riley Emerson. I know him from Paris…."

"Hang on!" She surprised him by not even questioning his request to speak to the owner.

"Riley? How are you? You still in Paris?" Josh's familiar baritone came across the miles like he was right there on the bed next to Riley. *Memories….*

"Hi, Josh. I'm okay. I just finished the pastry course the other day. Decided to try something new this time. I'm actually in Aspen, Colorado."

"Congratulations on surviving a second round of that special torture. So what's in Aspen? And why didn't you stop in New York on your way out west?"

"It was a pastry job at Antelope Inn, but that isn't working out."

"Good gig. I know the owner, Lincoln Mack. What can I do for you, or are you thinking of coming to New York now?"

"I am actually looking for another job around here, Josh. Do you happen to know anyone in Aspen or nearby?"

"I do. There's a guy I met a few months ago who's running the kitchen at Cascade, Pieter Van Loon. Got great reviews. Want me to introduce you? If he doesn't have an opening, he's likely to know someone in town who might."

"That would be fantastic. I really appreciate it."

"What are friends for?"

"Do you really want me to answer that?" Riley felt a tightness in his chest at the thought he'd let Josh get away.

"Probably not. But you need to visit New York. I'll show you my restaurant, and you can meet Micah and Ethan, my stepson."

"First chance I get."

"Let me call Pieter, then get back to you."

"Thanks."

An hour later Josh Golden called back with an appointment for Riley to meet Pieter Van Loon in the bar of Cascade. Riley got there early and was sipping Perrier when Pieter came out of the kitchen in a dirty apron and introduced himself with a handshake.

"Josh Golden said you're looking for a pastry job?"

"Preferably, but I'll take anything. I got my culinary cert—"

"I don't need your resume, Riley. Josh's word is good enough. I can probably squeeze in one more line cook until there's an opening in pastry. We can't pay as much as Antelope." He named the salary. "It's a good foothold in the local restaurant scene. There's a lot of seasonal turnover, but if you want to stay through ski season, you could end up with a much bigger role somewhere."

"Yeah, that sounds good. When do you want me to start?"

"Hang on. I said probably. I need to get final approval from the owner, but more importantly, you'll need to meet the sous chef. I don't want to bring someone in without him being in the loop."

"I understand."

"Let me get Phillip—the sous chef—out here to meet you, and I'll call Gaston, the owner. He'll love the chance to speak French, so you're probably good to go. Hang on here?"

"Sure." Riley sipped fizzy water and a few minutes later Pieter came out of the kitchen, followed by another man.

"Riley, this is Phillip."

They stopped in front of Riley's table, and he glanced up to find himself staring into the eyes of Denny's someone else.

Phillip turned the corners of his mouth down and looked like he'd rather set himself on fire than shake hands with Riley.

"Pieter, I'm not sure Aspen is the right fit for me. Thanks for your help." Riley held out his hand to Pieter, whose mouth was wide open. "Ask Phillip, after I leave."

Riley turned on his heel and walked as calmly as possible out to the parking lot. As he sat in the crappy rental car, he wondered how far to the nearest cliff so he could drive right off it into a painless future.

Chapter Two

BUT RILEY didn't drive off the cliff. He went back to the Red Roof Inn and parked the car so he wouldn't be tempted. He was hungry, and he walked a couple of blocks to a little diner he'd passed a couple of times now.

Diner food was comfort food and legitimate in a way microwave nachos could only dream of.

A meatloaf sandwich… mmmm. Riley could imagine the look of horror on his blue-blooded father's face if he knew Riley wanted to eat meatloaf.

"Why'd I spend all that money for your fancy Parisian cooking school if you can't understand the difference between meatloaf and pate de fois gras?"

Sometimes a man just needs a meatloaf sandwich.

He settled into a seat at the counter, and the waitress handed him a menu and a glass of water.

"Meatloaf sandwich, please." He didn't even look at the menu.

"A man who knows just what he wants." The waitress—Pauline if he could trust her name tag—winked. "I like that in a feller."

"If only I did know." He sipped water as she shouted his order to the cook through the window to the kitchen.

"Oh, what's the trouble?" Pauline glanced along the counter where only one other customer was seated.

Riley stared at her for a moment to discern what sort of answer she wanted: the truth or some palliative. She gave him her full attention. She was about fifty, with her hair pulled up off her neck and little extra padding around the middle. She looked exactly like Riley's ideal mother, the kind who baked cookies and gave hugs rather than leaving the kids to the care of a nanny who forced them to do calisthenics with the drive of a marine drill sergeant.

"Just lost a job and a boyfriend all at once." He hadn't meant to mention the boyfriend part, but she looked so kind he couldn't help it.

"Sorry to hear it. Both parts. You're not from 'round here, are you?"

He shook his head. "Just came to town yesterday to work at the Antelope Inn for the summer."

A bell behind Pauline announced that Riley's lunch was ready. Pauline served and then hovered while he took a few bites.

"Need anything with that?"

Riley savored the first mouthful. Good quality beef, a nice mix of seasonings, and a tangy slather of barbecue sauce. "Mmmm. It's perfect."

"Pauline?" The customer from the other end of the counter needed her and she left Riley.

He was finished with the sandwich and a few of the fries when she got back.

"Can I get a piece of that peach pie too?"

"Sure thing. A la mode?"

"Nope. I'm a purist."

She chuckled and served a giant slab of pie. "What kind of work you lookin' for?"

Riley picked up his fork and examined the pie before answering. "I was supposed to be the new pastry chef." He gave a wry smile. "Don't suppose you need a pastry chef around here?"

"Taste that pie." She nodded toward his plate.

He poked the crust with his fork: beautifully flaky. Then he took a forkful and closed his eyes as he tasted it. Perfectly cooked fruit, not too sweet. "Ahhh. Mmmm. Heaven." He grinned. "You don't need a new pastry chef, that's for sure."

"I bake the pies around here, uh…."

"I'm Riley Emerson." He held out his hand and they shook.

"Pauline Price. I wish I could offer you a better welcome to Aspen than the one you already got."

"Lunch here is a big help."

"Glad to hear that."

"Pauline, ma'am, can we please get the check?" A tall man in a booth on the other side of the restaurant shouted. He was in his late twenties or early thirties and wore a dark plaid shirt and a cowboy hat. He was sitting with a woman in her fifties. Either that was his mother or he had a serious May-December thing going on.

"On the way." Pauline nodded at Riley before she headed to the plaid cowboy's table. Riley watched her scribble on a pad as she moved across the room. She didn't waste a movement. The diner was well run, and even though it wasn't crowded, he suspected it was something of a local institution.

Riley watched the plaid cowboy stand to pull cash out of his back pocket. He sure filled his jeans out nicely. He was tall and slim. He helped his companion out of the booth, then tipped his hat to Pauline as he followed the woman toward the door.

"Thank you!" Pauline called. She came back behind the counter and rang up the bill. "That feller always leaves me a tip as big as the bill. He's a real gentleman."

"That he is."

"Is that so?" Pauline's tone was teasing, and Riley looked down at what was left of his pie, shocked that he'd expressed his admiration of the cowboy's ass so blatantly.

"Pardon me."

"Don't mind me. But, Riley, I've got an idea for you. Aspen's got a lot of seasonal workers, winter, summer, off-peak. Hospitality industry is big business here, you know?"

He nodded.

"This weekend is a sort of job fair for the ranches. Can't say there's any good jobs left, but there's half a dozen at least who come into town to hire folks for the summer. You should go check it out. Over at the Marriott tomorrow morning. If you go early, you got a better chance. Lots of the seasonal kids party late and don't wake up in time."

"You lost me at ranch…."

"You really aren't from around here, are you?"

"Cape Cod and New York City, but recently Paris."

"Quite the jet-setter? Well that explains your accent." She grinned. "Guest ranches—some folks call 'em dude ranches, but it's a dirty word to the ranchers—are pretty big business. Some are just for show, with horse riding lessons and fancy food. Others are working ranches that take paying guests to help cover expenses. But they're all out in beautiful country. Nothing like Cape Cod or Paris, though."

"You know what, maybe I need a big change. Thanks, Pauline." Riley finished his pie, drained his coffee, and left a wad of cash on the counter before she could even give him a check. "I'll see you for dinner and probably breakfast."

"Thank you, Riley!" she called as he opened the door.

He needed a good walk to counteract the huge lunch he'd just enjoyed, so he took a leisurely stroll around downtown. Aspen was a cute little town. Possibly the cleanest town he'd been in.

He was window-shopping when he spotted a poster with a rainbow border in the window of a western-wear shop:

Friday is Cowboi Night

10 p.m. - late

Club Rawhide

No doubt it was his kind of club, so he memorized the address and continued his stroll. He could tell the town was gay friendly from the laid-back attitudes of the same-sex couples he spotted strolling around downtown. It was one of the main reasons Denny had picked the Antelope Inn out of all the possible resorts they could have approached.

Denny and Phillip would both still be hard at work at ten on a Friday, so there was zero chance of running into them at Club Rawhide. Riley deserved a night out on the town.

At ten o'clock he stared at his reflection in the mirror. Or the top half of himself. The motel didn't have a full-length mirror in the room, but he thought he looked pretty good. He used some gel on his hair and wore brand new jeans and shiny black boots he'd gotten that afternoon. He even bought a hat similar to the one the plaid cowboy had been wearing.

He felt a little like John Travolta in *Urban Cowboy* only with tighter jeans. Someone ought to appreciate him—or at least his ass. He needed to let his hair down and take his mind off Denny. He didn't even need to go home with anyone; as long as someone was interested, it would be enough to restore his shattered confidence.

Besides, he had to get up early enough to get to the Marriott in time to check out the job possibilities on a dude ranch.

Estelle would love that image: Riley riding a horse around a real western ranch.

The picture made him laugh, and that felt great.

HE DROVE to Club Rawhide, which was about a mile from the Red Roof Inn.

The parking lot was half-full, and music spilled out of the side entrance as he made his way around to the front door. It had a countrified rock beat, but he couldn't name the song or the band. Living in France for the past four years meant he had lost touch with the American music scene.

At the front door a guy sitting on a stool collecting cover charges and checking IDs gave him a long look up and a longer look down.

"Hi, Riley," he said handing Riley's New York State driver's license back to him. "Twenty bucks."

Riley pulled the cash out of his wallet and handed it over. He was only a step inside when he heard the same man ask for ten dollars from the guy behind him in line. He spun around, ready to complain, when someone bumped into him from the side.

"Oh, sorry." The guy smoothed a hand on Riley's shoulder as he apologized, letting it linger for a long moment. Then tipped his hat and grinned as he moved toward the bar. "Lemme buy you a drink?"

"Sure." Riley followed.

Brian—as he introduced himself—bought Riley a bottle of some local beer, and they shouted over the thump of music and other patrons for a few minutes. "Wanna dance?" Brian asked.

"Sorry, not really."

"You sure?" Brian touched Riley's bicep, giving it a gentle squeeze.

"Yeah. Go ahead. Thanks for the beer."

Brian nodded and made his way along the bar until he found someone to dance with him.

Before Riley had finished his beer, someone else came up to offer him another drink.

"How about a Buckskin shooter?" the guy offered. He was a little older than Riley and had his shirt mostly unbuttoned. He kept staring at Riley's crotch and squeezing Riley's knee.

"What's in it?"

"What's not?" the guy replied, grinning. "Two shooters," he ordered, and the bartender poured a shocking variety of liquids into a silver mixing cup and shook it dramatically before filling two large shot glasses. Riley's new buddy handed over some cash and held his glass up.

Riley took his and they nodded.

"Down it," the guy said.

Riley took a tentative sip. It was strong but tasty, and he gulped it down, relishing the trail of heat as it slid down his throat. He glanced up to see his companion had only sipped about half his drink. He grinned at Riley. "Want another?"

"Not yet." Riley felt stupid he'd fallen for the ruse.

"Wanna dance?" the guy stepped between Riley's knees and placed one large hand on Riley's upper thigh, indicating he didn't really mean "dance."

"What do you want?" The guy leaned in and kissed Riley, hard and a little slobbery. His dark stubble scraped Riley's clean-shaven cheek, and he thought he might have lost a layer of skin. He ignored it and kissed back. This encouraged the guy, who immediately grabbed at Riley's dick through his jeans.

Riley wanted to feel wanted, but this wasn't quite it. "Maybe later...." He nudged the guy off him and slid down from the barstool. He was already a little unsteady on his feet.

COLBY ZANE arrived at Club Rawhide about eleven thirty, and the place was hopping. Guys mobbed the dance floor, and a few of the "cowbois" were already dancing atop one end of the bar, teasing and flirting with a mass of men waving dollar bills. He pushed his way through the crush of warm bodies and the aromas of aftershave and sweat. After getting a beer, he moved toward the edge of the dance floor.

There was a guy he met up with sometimes when he was in town. This time around Colby hadn't called ahead to make a plan, but if he ran into Paul then that would be one less thing to decide tonight. Colby wasn't in the mood to pick and choose. He had a lot on his mind, too many problems on the ranch to worry about, but Aunt Lynn didn't trust anyone else's driving so she'd roped him into bringing her to town this weekend.

Since he was here, no reason not to enjoy the experience to the fullest. His throat was dry, and he finished his beer in a few long pulls. He'd make the second one last longer. Once he got another bottle, he moved around the room nodding or making eye contact with a series of guys, hoping something would click with one.

There were some new men here since his last visit. A handful were older, probably wealthy visitors, while the rest were eager-faced young men ready to offer themselves to the highest bidder. Colby didn't want anything to do with either group. He was happy to stick to the locals, or other men who came in from the ranches from time to time for some companionship.

Paul was here tonight, already on the arm of another man, so Colby just nodded and smiled a friendly greeting. He was surprised when Paul whispered to his companion, then came up to Colby.

"Hey, cowboy. Didn't know you were in town." He gave Colby a peck on the cheek as he snaked one arm around Colby's waist.

"Last minute trip, just tonight. I didn't mean to pull you away...."

Paul shrugged. "You didn't. That's Roarke. He's down from Montana."

Colby nodded. He could guess Roarke wasn't out in his town, and weekends in Aspen or Vail might be his only chance for male companionship. "Well, you should get back. I'll try and let you know when I'm in town next time."

"What?" Paul leaned on Colby's shoulder to raise himself a few inches closer to Colby's mouth after a roar from the direction of the bar drowned out Colby's words.

"Never mind."

"You interested in coming home with me and Roarke?"

Colby glanced over at Roarke, who gave a sweet, shy smile. He was dark haired, on the burly side, and decent looking. He was in good physical shape, almost certainly a cowboy or wrangler from his stance and physique. "Gotta pass, Paul. I'm not really into threesomes."

"Only because you never tried one." Paul's voice was flirtatious, and he slid his hand along Colby's ass and around the front of his jeans in a way that made Colby seriously reconsider the invitation.

"Not tonight. I'm in town with Aunt Lynn, and we got errands tomorrow. But I'm sorely tempted."

"Next time?"

"We'll see." Colby grinned and Paul went back to Roarke, wiggling his ass in a shameless attempt to get Colby to change his mind. It almost worked. Another wave of noise from the bar swept through the rest of the place. The dancers usually generated a lot of excitement, and Colby wanted to check them out, after he made a stop in the men's room.

By the time he squeezed his way into the bar area, the crowd had grown. A couple dozen men ogled and felt up the paid dancers, who wore cowboy hats of various colors, leather boots and go-go shorts or G-strings. They were handsome guys in fantastic shape.

A blond dancer waved at Colby and blew him a kiss. Colby had gone home with Ashton one night the previous fall. Most of the guys were looking for cash to go home with you, but Ashton and Colby had clicked. It had been a big ego boost, but it hadn't been a great time. Ashton was hot as an August afternoon, but he'd turned out to be a high-maintenance, pushy bottom. Fucking him had been too much work for too little pleasure.

Tonight, Colby would stick to someone predictable. At the far end of the bar were a couple of local guys who wanted to try their turn at go-go dancing. The club let them on the bar during the cowbois' breaks. The three pros tipped their hats, wiggled their hips, and marched off down the jury-rigged steps, while two of the local wannabes hopped onto the bar at the other end and paraded toward the middle. A third man struggled to get onto the bar, and several patrons offered assistance, mainly in the form of grabbing his ass while pushing him up.

Another cheer went around the bar as the amateurs started thrusting to the bass-heavy dance track and pulling their shirts off. Colby noticed the guy at the other end was really unsteady on his feet. Too drunk to dance, and probably only up there because some dumbass friends of his dared him to do it.

But the guy was a looker. Not a local. He was wearing tight, slim jeans, a black shirt with pearl snaps, and brand-new boots so shiny they were blinding.

And he had on a new hat—a black felt Stetson. He clearly took fashion tips from *Urban Cowboy*, or one of the sales clerks thought it would be a hoot to sell the guy the most obvious tourist outfit. Colby shook his head as the guy stumbled.

Encouragement from the audience got him to unsnap the shirt. His skin was pale and smooth, almost hairless, at least at this distance. He had pink-brown nipples with large areolas. When he turned away, Colby noticed how great the jeans fit him. How would he look without them? Curiosity made Colby move down the bar.

The urban cowboy had undone his belt and zipper and guys were handing him money to get on with it. One guy handed him a shooter, and the guy sucked it down like water. Colby shook his head. This was going to be ugly. He headed back to the dance floor because he didn't want to watch this guy embarrass himself in public.

Ten minutes later Colby had danced with a likely prospect and was heading to the bar to get them both beers when a commotion in the corner near the back caught his attention. He usually stayed away from that side of the club because he wasn't into public sex, but something made him look.

It might have been because the drunk-off-his-ass guy was still on the bar and Colby suspected the worst. He wasn't far off. The Urban Cowboy was sitting at the edge of the bar with another guy behind him. His pants were around his ankles and his shorts were heading in that direction with the help of two other guys. A fourth guy was waving a pile of money.

"Who else wants to play? Twenty bucks!"

Shit. The guy had gotten himself into a game of what the locals called Geyser. The players put money into two piles, then had their turn sucking off the guy on the bar. They had thirty seconds. The one who got the guy off kept one pile of money and the "lucky" contestant kept the other half. It wasn't Colby's thing to play or watch, but plenty of locals liked it, though the contestant was typically one of the star fucker twinks looking for a sugar daddy.

The drunken urban cowboy probably wasn't capable of giving consent to a game like this. His head was lolling, and the only thing keeping him upright was the guy on the bar behind him.

Colby moved closer and had a momentary second thought. He'd never seen a drunk guy with an erection like that. Viagra aside—and this one was young enough not to need it—that was a real boner, and it was beautiful. No wonder there were a dozen guys lined up to play. Who wouldn't want a taste of that?

It didn't answer the question of whether the guy had made a conscious decision to play. By the time Colby made it to the end of the bar, the first guy was already sucking away to claps and cheers from the spectators. He wasn't likely to win, but he was giving it his all.

"Hey, this guy's totally out of it," Colby said to the man propping him up.

"Looks fine to me. Ask him." The second guy pulled the first one off and moved in for his thirty seconds of fun.

The third player was ready and waiting to start. "Dude, wait your turn."

"Just you wait a minute." Colby pushed the man behind the bar back with an open palm on his chest and leaned in to speak to the drunk guy. "You okay with this? All these guys on you?"

"Yeah." The guy nodded but his gaze was unfocused. "At least someone wants me." He sniffed at the end of the sentence and Colby made a quick decision.

"Break this up. Give everyone their money back. He's—"

"I'm fine. Thanks. You go next. You got a really pretty—"

And he puked all over the guy sucking his dick.

Colby tried not to laugh and failed. The guy stood up, roaring, and Colby made another quick decision. He grabbed half the cash, pulled the urban cowboy over his shoulder, and ran like hell for the door with a couple dozen angry men on his tail.

Chapter Three

COLBY RACED across the parking lot to the Marriott next door and used his magnetic card to go in through the side door. The men bunched up at the door, shouting, but none of them were guests and they couldn't get inside.

Colby stopped and put the guy down in the alcove next to a soda-vending machine. He got the man's pants back up enough to take him through the hotel. The guy leaned heavily on Colby, and he decided to put him back over his shoulder. They rode the elevator up to the fifth floor like this, along with a middle-aged couple who eyed them like the devil had just given birth to bunny rabbits right in front of them.

Finally safe in his room, Colby laid his guest out on the bed and went for ice, then offered the guy some water.

"Thanks." The guy drained the glass, then blinked a few times.

"I'm Colby. You feeling any better?"

"Hi, Colby. I'm Riley." He grinned, then his face went pale. "Oh God, where am I?" Riley rubbed the back of his head and had that green look like he might throw up again.

"Let me get you to the toilet."

"Okay." Riley let Colby help him into the bathroom, nearly tripping on his boots as they covered the short distance across the small hotel room.

Colby got more water and wet some towels for Riley.

"I'm okay," Riley choked out. "Leave me alone?"

"Sure." Colby sat on the bed, arms folded across his chest, while Riley heaved up far too many Buckskin shooters. "Let me know if you need anything, okay?"

"Yeah." Riley sounded like he needed help but didn't want to ask.

Who did? It was embarrassing enough in front of friends, but in front of a total stranger? Colby's heart went out to the guy, but he didn't know what he could do.

When it was quiet, Colby went back into the bathroom.

"Riley, let me take your boots and shirt and maybe your jeans so they don't get dirty."

"Okay, thanks." Riley nodded weakly and let Colby undress him.

Colby felt like a real perv as he looked at poor, vulnerable Riley on the floor, so he gathered the clothes and went back to the bedroom and inspected them for stains. He wiped some stray vomit off the shirt. The pants were clean enough for Riley to wear home later. Colby hung everything up in the closet.

He heard Riley getting more water and there wasn't any more vomiting. This was not how he pictured his night going. Sure, he'd left with a hot guy, though he hadn't expected to play nursemaid. But he still had done the right thing with Riley.

Colby undressed to his boxers and slid under the sheets. He could still hear music and raucous laughter next door at the club. Riley threw up again, and Colby consoled himself with the thought he was earning karma points he'd get a chance to collect at some point in the future. Hopefully in this incarnation and not when he was a mealy bug or a bighorn sheep.

The shower started, and he listened to Riley washing up. A few minutes later he came out of the bathroom wrapped in a towel. In the light coming into the room through the open curtains, he looked younger, and the damp hair falling into his eyes was damned sexy. The whole package was sexy as Riley stood at the edge of the bed, nipples hard nubs in the chill.

"I, uh. I'm sorry about this." Riley looked around. "Where're my clothes?"

"You got a car or did you take a cab?"

Riley looked confused for a moment. "Car. At the club, I guess."

"You shouldn't be driving, that's for sure. Stay if you want."

Riley was still unsteady on his feet.

"Look, it's a big bed. Stay here till you're steady enough to get home.

"Thanks… Colby."

"Don't mention it."

Riley dropped the towel and draped it over the chair to dry. In the dim room Colby admitted the view of naked Riley was excellent from all sides. Shadows from the moonlight accentuated a nice curvy ass and hips, and even soft his dick was beautiful. He tried not to think how it had looked when it was hard, or about the guys in the club who had been sucking it. He glanced away before Riley could notice the ogling.

Riley slid under the covers. The movement beside him made Colby think more ungentlemanly thoughts, and he realized how long it had been since he'd gotten laid. Hopefully karma would balance that out too. He could have been with Paul and Roarke right now, not babysitting this naked gorgeous guy he couldn't touch. Thankfully, Riley fell asleep quickly, but Colby listened to make sure he was okay before he closed his eyes.

WHEN COLBY woke, the first streaks of dawn were visible out the window. A movement behind him caught his attention, and he was startled for a moment to find he wasn't alone. Then he remembered the events of a few hours earlier.

"Uh, Colby?"

"Yeah?"

"That stack of money on the nightstand? Did I give that to you, or did you give that to me?"

Colby couldn't help laughing at the stricken tone of Riley's voice. He rolled over and came face-to-face with Riley, who smelled surprisingly clean for the circumstances, even his breath.

"You don't remember?"

Riley shook his head. "It must not have been worth as much as that if I can't remember." He gave a weak chuckle.

"The game in the club? The blowjob game?"

Riley furrowed his brow and frowned. "Oh, shit. It's coming back to me. I was playing the game.... I—aw, fuck."

Panic took over his expression, and Colby knew he'd done the right thing getting Riley out of there. Sober, the guy would never have agreed to that game.

"You made them stop, didn't you?"

Colby nodded.

"Then you brought me back here and nothing happened?"

Colby shook his head.

"Nothing at all?"

"Nothing. You weren't in any shape."

"Otherwise?"

Colby tried to tear his gaze from Riley's naked body, the sheets barely covering him. Riley noticed.

"Otherwise something might have?"

"I wouldn't have minded if something had."

"You stopped the game before...." He paused, then looked Colby right in the eye. "So, technically, you owe me an orgasm." Riley flashed a charming grin at Colby.

"I suppose I do, if you're keeping track." Colby sensed heat emanating from Riley's gaze and his body. Colby's cock responded to the immediate rise in sexual tension between them. "Did you want to collect on that right now?"

Riley reached out and traced Colby's collarbone. The electricity had Colby wide-awake and hard as a rock. Riley nodded slowly. "Would you mind if I did?"

Colby leaned forward and kissed him, softly at first, then when he felt Riley's cock pressing into his abs, hard and deep.

Riley let out a sigh and melted against Colby, sliding his arms around Colby's waist so they were chest-to-chest and their cocks nestled against each other.

They embraced, kissing, for a while. Riley tasted of toothpaste, which sure as hell beat the alternative. He smelled like hotel shampoo and soap, and his skin was smooth. In Colby's hands his ass felt as good as it had looked from across the room. And his cock felt like heaven as Riley bucked his hips against Colby's body.

"Wish you'd been the one to offer me a drink first last night," Riley whispered.

"Me too." Colby peeled back the sheets and surveyed Riley's body.

Riley stared at Colby, and somehow his fingers homed in on the little scars and marks that marred Colby's skin. Riley's touch was delicate, exploratory, arousing, and Colby let his body take over from his brain to enjoy the touches and take his own.

He rolled Riley onto his back and kissed him hard, then moved down to tease and taste each nipple, prolonging the journey to Riley's beautiful cock. Colby inhaled, sensing only soap and Riley's own scent. Not a trace remained of the men who'd pawed him over—and more—the night before. Still, maybe Riley's cock wasn't the best place to start, no matter how much Colby wanted to taste it.

"I like to bottom," Riley said, spreading his thighs so Colby had easy access to whatever he took a fancy to.

He wrapped one hand around Riley's cock and enjoyed the firm hot flesh in his hand while Riley stared up at him and reached to pinch one of Colby's nipples.

"You want me to do you first?" Colby asked.

"Before, during, after." Riley smiled again. He had a nice smile, a genuine smile now he wasn't completely shit-faced.

Colby remembered what Riley had said in the club "At least they want me." Or something to that effect. Someone's rejection had pushed him into dangerous behavior. Colby didn't want to be part of something self-destructive.

"You tell me what you like. What you *want*. Don't say whatever I want. Got it?"

Riley nodded, his lips pressed together in a more serious version of his carefree expression. "During. I like that best."

"Me too." Colby tightened his grip on Riley's cock and slid his hand from the base to the head, estimating its length compared to the width of his hand, like he might measure a horse. Just about two hands long. He smiled. Riley closed his eyes slightly as Colby played with his cock and explored his balls. With a fluid movement, Colby leaned down to suck just the crown of Riley's pretty dick into his mouth and savored the salty tang and the sweet, smooth skin. He liked the connection of having warm hard flesh in his mouth, knowing what he did with lips and tongue sent waves of sensation to every nerve ending in Riley's body.

Riley's nipples plumped even more, and his cock swelled in Colby's mouth.

"You got lube and rubbers, Colby?"

Colby didn't want to stop sucking to answer, but he did. He straightened up and pulled the necessary items from the nightstand. "Want me to slick you up or do it yourself?"

"You can do it." The words were a sexy invitation.

Colby drizzled lube on his hand and leaned back down to Riley's cock, this time tracing circles around his asshole until he felt Riley relax. Then he pushed in a finger and felt Riley's entire body react, contracting around his index finger for a moment before loosening again. He slid the finger in and out till Riley's hips went back down. The guy hadn't been fucked in a while, and Colby didn't want to hurt him. After he could get two fingers in, he pulled his hand away.

"You can do the condom for me."

"Sure." Riley changed position so he was kneeling in front of Colby and took half of Colby's dick into his mouth.

"Mmm." Colby liked Riley's quick, aggressive movement and put a hand through Riley's silky dark hair. Riley had him rock-hard again with a combination of sucking and tonguing, using one hand to cup Colby's sac and gently squeeze. He endured some disappointment when Riley pulled off, but it was to roll the condom down Colby's erection, which meant soon he'd have it deep in Riley's other end.

Riley turned around and pushed his ass up in Colby's direction.

In the pale dawn light, Riley's pucker glistened and opened up ever so slightly. Colby took aim and pushed right in, claiming Riley completely. The sharp intake of breath was particularly satisfying, just enough friction for Riley not to forget this too quickly, but not so much it would hurt.

"Oh ho," Riley said, then let out tiny grunts in time with Colby's sharp quick thrusts.

Colby squeezed and spread Riley's ass, shifting angles so he could go deep. Riley made lots of noise, which Colby loved, and clenched his ass at just the right time to add friction and sensation. They developed a good rhythm, working together, until the point when all pretense of a polite roll in the hay went out the window and Colby let himself go. Riley's bucking hips and moans drove him wild, and he was out of control as he pounded fast and deep. Riley's head banged into the headboard half a dozen times before Colby moved a pillow to protect him—and muffle the sound. Riley barely seemed to notice.

The only thing Colby didn't love about fucking Riley into the mattress was not being able to see his face. He was within an inch of finishing when he slowed his movements.

"Roll over," Colby said, panting.

Riley did as requested. His face was flushed, eyes half-closed and strands of hair at his temples damp. He looked so fucking gorgeous, already blissed out. And his cock was still dark and swollen, curving out and up toward his abs. Colby stuffed pillows under his hips, pushed Riley's thighs apart, and entered him again.

Riley's whole body shuddered, and Colby curved a hand around the base of Riley's cock, sliding up and down, eased by the remains of the lube he'd used earlier.

"Yeah, oh good. Good. Colby. Mmm. Yeah."

Colby tugged and stroked Riley while he watched pleasure wash over Riley's features. His swollen, kiss-bruised lips parted, his nipples budded, and the sounds…. People down the hall could probably hear Riley. People three floors up could probably hear him. Colby fucked him faster and slid his thumb along Riley's dripping cockslit.

Then Riley trembled and bucked his hips up and splattered a surprising number of pearly jets all over his chest, throat, and even his own face. The sight of it sent Colby plummeting over the edge, and he fought to keep his eyes open, wanting to see Riley's expression.

The next thing Colby knew, he was prone on top of Riley, holding on to him for dear life, unable to catch his breath. But it felt as if he were floating on the most amazing, beautiful cloud.

"I think I owe you some change," Riley said.

"Is that a compliment or an insult? My brain's not working too good right now."

"You don't need a brain with a body like that." Riley let out a husky, contented sigh and slid his hands appreciatively over Colby's ass. "But I meant it as a compliment."

Colby kissed him. He tasted like come. Riley had come on his mouth, in his hair, and in his eyelashes. Colby had never seen anyone come all over themselves like that except maybe in porn. Goddamn, it was hot.

"You been in any movies, Riley?"

"No."

"You sure?"

"You mean porn? Do I look familiar or something?"

"No, just you'd...." Colby stopped talking. Riley's smile had faded away. "Fuck. That was meant to be a compliment too."

"Thanks, I guess." Riley turned up half of his mouth, and Colby decided to call that a win.

He avoided further verbal faux pas by kissing Riley again and again. He wished he was twenty years old because that wasn't all he wanted to do to Riley again and again.

WHEN COLBY woke again, the sun was much higher in the sky. About ten a.m., he estimated. He rolled toward the middle of the bed, but it was empty. No sounds from the bathroom.

Riley was gone.

Colby scooted into the middle of the bed and pulled Riley's pillow against his chest, sniffing it, hoping to catch some lingering essence of his all-too-temporary bedmate. He had been looking forward to another round with Riley, a soapy, sexy shower and then breakfast or lunch, depending how long the other activities lasted.

Well, they'd spent a few incredible hours together. Colby finally accepted Riley wasn't just out getting coffee or donuts and hauled himself out of bed. He pissed, turned on the shower, and was about to step in when the steam on the mirror revealed a message:

Thanks for rescuing me, Cowboy.

No phone number or e-mail address.

Riley must not be into second encounters. Or he'd decided to go back to whatever jerk made him so insecure he was ready to let a roomful of strangers try to get him off. What might he have done after that if Colby hadn't "rescued" him? Rescued him right into bed with his legs spread.

Colby felt like a heel now, despite Riley's compliments and obvious enjoyment of their memorable fuck. He'd treated Riley no better than the other men—out to get what they could. No wonder Riley had split without leaving any contact information.

Colby finished his shower with two minutes of ice-cold water, like a penance, and was shivering by the time he wrapped the towel around himself and stepped out of the bathroom. The sentimental part of him hoped Riley might be sitting on the bed, waiting for him, but it was wrong.

A glance at the clock told Colby he was behind schedule. Checkout was noon. Aunt Lynn was busy all morning, but he was supposed to call her a little before noon to put their gear in the truck and see if she was ready to leave for home.

He packed his own gear up and brought it downstairs, then hit speed dial.

IT WAS a good thing Riley had set his cell phone alarm and put it on vibrate. Otherwise he would have never gotten out of bed with the plaid cowboy.

Colby. It was such a perfect western type of name. It didn't exactly suit the man, since "Colby" implied plain and earthy. Well, he was earthy, but there was nothing plain about him. Just thinking about him got Riley's motor running, and that would be a bad thing right about now.

He'd forced himself out of the sensual comfort of Colby's embrace, pulled his clothes on as quietly as possible, and tiptoed out of the room. The sun was blinding—and hot on his all-black ensemble—as he made his way across to Club Rawhide's parking lot, where he'd left the rental. Thankfully it was still there.

He felt sour liquid surge into his throat as he recalled his behavior in the bar the night before. Denny had him so fucked up, he'd gotten drunk and thrown himself at a room full of horny strangers who didn't have good judgment about boundaries.

If Colby hadn't come along, Riley would be in sorry shape, probably gangbanged and barebacked, and he wouldn't have remembered much about it. He wouldn't want to. Riley made a mental note not to accept any drinks if he went to a bar on his own again. He didn't think he'd been drugged, but he'd felt out of control in the worst way.

He'd let that dickhead Denny's rejection push him to a very ugly place. Even when he'd sobered up, he'd acted pretty slutty with Colby, telling him he owed Riley an orgasm. Kind, gentlemanly Colby, who hadn't tried anything with Riley, even though he could have. Riley felt Colby's eyes on him, knew Colby wanted him, but wouldn't take advantage of him like those horny losers at the bar.

That had been one spectacular orgasm too. Riley would remember that one for a long time. It would have been easy to stay and spend the day in bed with Colby. But he couldn't. He'd just remember a long, last, contented look at his slumbering cowboy.

He made it back to the motel and drenched himself in hot water, wishing he didn't have to wash away the scent of Colby or their time together. But he had to get his ass over to the summer job fair, and he wasn't likely to get hired reeking of booze and jizz, unless he wanted a job as a rent boy or at Club Rawhide.

Pass.

He put on a clean pair of dark pants, a nice button-down shirt, and combed his hair carefully. He slipped on the other pair of boots he'd bought the day before, buttery dark brown leather with a lower heel, much more comfortable than the pointy-toed black numbers he'd worn to the bar. These looked like the kind someone would actually wear on a ranch.

He dug around in his computer bag for the resume he'd printed the day before and headed back to the Marriott. He walked into the lobby slowly, glancing around, hoping he might run into his plaid cowboy, but Colby wasn't in sight.

Room 417, Riley recalled. He could stop in there after the job fair.

He found the ballroom set up with a dozen different booths for the local seasonal employers and the ranches. He realized that Denny had been smart about their summer jobs. He'd known the restaurant owners and arranged top-notch positions before the main summer hiring season began. All that was left now were the lowest level positions, most of which didn't require any culinary background.

If he couldn't get a decent professional job, he'd go home to New York or Cape Cod or the Vineyard and beg an old friend to take him on for the summer. He'd work catering on the east coast before he'd admit defeat to his parents.

Riley started with the farthest table from the door and went clockwise around the room. The first seven didn't have any kitchen jobs left. The next two had only one spot each and a stack of applications to sort through.

"You're overqualified for the openings we have left, Riley," the woman at table number ten told him. "I couldn't justify wasting your talents peeling vegetables and plating. And you're worth ten times what I can pay you. If you'd like to run the kitchen, you'll want to apply in January, for a position next summer. I'm sorry."

"I am too. It sounds like a fun position."

"Running a guest ranch kitchen is a lot easier than a restaurant. And you can't beat the commute. A five-minute walk with the most gorgeous views in the mountains."

"Next year, I'll plan better. Thanks for the advice."

"Good luck, Riley."

He got up and shook hands with the woman and moved on to the next desk, the Rocking Z Ranch.

The woman sitting there was on the plump side, with a strong face. She wore a buckskin jacket over a white blouse with lace around the collar and pearly buttons, like she was going to church. Her confident, rugged air blended with the soft, frilly look so she came across as Aunt Bea from the Andy Griffith show meets John Wayne.

"Good morning," she said. She eyed Riley up and down as if expecting the worst and not being particularly disappointed.

"Good morning, ma'am." Riley nodded the way Colby and some of the other men had, and the effect was startling. The woman's eyes lit up, and she even turned up one corner of her mouth.

"Have a seat, young man."

"Yes, ma'am. I'm Riley Emerson."

"Lynn Ann Hansley."

Riley sat and handed her his now-worn resume. "I'm looking for a job in the kitchen."

She let out a sigh and handed the paper back to him without even looking at it. "I'm sorry but we've got all the positions filled. I'm still looking for housekeepers, though."

He nodded and was about to get up when he glanced at the brochures stacked on the table and the photographs she'd set up. He picked up one of the photos. "Your place is really incredible. Are those real buffalo? I don't think I've ever seen a real one, in person."

"Where're you from?"

"Near Boston."

She nodded. "Thought it might be somethin' like that. How'd you end up out in Colorado wantin' to work in the kitchen of a guest ranch?"

"I'll spare you the ugly details, but I was supposed to be working at Antelope Inn. I had to change my plans when my, uh, love life hit a snag."

"You were gonna work at Antelope Inn? Chopping and slicing?"

"No, ma'am. I was supposed to be the new pastry chef, but I don't mind chopping and slicing. I could even learn to make beds…." He looked at the snow-capped mountains in the photo and the grassy fields with buffalo roaming and wondered if that would be better than going back to the east coast with his tail between his legs. The air would be fresher, and he'd probably rather spend time with Aunt Bea Wayne than listen to his father say "I told you so" until Riley found a job worthy of his credentials.

"Pastry?" Aunt Bea grabbed at the resume again and nodded as she skimmed it. "Core-don Bloo?" She didn't even attempt the French pronunciation. "You know what gluten-free is?"

He nodded.

"You know how to make gluten-free bread that doesn't taste like dried-up wallpaper paste?"

"Yes. I—"

"You're hired."

"Really?"

"Yes. I'm supposed to be meeting two prospects for running the kitchen, but I know neither of them can even spell Core-don Bloo much less say it. I know I musta mangled it something fierce."

"Well...."

"Anyhow, I suspect you know your way around running a real kitchen and cooking just about anything, right?"

"Yes." It wouldn't do to sell his skill short. "How many kitchen staff?"

"Four, for twenty guests and fifteen staff, plus the family now and then, which is another seven."

He did some quick calculations. "How many different main dishes do you intend at each meal?"

"Why, one. It ain't no restaurant with a menu. It's a ranch, a working ranch with some pampered guests. But you just cook and they eat. Some of the guests need gluten-free and that throws a real monkey wrench into the works. I was thinking of getting them all in at once. Havin' a big "Gluten-free Week" and they can all show up and my kitchen staff doesn't have to do lots of extra work."

Riley wasn't sure if he was supposed to laugh, so he just nodded. "With four people I could definitely do a couple of different dishes at each meal, plus any special requirements. I can work up some sample menus and costing, and you could decide what works in your budget. I'll need some budgeting information and—"

Aunt Bea's eyes lit up again. "Look, Riley, honey. That sounds great. I trust you. There'll be time to go over everything later on. But I haven't said what the pay is yet. You may not be so eager once you know." She told him the weekly rate.

"I get room and board for free?" He was calculating. The monthly pay was less than a quarter what Antelope Inn had offered him, but he wouldn't have to pay the exorbitant rent on the fancy apartment Denny had chosen, right in town.

"Yes. And of course you can ride horses or go on the excursions on your free time. Or come into town with the other staff."

Riley could save everything he made. He looked at the photographs again. "Where do I sign?"

COLBY HAD all his gear in the truck when he called Aunt Lynn's cell phone.

"Good morning, sleepyhead. You awake?" she asked with a hint of a chuckle in her voice.

"Been up for a while. How's it going?"

"Just great. I'm just finishing up with the hiring and planning. My bags are at the front desk."

"I'll put them in the truck and meet you in the ballroom."

"Perfect."

Colby went inside and collected his aunt's overnight bag. She'd have some brochures and photos and things in the ballroom he'd need to pack up too. A group of people came out as he entered, including a guy wearing a black felt Stetson. The sight made Colby's chest tighten as he stared at the man, but it wasn't Riley.

He made his way to the Rocking Z table in the ballroom, where Aunt Lynn had collected all her paper and recruiting crap, as he called it. Thank God he didn't have to try to figure out who to hire for the summer. He left that side of things to his aunt and cousins, who ran the guest ranch.

Colby and his uncle did the real ranching, with the help of his cousin Rachel's husband and their hired hands. They took on two extra men in the summer, and everyone had one shift a week with the guests, in addition to the wranglers Lynn hired to work with the guests.

"So you filled all the spots?"

"And how. I got the housekeepers. I hired two extra this year. I know from experience at least one won't show up and one will be as useless as teats on a bull." She put the papers in a small box, and Colby tucked it under his arm and swung her bag over his other shoulder.

As they headed for the parking lot, she was still going on in her usual chirpy tone. "And I got us a real-live gourmet chef."

"Did you now?"

"Yes, sirree. Trained in Paris at the Core-don Bloo and ev'rythin'. Even knows what gluten-free means. Paris...."

"Now why'd you go and do that? What's wrong with good old American cookin'? We don't need no fancy Core-don Bloo nothing."

"I know that. He's gonna do the chuck wagon meals and serve hearty western fare. But if we want somethin' fancy for an occasion, like with that ol' moneybags investor coming in a couple of weeks, we can do something really special."

Colby snorted. Aunt Lynn had run the kitchen herself with no trouble. Why'd she suddenly decide to hire in some foreigner? He put her stuff in the back of the cab and helped her up into the front seat. He noticed she didn't bend as easily as she used to, and she needed a little leg up now and then.

Chapter Four

RILEY WASN'T sure he'd made the right decision about taking the job at Rocking Z Ranch for the summer. It wasn't the Antelope Inn or Cascade. It wasn't going to look good on his resume when he tried to get his next serious culinary position. But for his soul, it felt like the only possibility.

Denny and Phillip had wrung the heart out of him. He needed some time and space to heal and decide what the right next step was for him. He could always go back to Paris, and he could probably get a decent spot in New York. He'd gladly live in either city.

But the drive out to Aspen from Denver, through rugged mountains and the majesty of nature, had touched something inside he'd never known existed. It felt right. And if it wasn't, he only had to manage a few months. He wasn't moving out to the middle of nowhere for the rest of his life.

As he headed south early Wednesday morning on the two-lane highway toward the Rocking Z Ranch, he felt a level of excitement he hadn't known in ages. Not even the previous week when he'd been on the way to meet Denny. Only now could Riley admit he hadn't been as completely stoked as Denny about their summer plans. So excited he'd left Paris a month before Riley so he could arrange their apartment and get started at the Inn. Looking back, Riley should have seen it all unfolding.

The whole Aspen idea had been Denny's. He'd grown up nearby and spent the "seasons" working and making money from the constant flow of wealthy tourists and part-timers. People who greeted you with a folded bill rather than remembering your name. Riley knew these people well. He—or his family—was part of that group. They'd summered on the Cape or the Vineyard, and more recently in the Hamptons after his father's business resulted in a move to Manhattan.

But it wasn't Riley's idea of a perfect summer. He'd wanted them to do a trip through Asia, eating their way from country to country, experiencing something new and exciting around every corner. Denny wasn't interested in new; he seemed drawn to the familiar and safe.

Riley might be the only one in the world who thought cooking at a dude ranch—guest ranch as he had been cautioned to call it—would be new and exciting. But it was.

It had to be.

It would be. He'd spent every waking moment since Saturday researching campfire cooking and chuck wagon techniques. He'd never actually done any of them, but he had enough of an idea how it should work. Cooking was cooking. All he really needed were a few adjustments for equipment. He'd do some practice runs in the week before the first guests arrived, and it should be a picnic, literally.

Well, not quite *every* waking moment. The remaining time had been spent wandering around Aspen and lurking at Club Rawhide hoping Plaid Cowboy would show up. He even took all his meals at the diner with Pauline and grilled her about the sexy rancher.

"Don't know which ranch he's with. Comes in here once a month or so, sometimes more during the summer. Depends on how busy the ranch is, I guess. I'll keep a look out for him and e-mail you if he comes in again, how's that?"

"Thanks, Pauline." Riley had been surprised at her eagerness to help him in his hunt for a long, tall, plaid version of Cinderella.

Only Riley had been the one to leave when the alarm clock struck. Technically that made *him* Cinderella, but he liked the way it sounded the other way round.

Well, he was on his way to a new chapter in his life on a ranch with buffalo roaming, and a summer of farmhouse dinners and the occasional loaf of gluten-free bread.

And a bunkhouse full of cowboys, at least in Riley's fantasy version of the Rocking Z. It hadn't been that much of a fantasy. He'd pored over the ranch's website and noticed quite a few hunky guys on horses in the photos.

He even figured out why it was called the Rocking Z. The Zane family had obtained the land in 1873, and passed the ranch down through the generations. Now Lynn Ann Hansley and her husband ran the ranch, along with their two daughters. Born a Zane, Lynn inherited the ranch as the only one in her generation.

Riley would be there soon enough.

COLBY HADN'T expected the memories of Riley to linger so long. He thought about Riley just before he went to bed, and when he awoke in the morning, he reached out just before he opened his eyes. He was alone.

Sometimes he'd get a flash in his mind's eye of Riley's smile or hear his laugh. Colby knew Riley wasn't anywhere near as promiscuous as he'd seemed at the bar. He'd been so embarrassed at the memory of what had happened. That attracted Colby to Riley as much as his good looks and their compatibility in bed. It had been fun and easy to… he didn't want to say "fuck Riley" because that seemed too base. It hadn't been making love. It was somewhere in between.

On Monday, Lynn, Rachel, and Alicia couldn't talk about anything else but the imminent arrival of the summer staff, including that new chef. Colby couldn't listen to another word. He had just a couple more days till they'd be overrun with summer staff and guests, and the only place to get any peace was far from the house and guest cabins.

After lunch, Colby took his bay cutting horse, Hickory, out to Big Dipper. Everyone else called it Pasture 4 or West Pasture, but to Colby, it would always be Big Dipper. As a kid, his dad had laid out the map of the Rocking Z, and Colby said that pasture had a funny shape so it looked like the Big Dipper.

Dad gave Colby a pencil, and he crossed out Pasture 4 and wrote in Big Dipper. During the recent talk about selling some acres, Uncle Jake had pulled the map out. Colby's childish printing was still there, in faded pencil. He got a huge knot in his throat as he recalled that day with his father. It had been one of their last together.

Feeling sentimental, he steered Hickory north to a little rise, just high enough to give a nice view of most of the Z and the spectacular backdrop of the Rockies in the distance. At the top, he dismounted and dropped a rein so Hickory would stay put. On foot he crested the rise. He hadn't been here for a long time, but for some reason he felt the need today.

At the top the sun glinted off a granite gravestone. He wished he'd thought to bring some wildflowers along as he settled himself on the grass. As he read his parents' names he tried to remember their faces. It had been more than twenty years since they'd died. December 23 of his eighth year. It was all a blur now, and he wouldn't remember anything if Aunt Lynn hadn't explained what happened.

"Why are there three hearts on there?" he had asked as he'd traced their names and the entwined hearts when the stone was installed.

"Because they loved each other more than just two hearts could hold."

It was only years later, just before he went away for his first year at Colorado State, that he learned the whole story.

"There was an accident that night as your dad was trying to get your mom to the hospital. It was dark and icy and another car skidded across the road and hit them."

"Aunt Lynn, I know all that."

"Did you remember that your mom was pregnant? That you were going to have a little sister?"

"No." How could he have forgotten that?

"She was supposed to go stay at the hospital before the baby came, but she wanted to have Christmas here on the ranch with you and your dad. She went into early labor and your dad...." Aunt Lynn cried that day as she told Colby the whole story. She still cried when anyone talked about that night.

Colby leaned forward and traced the hearts like he had a hundred times before. One for his mom, one for his dad, and one for the little sister he'd never known.

Mom hadn't grown up on a ranch, but he knew she loved this place as much as his dad had. As much as Colby still did.

"We won't sell out. Not as long as I have a say. I'll find a way. I promise."

Chapter Five

COLBY HAD stayed out in Pasture 7—Fat Creek Pasture—as long as he could on Wednesday. If he came in much before dusk, Aunt Lynn and Rachel would rope him into helping get the new staff squared away. They were an intrusion on the real work of running the Z, and even though the guest ranch helped pay his cowboys' wages, he didn't have to like the whole damn operation and the extra fuss it kicked up for everyone who lived and worked here year-round.

As expected, when he and Hickory trotted around the bend and the home buildings came into view, he saw the commotion hadn't yet subsided. He took his time cooling Hickory and brushing him until his bay coat shone, then turning him in to the Little Home Paddock for the night with the rest of the working horses. Colby lingered, making sure Hickory had a bit of hay and plenty of water, until his rumbling stomach turned traitor and he debated how long he could last without food. Could he make it till the welcome dinner was over? A rumble as loud as an avalanche answered that question.

Colby gritted his teeth and made his way up the path toward the bunkhouse. Kit Merritt raced up before he'd even opened the screen door.

"What's up, Kit? The wranglers arrive okay?" Wranglers handled the horses for the guests, but they stayed in the bunkhouse with the ranch hands, except for Rita. As the only female wrangler she stayed in a staff room shared with another guest ranch employee.

"Yup. I helped show them around, and they're going up to the house for dinner now."

"The house? Why not the dining hall?"

"Aunt Lynn's taking care of everyone up at the house tonight to keep the dining hall clean for the new chef. They're expecting Marcus back any minute."

"Where *is* Marcus?"

"Uh, well... Aunt Lynn asked him to go pick up the new chef, cause he—"

"New chef? Marcus is my foreman. He ain't no chauffeur."

Colby fought the urge to punch the doorframe. He'd done it once before and broken the door. Then he had to spend a morning repairing it when he had better things to do. Lesson learned. But he was still pissed off that Lynn had Marcus off on some guest-ranch errand.

Kit was quaking in his worn boots. "You should come up to the house, then. Dinner sure smells delicious."

Colby stormed up the path to the main house, leaving Kit standing at the bunkhouse door. He went around the back way, through the yard, past several picnic tables and a dozen or so strangers, and yanked open the kitchen door. Delicious aromas of roasting beef and corn bread slowed him for a moment, but his brain took control back from his nose and stomach.

"Lynn? What's up with Marcus?"

She was at the stove stirring something. At his voice her shoulders crept up her spine and she turned around. "Oh, Colby, honey, I coulda used your help a few hours ago. I tried the radio, but you didn't come in. So I went to Marcus."

Colby had been on a section of the ranch that didn't always get radio signals. He knew where the radio didn't work and tried to be in those spots when avoiding things like guest-ranch nonsense.

"Why'd you need help? What happened?" Her words changed his mood from anger to worry. "Is someone hurt?"

"I don't think so. The new chef had some car trouble, so I asked Marcus to help him out. Somewhere near the pass on 82. Hopefully they got his car running again, otherwise Marcus was going to try and tow it back here."

Colby counted to five before answering. It kept him from saying the first thing that came into his mind about this high-maintenance new chef. "What was he doing on 82? It's too early in the season for damn French fools to be driving up there. Probably still snowing."

"He's not French. Just studied there. But I guess that's my fault, not giving him the warning and proper directions. He called on someone's satellite phone from the scenic overlook parking lot, or we—"

"He sounds like far too much trouble already, Lynn. You sure he's worth it?"

"Maybe, but I hope he's okay. He isn't from 'round these parts, and he might not have a warm enough coat. You know how the weather can sneak up on us too. Shame on you, Colby Zane."

Colby looked at his own dusty boots for a moment, cheeks heating like a five-year-old being scolded by Auntie Lynn for pulling his cousins' hair or riding off across the pasture out of Uncle Jake's sight again. He took in a few breaths before he could face her again.

"You're right. I wasn't thinking." It was customary for ranchers to help each other out in an emergency, and that should extend to their staff, even French fools.

"Go wash up for dinner." She turned back to the stove to stir the pot of beans.

His cousins, Rachel and Alicia, came into the kitchen and started taking dishes out to the tables set up behind the house. Colby realized he didn't have time for the shower he desperately needed. He scooted out of the kitchen into the downstairs bathroom and washed his face and hands. He smelled like he'd done a decent day's work, but nowadays no one appreciated that. As he sat down at the table next to Rachel, she crinkled her nose and gave him a little wink before she started passing dishes around.

On his other side sat a blonde girl wearing a sleeveless top with nothing underneath. He couldn't help noticing that because she leaned over a lot.

"I'm Katrina. I'm helping in the kitchen. Or I will be." She introduced herself to Colby.

"Nice to meet you, ma'am," he said and turned his attention back to the beef stew and corn bread.

"'Ma'am.' That's so sweet. I didn't think cowboys were as polite as they seem in those old movies." She laughed and kept touching his elbow.

Across the table, his younger cousin Alicia twisted her mouth into a smirk. He shot her a deadly glare and she winked at him. "Katrina, that's my cousin Colby. He runs the ranching side of the operation."

"You mean all the horses and cows?" she asked, her eyes wide with curiosity that couldn't be genuine.

"Yup." He pushed a large hunk of corn bread in his mouth so he wouldn't have to keep making small talk and Rachel kicked him under the table.

Once everyone had finished dinner, Aunt Lynn and Uncle Jake stood up on the benches on the first table.

"Jake and I would like to welcome all our new staff members to the ranch. For those of you returning, welcome back. We missed you! Now I'd like y'all to each stand up, introduce yourself and say where you're from, what you'll be doing here, and maybe tell us what you expect from your summer at the Rocking Z."

Colby groaned and wished he'd had the forethought to grab some beer before he came out to dinner. He glanced toward the kitchen door, wondering if he could get past Aunt Lynn without being noticed. She called on the first person sitting on the other side of the backyard, and Colby got up slowly and hunkered down as he made his way to the kitchen, hoping she wouldn't notice. It wasn't dark yet, and Aunt Lynn had an eagle eye.

"Colby, why don't you go next?" She'd caught him, and he straightened up and touched the brim of his hat and meekly went back to his seat.

Katrina squeezed his elbow when he sat down again. "You are a sneaky devil, aren't ya?"

"Not near sneaky enough." He stood up. "I'm Colby Zane and I—"

He didn't get further than that because a commotion of honking coming from the front of the house interrupted him.

"That'll be Marcus," Alicia said. She and Rachel stood. "Let's make sure the chef made it here safe and sound." They went around the side of the house, and Aunt Lynn hopped down off the bench and went after them, first excusing herself to the staff.

Colby figured this was as good a time as any to make his break for it. He was heading toward the kitchen door when Lynn grabbed hold of his elbow and stopped him in his tracks, just a few feet from the promised land of the door.

"Come on and help."

"I'm not part of the kitchen crew. He's your responsibility. I'll go and collect my cowboy, though."

"I s'pose I can't really ask for more'n that." Lynn still had his elbow in a pincer-like grip. "You promise me right now you'll be nice to the chef, or you can cook your own meals the rest of the summer."

He let out a snort until her grip tightened even more. "Okay, yes, ma'am, I'll be nice."

Aunt Lynn nodded and let go. Colby rubbed his smarting elbow as she preceded him around the side of the house to the driveway. He spotted Marcus hopping down from one of the ranch pickups, a powerful dually that could tow a six-horse trailer. At the moment it happened to be towing a craptastic little hatchback of indeterminate make and model. One of those things with fake wood paneling on the side. It had to be near as old as Colby, and probably older than Marcus.

Marcus went around in front of truck and the passenger door opened. Colby felt a spark of momentary curiosity about this legendary chef his aunt had been talking about since they left Aspen. He'd grown to the size of Paul Bunyan, at least in Colby's imagination. And Colby was pretty sure this guy was going to be his least favorite person on the whole ranch, behind even the clingy, braless Katrina.

The chef put one foot down on the running board, still a couple of feet from ground level. Fancy brand-new boots were all Colby could see. Guy had probably never been on a ranch or near a cow in his entire life.

But the boots looked familiar. By then the guy had dropped down to the ground and Colby saw only his ass in perfectly fitted denim jeans. He had that going for him at least: a nice tight, curvy ass that Colby wouldn't mind staring at all summer.

Then the guy came around from behind the door. He was rushed by Lynn and her daughters and it was a minute before Colby got a good look at him.

There, ten feet away on Colby's own ranch, was his lost urban cowboy.

This might not be the worst fucking idea after all.

RILEY STEPPED out of the cab of Marcus's truck feeling like an absolute fool. It had been embarrassing enough to get stuck in a blizzard at the top of the pass in the first place. Calling Lynn had taken bravery he hadn't known he had, but he needed to explain why he'd be late. Then showing up with his disabled vehicle in tow while everyone on the whole ranch watched his arrival was absolutely mortifying, but Lynn and her daughters gave him an unexpectedly warm welcome.

As soon as they moved back to let him breathe, Riley had the wind knocked right out of him again, only a dozen times worse.

There, a few feet away stood the plaid cowboy.

And didn't he look exactly like dessert in his dusty boots, worn jeans, and light chaps that only emphasized how well he filled out said jeans. The only problem was the scowl on his face, but as soon as their gazes met, Colby's lips curved up in a slight smile. His eyes flashed immediate—and intimate—recognition.

It took all of Riley's willpower not to throw himself into Colby's arms and dive down his throat. He wanted strong arms around him and soft lips pressed to his, while hard flesh....

"Riley? You must be worn out. Come on and get some dinner, and something to drink." Lynn was talking, hooking her arm right through his and walking him right past Colby, who followed their progress with a wide-eyed gaze, mouth a thin, pale line bisecting his face.

"Yeah. That sounds great." Riley glanced over his shoulder, but the two daughters had fallen in behind him and blocked his view of Colby. "I'm parched."

"You're just in time. We're having a little welcome and orientation dinner out back. You take a few minutes to wash up inside, then come out back."

Riley glanced back before he entered the house, but Colby was gone. They hadn't bothered to introduce Riley to him. Did that mean he was just a hired hand? Riley didn't know whether Colby was out here on the ranch, so it was probably a good thing he hadn't flung himself into Colby's arms or done anything super gay or potentially dangerous like that.

But the spark of recognition warmed Riley's insides, and he hoped Colby would find a way to talk to him soon. Tonight.

After a much-needed pit stop, Riley walked through the house, barely noticing a thing about it, not even the kitchen, and stepped out into a large flat grassy yard covered with picnic tables seating a few dozen people. Large serving dishes still emitted luscious aromas, and Riley realized how long it had been since he'd eaten a real meal—the Power Bar and bag of stale peanuts Marcus found in the truck's glove compartment didn't count.

"Come on and set yourself down and eat." This was Rachel. She put him next to a slim young woman in a lacy sleeveless top and no bra, then handed him a plate and started heaping food on it.

At one end of the set of tables, a man Riley recognized from the ranch's web site as Jake Hansley, Lynn's husband and Rocking Z's owner, stood on a bench addressing the group.

"Okay, last table, then we'll get to our late arrival."

Two people stood up and shuffled nervously and glanced at each other a few times as they introduced themselves, then Jake called out, "Our brand new Parisian chef has just arrived!"

A round of applause went up around the yard, and a few people clinked silverware on glasses.

"Riley, I'm Jake Hansley. How 'bout you tell the rest of the staff all about yourself and how you found yourself here on the Rocking Z?"

All heads turned to stare at Riley, and he felt more self-conscious than he had in years. He stood up and smiled, letting his gaze sweep the tables, but the one face he hoped to see wasn't there. With that knowledge, Riley suddenly felt like a balloon that had all the air let out of it: kind of flat, deflated. A chill gust passed him, and he wondered if that was real weather or just disappointment. He shook off the flurry of emotion and nodded.

"Hi, everyone. I tend to avoid making grand entrances unless I'm serving up something incredible, and I promise to do that as often as possible." Laughter bubbled through the yard and smiles appeared on faces, bolstering Riley's flagging mood, save for the one voice that announced "He's not French!"

"I'm Riley Emerson and I have two degrees from Le Cordon Bleu in Paris." He consciously stopped himself from saying "Core-don Bloo," but he grinned as he thought of Lynn's excitement. "I did both the regular cooking program and the pastry program, so I can probably cook just about anything you can't pronounce. I'm looking forward to the chance to prepare some more down-to-earth dishes here for the staff and the guests. That's pretty much how I ended up here—looking for a little bit of adventure. I can't wait to meet my new crew and start trying out a few new recipes. I'm counting on you to be our taste testers."

That last line got everyone clapping, hooting, and hollering, and Riley nodded again and decided to stop talking. He sat back down, face warm and heart racing like a Metro train as adrenaline washed over him.

"You take your time finishing dinner, then we'll show you to your quarters. We can save the kitchen tour till the morning if you're tired." Lynn said.

"No, I'd like to take a look tonight, and meet my crew so we'll be ready for breakfast tomorrow morning."

"All right, son. I like that kind of enthusiasm!" She clamped a hand on his back much harder than he was expecting, and he dropped his fork. "Sorry 'bout that. Just leave it. We'll get it when we clean up."

Riley thanked her and dug into the beef stew with a clean fork from a plastic cup on the table. The stew was a bit salty, but the beef was tender and flavorful. If this was beef from their cattle, it would be a pleasure cooking here this summer. He had plenty of ideas to punch up the traditional dishes, and his brain immediately started analyzing the beef stew as he chewed. A bit of wine would be a nice touch. Some fresh herbs. Edamame instead of peas? He'd give that a try. Then he took a bite of corn bread, and more ideas flashed across his brain. He washed everything down with fresh-made lemonade that was a bit too sweet for his taste.

Well, Rome wasn't built in a day.

COLBY WATCHED his aunt and cousins herd Riley into the house and took the first opportunity to go upstairs and into a nice hot—make that cold—shower.

"Boss, what should I do with the chef's bags and things?" Marcus asked before Colby had made it ten feet. "And his car?"

"Luggage?" Colby's first thought was to leave everything here in the middle of the driveway, rather than have his foreman do the new chef's work. Then he remembered it was Riley. Plus there was his aunt's admonition to be nice. She needn't ask twice. "Put the luggage in whichever room Lynn assigned him."

Marcus blinked at Colby a few times before nodding. "Whatever you say."

Colby realized he'd made such a complete about face regarding this new chef, whom he'd complained about until the moment he arrived, that even Marcus noticed the difference. He couldn't be seen to be too nice to the guy in front of the staff. And Colby shouldn't be expecting his people to treat Riley special, even if Colby wanted to.

"But just unhook the car and leave it in the driveway, but out of the way. What's wrong with it anyway?"

"Busted hose on account of the altitude, I think. Shouldn't be too hard to fix, but it was faster just to tow it down the mountain before it got any colder."

Colby nodded. "Fine. Jake can help him sort it out tomorrow. Thanks for your help. You make sure and get yourself dinner and then relax. We'll go over tomorrow's plans over breakfast."

Marcus stared like he'd seen a three-headed calf doing a square dance, and Colby realized he'd been too damn nice again. Was the Riley effect good or bad? He'd figure it out later. First, he needed to clean up; then he'd find a way to have a private chat with Riley.

Colby went in through the front door and took the stairs three at a time up to the third-floor bathroom. He peeled off every stitch of dirty, sweaty, stinky clothing while the shower got good and hot. Usually he didn't care how he looked or smelled at the end of the day, but he preferred not to give Riley a malodorous welcome. He'd soon see—and smell—the real Colby, but for tonight at least, Colby would make a little extra effort.

If Colby had any say in it, they'd be spending time together. He had to talk to Riley—alone. And the conversation was likely to go better if he looked and smelled his best.

He finished off with a couple of minutes of cold water, for good measure. He turned off the shower and used his hands to squeegee away most of the water from his legs and body before wrapping himself up in a thick, clean towel.

Even though he had a bedroom here in the main house, he usually showered in the ranch hands' bunkhouse right before dinner, and he often slept out there too, especially when he needed an early start. He might be the boss, but he didn't want to give his ranch hands the impression he thought he was better than they were. It was a particular challenge being part of the family. But tonight he was grateful for the nice hot shower, the fancy shower gel, and the privacy.

He scrubbed at his hair and skin with the plush towel, then realized he hadn't brought in any clean clothes. He wrapped the towel around his waist and padded down the hall carrying his boots, which he left outside as he went into his bedroom.

Three large suitcases sat between the bed and the dresser.

What the hell?

He grabbed the bright green tag on the first and spotted Riley's name and an address in Aspen. Why had Marcus put Riley's gear in Colby's bedroom? What did anyone know about him and Riley? Was this some kind of joke?

Then he remembered something Alicia had said that morning at breakfast about the room over the staff kitchen needing some plumbing repair and the chef needing another room for a night or two. Colby told her not to put him in the ranch hands' bunkhouse, and this was probably her way of getting back at him.

He better get dressed and out of here before Alicia, Lynn, or Rachel showed up to give Riley a tour of the house. Colby draped the damp towel on the back of the chair and leaned across the suitcases to find a pair of underwear in the top drawer.

That was when the door opened.

Colby turned to see Riley standing in the doorway, thankfully alone.

"Well, most places leave a mint on your pillow, but I think I like the way they do things out West a whole lot better."

RILEY COULDN'T help admiring Colby's very shapely bare ass as he bent across the suitcases. He shut the door behind him so Alicia and Lynn wouldn't try to follow him in. He stared at a buck-naked Colby standing at the foot of his bed. Colby had a pair of underwear clutched in one hand and used it to cover himself up as he stared back at Riley.

Riley pointed his chin at Colby. "Is that so I can't see how happy you are to see me? Or because you aren't happy to see me?"

"I... uh... I am.... Fuck." Colby let out a noise like a suppressed laugh, or at least Riley hoped it was a laugh. "I'd be glad to see you if I wasn't so surprised." He looked down at himself but didn't let go of the wadded up shorts pressed against his dick.

"Surprised? I'm the one who's surprised. I didn't know you worked here."

"I guess I didn't introduce myself properly. Colby Zane. Z as in Zane."

"Riley Winthrop Emerson." He cringed. Why had he used his full name? "I'm the man with three last names. It beats having three first names and being thought a serial killer." Colby laughed, thankfully not scared off at hearing the well-known Boston Brahmin families Riley sprang from. "But you must have known I was coming."

"Aunt Lynn just kept calling you 'the chef.' She never mentioned your name, at least to me."

"Does everyone call her Aunt Lynn?"

"Pretty much, but she really is my aunt. She's my father's sister."

"Don't take this the wrong way, but I don't really want to be talking about your father while you're standing there naked three feet from me."

"You're still three feet away. Where's the harm?" Colby grinned.

Riley closed the distance. "So why didn't you say anything when I arrived? Does your family know you're gay?"

"Oh, yeah. That's not even an issue. I just didn't get a chance, what with the cousins dragging you into the house. I figured it was my chance to get a shower. Been in the saddle all day and I didn't smell too fresh."

"You cleaned up before you would talk to me?" It was such a simple thing, but it warmed Riley's heart as much as the rest of him. He'd had more than his share of unwelcome arrivals—like finding Denny with Phillip in Aspen. But

Colby, Riley's one-night stand, felt the need to have a shower before even saying hello.

Colby shrugged. God, he was adorable, especially with the little pink blotches on his cheeks.

Riley stepped forward and took a chance. He tugged the underwear out of Colby's hand. "Well, if you're so happy to see me…?"

Colby responded by pulling Riley into his arms so fast and so tightly, he could barely breathe. When Colby's lips pressed against his, Riley opened his mouth and gave Colby his own special hello. They held each other close for a few moments, kissing hungrily, making soft little moans, and it didn't take long before Riley discovered how glad Colby was to see him. And he was just as happy.

He reached down to wrap a hand around Colby's cock, nice and thick and hard, and pressing against Riley's belly.

"Now that's not fair." Colby stepped back half a pace and went for Riley's belt. "Let's even this up."

Riley wasn't about to complain. Only now he wondered how *he* smelled after a day of rising early, getting caught in a snowstorm, and then being rescued and towed. But from the way Colby pulled him close and pressed his mouth against Riley's, he couldn't have smelled too bad at all.

He inhaled the clean, fresh-washed scent of Colby's skin and hair and let himself fall into warm, strong arms. He closed his eyes, opened his lips, and let go.

"Riley?" It was Aunt Lynn calling from the hallway. She knocked once and opened the door without waiting for a response. "Let's give you the cook's tour—literally." She chuckled and Colby stepped back as if struck by lightning as the door opened.

From the corner of his eye, Riley saw Colby grab for his towel. "Yes, Aunt Lynn, just—"

"Now, Colby, didn't I mention Riley was gonna be stayin' in your room?" She let out a good-natured chuckle, showing no embarrassment or concern at catching Colby in a towel. "You won't mind bunking with cowhands a few days, will you?"

"No, ma'am. Just grabbing a few things." He gave Riley a sly wink that Aunt Lynn either didn't catch, or didn't acknowledge.

Riley was ready to get back to grabbing a few things himself, but he couldn't refuse Lynn's offer.

"Sounds good. Sorry to disturb you, Colby."

Riley nodded and followed Aunt Lynn down the hall, with a quick glance back at Colby. At least Colby knew where Riley would be for the next couple of nights. The thought made him smile as he headed down the stairs and out the door.

Chapter Six

RILEY'S FIRST morning at the Rocking Z was easy enough. Aunt Lynn had offered to cook the staff breakfast while Riley got himself settled into the new kitchen facilities in the dining hall, located in a building between the main house and the barn. He was grateful for her assistance. He was used to rising early; it was standard for the pastry chef. Arriving at the kitchen in the dark was nothing new for anyone who baked bread and croissants for a restaurant or patisserie. He should have no trouble having the crew breakfast ready by six every morning.

What hadn't been easy was lying in bed the night before, naked, staring at the ceiling. Riley had showered after his tour with Lynn and was ready and eager for Colby to make his way back to his own bedroom once the coast was clear. Even though the sheets were freshly washed, Riley imagined they still held something of Colby in their scent. He thought about the night they'd spent together in Aspen, eager for a repeat, especially when neither had been drinking.

The memories had Riley hard and ready, but he didn't give in, expecting Colby to make an appearance.

The red numerals on the digital clock mocked his need and loneliness, and at 3:42 a.m. he gave in and jerked off. The next thing he knew it was 6:38 a.m. and pounding on the door awoke him. He snapped up to a sitting position, still brushing hair out of his eyes.

"Yes?"

"Riley, I'll put leftovers from breakfast in the kitchen fridge, but you come on down whenever you like." Aunt Lynn's tone was cheerful and not a rebuke for oversleeping.

"Thanks!" He heard her heavy footsteps making their way down the stairs before his brain was lucid enough to form an actual excuse for sleeping through the alarm. "Fuck." He let himself fall back down on the pillow and stared at the ceiling again. He couldn't afford to get fired the first morning on the job.

Maybe Colby was still downstairs having breakfast. Riley dressed in record time, but by the time he got to the kitchen found only Lynn and Rachel sipping coffee from chipped green mugs with the ranch logo.

"Hope you slept well," Rachel said, standing as he entered the kitchen. "Let me get you some coffee."

All this hospitality overwhelmed him. It was such an alien atmosphere compared to a restaurant, where he really would have been sacked for showing up late the first day. "I can—"

"Nonsense. You don't know your way around just yet." Rachel poured coffee and handed him the mug. It smelled delicious. "Milk and sugar on the table."

Riley sat down and reached for the milk jug.

Lynn grinned and slid it over to him. "It's from our cows. Still warm."

It *was* still warm. The thought creeped Riley out a little, so he decided to have his coffee black this morning.

"I thought I could offer some suggestions for this first week before the guests arrive," Lynn said. She got up and brought a battered hardbound book over to the table. "These are some of our family recipes, and we've been using them for the staff for years. Till now we've served the same food to the guests, but I'm sure you'll want to do things your own way once you get settled in."

Riley slid the book close and began flipping through the pages. It was a scrapbook, with some recipes handwritten, and others on 3x5 cards that were pasted or taped in. Most of the pages were worn and more than a few had food splatters. Old-fashioned biscuits, chicken and dumplings, five kinds of chili, fruit fritters, and so many more. The names sounded homey and comforting. They used few ingredients and looked simple enough.

"Wow, what a great family history these old recipe books can be." Riley wasn't sure he'd make any of them, but he understood the heritage these recipes represented. "Any particular favorites you want me to serve?"

"That's very thoughtful of you," Lynn said with a smile that made her eyes twinkle. "I've always loved the chicken and dumplings, and Jake adores barbecue ribs. I can't make 'em too often, except now he's supposed to be watching his cholesterol, so I only make them for special occasions. Rachel?"

Rachel flipped to a few of her own favorites, but Riley really wanted to know which ones Colby most enjoyed. He couldn't wait to find the perfect dish to feed his new cowboy.

Assuming Colby *was* his new cowboy. Had he just been leading Riley on with that kiss the night before, or was there some other reason Colby hadn't come to tuck Riley in properly? He supposed a lot of it had to do with being in the main house, where Colby's family might catch him slinking around in the hallway. And Colby probably had to get up early. At least Riley would see him at lunch or dinner.

"Riley?" Rachel's voice reminded him he wasn't alone.

"Yes?"

"Here's the head count for lunch and dinner today. I've got all the pantry staples in the dining hall kitchen, so you'll need to let me know what else you're gonna need. We call in the orders on Mondays and Thursdays, and they're delivered the following day. If you need something sooner than that, well, you're outta luck. It's a three- or four-hour round trip to the nearest store, so you can't run out for a special ingredient."

"We make do with a lot of substitutions." Rachel grinned. "Mom's an expert at that."

"I can't ask the neighbors for twenty cups of sugar?" Riley was pleased when they laughed at his feeble joke.

"I'll get you the budget details and leave you alone to plan out the next week's menus, then we'll call in the orders around ten. Will that suit you?"

"Sounds good."

Rachel and Lynn stood up, and Riley started to rise. "No, you finish your coffee and help yourself to anything in the fridge. Rachel's got hiring paperwork to attend to, and Alicia and I have staff training. You don't need to be on our schedule right now. We'll all settle into a new routine in a few days. We're so glad you're here, though." Lynn patted him on the arm and followed Rachel out of the kitchen.

It was barely seven. Riley had three hours to get his menus set. He raced upstairs to grab his recipe book and the new chuck wagon cookbooks he'd gotten in Aspen and settled in for some fun.

WHEN HE met with Lynn he handed her the week's menus.

"I don't need to micro-manage you. I'm sure it's all going to be delicious. Especially if I don't have to cook everything." Lynn chuckled. She glanced at his shopping list and they put together the food orders. She phoned them in to her supplier Ralph Meary, reminding him that Riley would be doing his own orders going forward.

"You'll get to meet him tomorrow when he delivers."

"He drives the truck too?"

"His son, Steve, drives the truck, but Ralph never trusts him to get the orders straight. In truth, Steve's never made a mistake. Ralph just likes to meet the customers and chitchat. It's the best way to get feedback on prices and quality, he says. There's a new supplier working out of Clearwater—that's the nearest town, two hours by car—but he's too cheap. Doesn't have the quality Ralph offers. I'd rather spend a bit more and get what I'm paying for."

"I agree. But I'll be careful to stay in your budget."

"That's all I ask. You'll have a bit extra to spend when the prospective investor comes out during Week Two." She paused, probably spotting Riley's blank face. "We number the weeks. Week One is the first week we have guests. I guess we're in Week Zero now. Anyhow, I'd like you to prepare something really memorable while he's here. We need to pull out all the stops."

"Investor? Are you selling?" Riley felt a twinge in his gut.

"Not really." Lynn shrugged. "We're not selling any land. The idea is for him to buy into half of the guest ranch business. We need capital to make some improvements so we can charge a lot more. Right now the guest side is covering the losses on the stock business."

"Losses?" The twinge became a recurring sharp pain.

"Beef prices have been high lately, but they were low for a long time. The upkeep on a place like this is overwhelming and we couldn't always cover the bills. We've cut the size of the herds to keep expenses down, but the fixed costs are still killing us most months. We've had to make some cost-cutting moves as well as look for new ways to bring in more revenue."

"Same old story." Running a restaurant was pretty similar in regards to high fixed costs, like rent.

"I suppose it is. I suspect we'll end up selling off some land before too long. Unless of course we get the guest ranch to a more exclusive status. This guy, Wellington, says he knows a lot of wealthy folks from the east coast who'll pay dearly for a week or two out on the range, as long as it's fancy." She chuckled. "We're aiming to be the most luxurious cattle ranch in Colorado. Have you ever heard anything so danged ridiculous? Luxurious?"

Riley joined in with her laughter. He could tell she had mixed emotions about the situation, but selling part of the business to rich Easterners must be far preferable to selling off the beloved land. Her family had been here practically since the West had opened up—if the web site was to be believed—and even if that were an exaggeration, he could already see how attached to the land this family was.

COLBY DIRECTED his palomino mare, Twenty-four, along the fence in the eastern pasture. It was over an hour's ride from the main buildings, and he was supposed to meet Marcus here. Ted Green, the neighbor to the west, and owner of Greenland, had called during breakfast to complain that the fence was down and Rocking Z cattle were chomping their way into Greenland's pastures.

Still half a mile away, Colby could see Marcus's truck parked near the spot in question. He was digging postholes but wouldn't be able to finish the job until Colby arrived to herd their cattle back through the fence.

"You took your sweet time!" Marcus shouted as Colby approached.

"You're working too fast." Colby nodded and grinned. He pushed Twenty-four through the fence and started to round up the cattle scattered on the other side. "How many we have in this pasture?" Colby knew to the head where every animal was supposed to be, but he liked testing Marcus and the other ranch hands.

"Two fifty. How many did you pass on your way here?"

"Only seventeen. Plenty of work for me." He touched his heels to his horse's flanks and loped toward the farthest cow he could see, bringing the mare back around to group the cattle into a mass and head them back to Z territory.

He heard a few canine yips as Daisy, one of the herding dogs, raced up to him. She must have come in the truck with Marcus. She was an Australian shepherd and would do at least twice the work of Colby on his horse. Daisy nipped at a few slow-moving cows' heels and ran off into the distance to search for more as Colby got this mass moving through the open fence.

He counted 113 head as they made their way past Marcus.

"Still looking for another hundred and twenty," Colby shouted and Marcus nodded.

"Want me to drive on ahead?"

"You know Green would shoot both of us on sight if we drove across his pasture. The cattle have done enough damage."

"It would almost be worth it, just to see his ugly mug."

"I shouldn't agree with you, but I wouldn't mind seeing that either. Just not today." Colby clicked his tongue and reined his mare after the rest of the roaming cattle.

The Rocking Z and Greenland had been in a land feud for years. Some said it happened when Colby's father wouldn't marry Green's daughter, preventing the two ranches from merging into one behemoth. Aunt Lynn wouldn't confirm or deny the theory. But whatever the cause, Greenwood made life difficult on a regular basis for the Z. Colby fully expected a bill for use of the pasture once they got their stock back home. It was exactly the kind of thing Greenwood would do. Bastard.

Today, the intrusion into the relative calm was that Colby had to leave without breakfast. Jake had handed him a cup of coffee as he relayed Green's complaint, and Colby saddled up and was on the trail before getting to see Riley.

He needed to explain why he hadn't come back the night before—wanting to avoid any chance of running into family outside of Riley's room. Now, Riley might think Colby was actively avoiding him.

Unfortunately, that was life on a ranch. Unpredictable and impossible to schedule.

Daisy had rounded up another twenty head, and Colby brought them over to Z land while she raced around gathering another bunch. Good working dogs like Daisy were worth twice their weight in gold. He'd ask Riley to cook up a special treat for her at dinner. At this rate, it didn't look like they'd be back for lunch.

It took another hour and a half to locate and move the remaining strays. Then Colby and Marcus ate sandwiches and fruit, washed down with water from the cooler Aunt Lynn had packed them as soon as Green had called. They spent another two hours repairing and reinforcing the fencing along the border with Greenland, and then Marcus drove off and Colby rode back to see what fresh disaster awaited him.

RILEY SPENT the morning checking out his new kitchen and meeting his staff. Two of them, Chuck from Georgia and Katrina from Minnesota, knew little more than how to boil water, but made up for it in enthusiasm. Typical summer-job kids. He'd had plenty of them in other restaurants he'd worked. By the end of the summer, one of them might decide he loved the kitchen and would look for another culinary job, but the other would just get through their work as best they could, always thinking of how they'd spend their free time.

The third member of his staff could have been Riley eight years earlier. Willa knew her way around a kitchen, from the ingredients to the tools, and actually knew how to cook. She'd make a great sous chef, organizing the other two in the easiest tasks in the kitchen while Riley handled the difficult dishes.

For the first staff lunch, Riley chose what should have been a fairly foolproof menu of pasta with a creamy sauce containing matchstick carrots, yellow pepper strips, and peas; a four-melon salad; plus some double chocolate-chip cookies and pound cake he could make in his sleep. The pasta was a pretty dish with all those crunchy multi-colored vegetables and it should make an impression. The main dishes had a lot of ingredients that required chopping, a good opportunity for his new team to get used to the workspace, and to him. He walked around behind each of them to watch them as they chopped up fruit and vegetables.

"Katrina, try and get those slices and cubes even. It looks like Picasso chopped this." He pulled out two pieces of honeydew of widely varying sizes. "Watch." He grabbed another piece of fruit and showed her how to slice it first in one direction, then after lining the slices up, the other, to form more uniform cubes.

"Okay." She tried on another piece with similar results. "Why does it matter? Everyone's just going to chew it up."

At one end of the table Willa was busy producing beautiful cubes of watermelon. She glanced up but didn't join the discussion.

Across the table Chuck snickered. "Presentation is as important as taste." He spoke in a high-pitched voice, perhaps his Julia Child impression.

"That's part of it, Chuck," Riley said. "But more importantly, when you're cooking, pieces of similar size take the same time to cook. A big piece like this"—he pointed to one of Katrina's—"would be raw, while this little guy would be dried out or burned."

"But we're not cooking the fruit salad," Katrina said. "Are we? That would be kind of… interesting."

"You think so?" Riley asked, pleased she had an opinion about something new to her. "Maybe we can try that when we have more time."

"Cooked fruit salad?" Chuck made a puking gesture, complete with sound effects. Katrina laughed. Willa ignored him.

"Every chopping job is a chance to practice," Riley said. He was busy chopping onions, fire-roasted tomatoes, mango, chilies, and herbs for the salsas he would have out on the tables at dinner. One would be sweet, with the mango and chili, the other more traditional and savory.

He speed chopped an onion, and Katrina's eyes widened. "I don't expect you to do it that fast, even by the end of the summer. I've had a lot of practice."

"I can do that." Chuck grabbed a piece of honeydew and chopped at it quickly, imitating Riley's technique. "Oh, ow, ah!" He grabbed for the fingers of his left hand, spinning around.

Katrina shrieked as Riley raced around the table to see how much damage Chuck had done. God, he hated blood. At least he knew the first aid kit was freshly stocked. He put one hand on Chuck's shoulder, and Chuck spun back around waving his finger and laughing. "I'm bleeding, but it's just a little cut." He did a decent Dan-Ackroyd-doing-Julia-Child impression from the old *Saturday Night Live* episode, but in fact he hadn't even nicked himself.

"That's funny, Chuck," Riley said, not at all amused. "But don't forget the boy who cried wolf."

"Whatever that means," Chuck said under his breath. Katrina laughed again.

Riley hoped Katrina wasn't dumb enough to fall for Chuck's stupid antics. Had he ever been young enough to find such behavior charming? He hoped not.

But there must be some reason he'd fallen for Denny. In retrospect, maybe it wasn't so different from Chuck and Katrina.

"Done with these watermelons," Willa said. "I left big enough pieces of some rinds so we can assemble the salads in them and just refill as they empty." She pointed to the hollowed-out shells of two medium-sized watermelons. "Then we can give what's left of these to the dairy cows or the compost. No waste." Willa was from California, Berkeley to be precise, and it was evident from nearly everything she'd said that morning.

"Brownnoser," Chuck whispered out of the corner of his mouth.

"Chuck, we can make working in this kitchen fun, or it can be very unpleasant. I can go both ways."

"Both ways, really?" Chuck said with extra smarm, then stopped himself as he saw Katrina frowning. "Oh, sorry. Really." He looked a little shaken, but Riley wasn't about to let him off the hook.

"So, there's plenty of knives in classic TV and films, besides that old SNL gag." Riley waved his chef's knife, then sliced it through the air quickly. "Samurai tailor? That was a good one." He made another imaginary slice in the direction of Chuck's crotch. "And then, the mother of all knife films, *Psycho*." He made stabbing motions and enjoyed the way Chuck got very pale. Then just as quickly, Riley went back to chopping onions.

Chuck kept his head down the rest of the morning, and Katrina didn't seem to find him quite so interesting after that. Her chopping skills improved as she concentrated. "Riley, is this any better?" she asked, seeking his approval.

"Good job, Katrina. Willa, can you assemble the fruit salad? Chuck, get the water for the pasta boiling while I just add some fresh herbs to the sauce." He grabbed a few small spoons and offered each of them a taste."

"Oh, wow, that's good," Katrina said. "Pretty, too. Now I see what you mean. I'll try harder with the chopping."

"It takes a lot of practice to get it perfect. You'll get the hang of it soon and it will be second nature."

All he needed was for the staff to come in; then he'd throw the pasta into the water and have everything ready to serve. He peeked out the kitchen door to see the tables full. But the one face he was most looking forward to wasn't there. Hopefully Colby was just running a little late.

Katrina, Chuck, and Willa proudly served up their creations to the housekeeping staff and the wranglers, as well as the ranch hands and the whole Hansley family: Aunt Lynn, Uncle Jake, and their two daughters. Lunch for about twenty-five people was no sweat for Riley. He was glad to be back in the kitchen, even if he felt like a babysitter. It was only the first day. Chuck would shape up or Colby could retask him to shovel horseshit.

When they put out trays of the pasta in the sauce and the melon salad, Riley was thrilled to hear everyone mention how pretty everything looked. He came out of the kitchen to see if people enjoyed the dishes. He noticed all the pasta and most of the fruit was gone. That was a good sign.

The housekeeping staff was vocal in their praise of lunch, but the ranch hands and the wranglers were too busy eating to talk, even to each other.

"What's next, Riley?" Lynn asked.

"I've got more fruit salad. It's too hot for any heavy desserts, but I've got some fresh-baked cookies and—" He noticed Lynn frowning. It was the first time she hadn't been all smiles and cheer.

"Let's take a look." She stood and hurried toward the kitchen as the ranch hands started grumbling.

"W-what's wrong? I thought everyone liked lunch."

"They did. What they had of it." She stopped and frowned again. "Riley, the ranch hands work real hard. They need a lot of food. Real hearty, stick-to-your-ribs food. Meat and starch. Pasta and fruit salad is like an appetizer to them. Where's the meat?"

"I—uh—didn't make a meat dish."

It didn't take Lynn long to find a solution. "Chuck and Katrina, come with me to the house. We've got leftover beef stew and corn bread. It should be enough for the ranch hands." She turned to Riley. "How about you and Willa slice up some bread and find some rolls in the pantry. Put a basket with bread on each table and some butter. Then dish up the rest of the pasta and fruit to keep 'em occupied till we get back with the stew and heat it up."

Riley just nodded and watched Lynn rush out the door with Chuck and Katrina. Willa headed for the pantry, and he stood in the middle of the kitchen realizing he might be in way over his head here. He didn't have a clue what the staff needed, and now he wasn't sure he knew what the guests would want either.

"Riley, help me get this stuff in the baskets." Willa opened bags of dinner rolls and started slicing loaves of bread.

He snapped out of his fog and helped her. Then they put out the rest of the lunch they'd prepared. By the time that was gone, Lynn and the others had arrived with bowls of stew. Riley brought out platters of cookies and sliced up buttery pound cake. It took only another ten minutes before every plate, bowl, and platter was picked clean and the hands shuffled out of the hall. When Riley went back out it looked like a swarm of locusts had descended and fled after leaving not even a watermelon cube in their wake.

While the kids did the dishes, Lynn sat in the dining room for a chat with Riley.

"Honey, I can tell you're a skilled and thoughtful cook. That'll do us proud when the guests arrive. They'll be pleased with your fancy little touches. As long as you have some real hearty dishes for the kind of appetite the hands have, you'll be a success. Now, let's have another look at what you've got planned."

They went over every menu in detail, including quantities. Lynn suggested some changes, additions and nearly doubled the quantities.

"This isn't a fancy place with big plates and tiny portions. You need to fill in the empty spaces. Once the guests arrive all the staff will be ravenous. Housekeeping's hard work too. What would you like to eat after cleaning up after a bunch of messy folks?"

Riley took notes and swore that he'd never make a mistake like this again.

Now he was glad Colby hadn't seen his massive failure. He still glanced toward the barn and the bunkhouse, expecting Colby to come around the bend and swing into the guest dining room at every crack of twig or rustle from one of the penned animals. But he never did.

The guy has to eat, Riley reasoned after Lynn had left him to help his staff finish the cleanup. Colby would have to turn up for dinner. It's not like he could stop for takeout on the way home.

Fifteen hours ago, Riley had never thought he'd see his plaid cowboy again, and he'd been fine with it. But now he'd found Colby—kissed Colby, or more accurately been kissed by Colby again—Riley couldn't stop thinking about him.

He better make something fantastic for dinner. And lots of it.

BEFORE COLBY even got back to the barn he got a call that a cow had gotten caught in a gate two paddocks away. He met Tommo, one of his ranch hands, there and hopped off Twenty-four to inspect the cow's injuries. Colby tethered her to a fence post with a halter he kept in his saddle pack, and she was calm and well behaved.

"Should we call the vet?" Tommo asked, crouching next to the cow as Colby skimmed his fingers over the gash in her side and the swelling on one leg.

"I'll clean the wound, but it doesn't look too serious. I'd prefer to bring her into Home Paddock to make sure, if she can get there under her own power. If not, then I'll get Marcus to pick her up in the truck and we'll definitely call the vet."

Tommo nodded and helped keep the cow from moving as Colby tended her cuts, which were superficial. She could walk, so they gently herded her in the direction of home. When she developed a slight limp before they arrived, Colby called the vet and arranged a visit for that afternoon. The end result was a hundred-dollar vet bill, but the cow would be fine in a few days.

Colby glanced at his cell phone.

"You got a big appointment or somethin'?" Marcus asked as he walked up to the paddock fence. "You musta checked it five times while we were out collecting cattle this mornin'."

"Naw. Just checking to see where the next emergency will be." In truth, Colby was pleased to find it was five thirty. Dinner was at six fifteen. Plenty of time for a good shower before dinner. He'd missed seeing Riley at breakfast, and as usual never made it back in for lunch, but nothing was going to keep Colby from the dining room tonight.

He made sure his horse was fed and watered, then cleaned and put away his tack before making his way to the bunkhouse. He'd forgotten the guest ranch wranglers were around and had to wait his turn for a shower in one of the three stalls. He made small talk with two new wranglers, Ted from Texas and Brian from Florida, both in their early twenties. Colby had done phone interviews with both men before they had face-to-face interviews and riding demonstrations in Aspen the week before Lynn had hired Riley.

He couldn't wait to see Riley that evening. He'd find plenty of ways to make up for not visiting him the night before. They'd just have to be very quiet. Warmth spread through his lower regions at the thought, and he hoped no one else had noticed.

When his turn arrived, Colby spent a few minutes under cold water, wanting to cool off after a hot, sweaty day and those daydreams about Riley. Then he put on the best pair of boxer briefs he had in the bunkhouse and a clean pair of jeans. He didn't have any nice shirts here, but as long as it was clean, he couldn't ask for more. He slid on his "indoor boots" and made his way toward the dining hall, situated halfway between the barn and the main house. Delicious aromas greeted him even before he arrived.

Uncle Jake was coming down the path from the house as Colby stood outside watching Riley carry a platter piled high with what looked like chicken. He saw Riley glancing at the staff as they lined up for food. "Evenin', Jake. Dinner smells good from here. I can't wait to taste what Lynn's fancy Parisian chef cooked up for us."

Jake shrugged. "Don't have a clue. Tonight it's Lynn's beefy mac casserole for us. Family meeting, remember?"

"Is that tonight?" Colby glanced at Riley and willed him to look toward the gate so Colby could give him a wave, some acknowledgment.

"Nothin' for it but to discuss the situation, I'm afraid. Better to get it over with before any guests start arrivin'."

"I suppose. Let me just grab a plate from in there...."

"Dinner's on the table. Your aunt will be hurt if you bring in something else. C'mon, we'll be late." He touched Colby's elbow.

Colby nodded and gave Riley one last glance before he headed to the house and the unpleasantness that would follow.

THE FAMILY assembled in the large dining room, where Lynn and Alicia hovered around the table, passing platters of food. Colby and Uncle Jake were the last to arrive. Only then did Lynn settle in and help herself to food.

After ten minutes of pleasantries and discussions of the day's problems, Uncle Jake stood. Everyone else stopped talking and gave him their full attention.

"I know it's not a topic anyone wants to discus, but we have to. I've spent a few days going over the books again and the situation's just not improving. We need to make some important decisions."

Colby glanced away, not wanting to meet anyone's gaze. He wished he didn't have to be here. He didn't want any part in the decisions. Let everyone else decide; he'd done more than enough to cause the problems. He didn't trust his judgment in getting out of them.

"Even with beef prices recovering, because of losses already piling up due to the number of stock we lost over the winter, we're facing a serious shortfall this year. If we want to keep going here, something big is going to change." He shuffled from foot to foot and glanced around the table, letting his gaze rest on each person for a painful few seconds. Colby felt the color rise in his face and stared at his plate.

"First let's vote to see if everyone wants to keep the ranch. We could easily sell it to a number of prospective buyers and all walk away very comfortably. Should we sell? Show of hands."

No one raised a hand.

"Who wants to keep going, then?"

Everyone raised a hand.

"Fine. Now the choices: either cut costs or bring in more money, or both. We can sell a portion of pasture land to Green—"

"We can't carve the place up!" Alicia said.

Uncle Jake raised a hand. "Let's save the discussion till I'm done setting out the lay of the land."

"We can sell off some land to Greenland. We can cut some staff. We can take on more paying guests. Or we can get an investor either in the ranch or in the guest operations." Jake paused. "Y'all think about those options for a few minutes, then we'll go around the table and hear your thoughts before we vote."

Colby was relieved that Uncle Jake didn't linger over the causes for the financial situation: Colby's bad decisions over the winter, designed to cut costs.

Thankfully, Uncle Jake started at the other side of the table, with Aunt Lynn.

"Well, none of those choices will be easy, but I'm against selling any land. What happened this year won't happen again. It's a one-time loss. I don't want to make a decision based on that." Gratitude swept over Colby that Lynn hadn't named names. "Selling land can't be undone. All the other options can be reversed."

A chorus of approval sounded around the table, and even Colby joined in.

"As for what I suggest," Lynn continued. "I don't see any problem with taking more guests. But we'd need to build more rooms, so there's an investment required. We could also charge more, now that we can offer some fancier food than I can cook." She grinned as she waved a hand over her beefy mac casserole and the half-eaten plates of food in front of everyone but Colby. He'd cleaned his plate, ravenous after a busy day on the land.

Alicia chuckled. "I admit I snuck in and got a piece of Riley's chicken and some spicy chocolate cake. It was like something you'd get in a fancy Aspen restaurant."

"That explains why no one's eating much tonight." Lynn made a disappointed clucking sound.

"It could also be the topic of discussion," Rachel added as she scooped up some food from her plate, then swallowed a heaped forkful of casserole, clearly trying to humor her mother.

"Alicia, you're next."

"I think that new chef's dishy." Everyone laughed at her unintended pun. She was twenty and still a little boy-crazy. Not that she'd get far with Riley. "And his food's delish. But I don't understand how we can justify his wages when we're underwater. Sorry, Mom." Lynn gave a nonchalant shrug and Alicia continued. "I don't want to sell off anything. I guess having more guests is the best option, but I don't know how we can pay for that."

"Thank you, Alicia. Rachel?"

"Yes, Ms. MBA," Jake said, relieving some of the tension around the table.

"You all know I'm for expanding the guest ranch. I really don't want to sell, but I think it's an option to fund building another set of guest rooms. It would also cut our ranching costs since Colby would have less land to keep up. How much land do we really need to run this place? It's more expensive than ever to have huge herds, and that's just more of a risk, more uncertainty. Something else could go wrong tomorrow or next week and we'd lose another few hundred head. The guest business is more of a steady stream, and if we don't book every room for the season, we also don't have any additional costs at all. Less food and fewer housekeeping and kitchen staff."

Murmurs of assent bubbled around the table.

"But like Mom said, you can't undo selling. I've spent a lot of time away from here, so I'm not as attached to the land and the stock as Mom or Colby, but I know what they think about it. I'd much rather find an investor to fund the expansion, in return for stake in the guest ranch business *only*. We put into the contract that we have the right to repurchase, just in case things don't work out, or our finances improve dramatically." She took a sip of water and carefully wiped her mouth on her napkin before continuing. "As you know I've already contacted a few prospective investors and there's a high level of interest among them. I know we haven't made any final decisions, but Mr. Wellington will be taking a look at the property soon. I think we should wait to see what he has to say before we take a final vote on the matter."

As usual Rachel had a well-prepared and persuasive argument. Colby couldn't fault her ideas or her delivery, as much as he hated the idea of anyone else owning even a portion of anything on the Z.

"Colby, what are your thoughts?" Uncle Jake asked.

Colby's heart threatened to tear a hole in his chest. "I'll be happy going along with anything that doesn't mean selling land, stock, or cutting my staff. We're spread thin enough as it is, which is why we lost so many this winter. I guess I'd go along with the investor if that's the only option."

"Any other comments or responses?" Uncle Jake asked.

"Daddy, what do you think?" Alicia asked.

"I'll keep my thoughts to myself for the time being. As the tie-breaker vote, I don't want to influence anyone else." He grabbed his hat off a peg on the wall. "Cast yer votes." Everyone wrote on the little white cards Lynn handed out, then Uncle Jake collected them.

"I should clear these plates," Lynn said, picking up Uncle Jake's plate, then Colby's.

"Mom, you're dragging out the suspense!" Alicia shouted, but she helped clear the table.

Finally everyone was seated again.

"Let's take a look here." Uncle Jake pulled out the first piece of paper. Colby could tell from the way it was folded it was his. "Investor." He took out the second card. "Sell some land." Colby bit his lip and glanced across the table. Who had voted for that? Well, one vote to sell wasn't the end of the world.

Uncle Jake grabbed the third card. "Sell land."

Colby's gut did flip-flops, and he thought he might be sick. If the fourth vote was to sell, they were sunk. Uncle Jake's vote wouldn't matter against a three-to-one majority. Please let it be investor, Colby prayed silently to whatever god looked down on ranchers and cattlemen.

"Well, we got ourselves a real horse race here," Uncle Jake said, though he looked mighty surprised. He reached for the last card. "Investor."

Colby let himself breathe again. He didn't think Uncle Jake would vote to sell; he'd worked the land as if it was his own. Then again, he hadn't grown up here. He'd married into the land, Lynn's family land. Colby's family. Oh, God, Colby hadn't ever thought it would come to this. He loved this place, loved the land, the stock, the work. It was his only connection to his parents. What if this place got carved up and sold off piece by piece as finances deteriorated? Colby had made an already bad situation worse. This was all his fault. How on earth could he fix it?

Uncle Jake. "Well, I'm the tie-breaker after all. I can see both sides, quite honestly, as much as I love this place. I know some of you are gonna want to slice and dice me, but I'm reserving my vote until we meet Mr. Wellington."

"What?" Colby couldn't rein in his emotions a moment longer.

"Colby, I understand what you're going through. We have to give up something, some part of this place, with either choice. Either our land or our control over part of the business. Both are difficult to accept. I want to see what we're getting into if we work with this investor. And he may not even be interested. I'm not prepared to vote yet. Comments?"

No one else said anything and Colby didn't trust his voice or his temper.

"Fine. Meeting adjourned. Oh, last thing on the agenda. Dessert."

Colby snuck out of the room as everyone else turned their attention to the pie Rachel brought in from the kitchen.

That wasn't the dessert he craved.

Chapter Seven

IT WAS still light out when Riley and his crew finished cleaning up after dinner. A thick crescent of moon looked old and faded in the approaching dusk as he ventured outside the dining hall building.

In one direction the path led to the main house, and in the other, toward the barn and corrals. At least he thought they were corrals. Should he go look for Colby, or would that be too stalkery? A quick stroll couldn't do much harm; he'd just say he was looking around, getting his bearings.

So with some trepidation, Riley went left, toward the horses and cows. That reminded him of the Rocking Z brochure; he hadn't seen any buffalo yet. Where were the buffalo?

As Riley approached the barn, he noticed Marcus, who gave a friendly wave and disappeared inside before Riley could ask if Colby was around. The barn door opened again, startling Riley and making his stomach do unpleasant flips and flops. Several of the ranch hands and wranglers came out, then headed in the direction of the bunkhouse. But Colby wasn't in that group.

Never mind. I'll head in the other direction. No one will know I'm looking for him.

As soon as Riley turned, his mouth dropped open, completely involuntarily. He was facing west and he was treated to the beginnings of the most beautiful sunset he'd ever witnessed. Mesmerized by more shades of pink and gold than he could count, he headed away from the barn and onto a path that led up a slight incline.

From the top he could see out across the lower valley, a brown-and-green patchwork of pastures and croplands, ringed by the Rockies and all under the darkening dome of brilliant blues, fiery reds, glowing pinks, and now regal purples.

During his life, Riley had seen plenty of important paintings—in museums, in the homes of his parents and their friends—but Monet, Turner, and Van Gogh didn't come close to a Colorado summer evening. It just about took his breath away. It certainly chased away memories of all the dumb stuff he might have said or done. He filled his lungs with clean air and turned back to the trail for a moment, hoping no one else would arrive to spoil the moment.

No one was there. All Riley heard was a horse whinnying, a few cows, and some cheerful songbirds, celebrating that they'd made it through another day without becoming a predator's dinner.

Riley had made it through a day too, not unscathed, but still standing.

In the distance, he heard shouts and laughter, probably the staff relaxing at the end of the day. The noise shattered Riley's peace, and he headed back toward the house, walking slowly.

He entered through the kitchen door. The lights were on and there were dishes and platters on the counter, but the downstairs was deserted, perhaps for the first time since he'd arrived. After making his way upstairs, he took a refreshing shower, washing away the cares of the day and getting squeaky clean for what he hoped was Colby's impending arrival.

Back in the bedroom, he finished drying off and looked in the mirror, vowing to get some exercise this summer. He dug around in one of his suitcases for suitable attire for bed. Should he wear something sexy? He didn't want Colby to think he was slutty by wearing some tiny thong, so he tossed that back into the case. All his boxers were boring and might turn Colby off. He had some cute pink trunks that weren't too slutty.

What would Colby like?

The answer was so obvious. Riley smiled and shut the case, then slipped under the sheets wearing nothing at all.

The clean, crisp cotton felt cool against his skin, and he lay on his back. He could see the tail end of the sunset through the window behind his bed. With a sigh he stretched his arms over his head and slowly lowered them.

Today hadn't gone quite as he'd imagined, and he still didn't know what might happen with Colby. But he could count on another beautiful sunset every single day, and that was more than good enough.

COLBY ESCAPED upstairs without attracting notice, or so he hoped. He would have taken the stairs two at a time, but he didn't want to make too much noise. Aunt Lynn would remind him he was sleeping in the bunkhouse with the ranch hands and wranglers until Riley's quarters were ready.

He was out of breath by the third floor, but it was anticipation and not exertion. And a little uncertainty. Would Riley want a repeat of their previous night together, or had Colby misinterpreted his reaction the night before?

His body temperature rose as he recalled their kiss and the way Riley's erection felt against his thigh. Colby felt himself hardening at the memory, and he waited a moment on the landing to calm his nerves and his body.

Outside Riley's room, Colby raised his hand to knock, then paused. He counted to three—didn't make it to five—and rapped twice. *Tap-tap.* No answer. He put his ear against the door and listened. Nothing. Absolute silence.

"Riley? It's Colby." He kept his voice low, but from his own experience, anything above a whisper filtered into the room. And out.

Riley wasn't there. Colby's mood deflated along with the remnants of his arousal. He went back downstairs, skirting the dining room to avoid getting roped into a family discussion. A group of summer staff were sitting around a fire pit, talking and laughing. One girl strummed a guitar absently while staring at the guy sitting next to her.

But Riley wasn't part of that group. On his way back to the bunkhouse, Colby noticed the lights still on in the staff kitchen and went inside.

A slender blonde in her twenties was making an inventory of ingredients. She turned and greeted him. "You've missed dinner, but I can get you some leftovers. I'm Willa, by the way."

"Colby Zane." He held out a hand. Willa shook with a firm grip.

"I know. Your uncle introduced you last night at the dinner."

"Right."

She gave him an appraising glance which he didn't return.

"Is Riley still here?"

"Nope. Left right after we finished the dishes. Like a bat out of hell," she added with a pleasant laugh.

Colby nodded. "Thanks." So Riley had some after-dinner plans that didn't include Colby. Served Colby right for not making more of an effort. No matter how legitimate his reasons, he should have found a way to apologize to Riley and arrange a rendezvous of some sort for tonight.

"Should I let him know you were looking for him?" Willa asked. He could see from the little smile playing at her lips she might suspect the nature of his interest in Riley, and he didn't care whether she knew. But he liked the way she didn't make a fuss about it or make a joke.

"That's fine. I'll catch him up at some point." Colby left the kitchen and headed down the path toward the bunkhouse, grateful for the refreshing breeze. The moon was bright, like a giant pearl in the clear sky. Laughter and guitar music drifted over from the group of kids, and he felt lonelier than ever.

Usually he loved the quiet of the night, the respite from the busy days that were never long enough to do everything that was required to keep a place like the Rocking Z running properly. His bones ached now that the adrenaline of seeing Riley was gone.

At the bunkhouse door he stopped. He wouldn't make the same mistake he'd already made twice, first at the hotel in Aspen and then last night. Nope. He turned and went back to the main house, stopping in his uncle's office to search for a pen and some paper. He sat down at the old-fashioned mahogany desk that had once been his dad's and his grandfather's.

It took a while for the right words to come; then he penned them and folded the paper.

Pleased with his decision, Colby relaxed for a few minutes in the comfortable chair that squeaked when moved. He'd sat on his granddad's lap, and then on his father's, as they'd done paperwork or written checks.

Would it be his someday? Not just the desk and the chair, but the Z? Would the ranch still be here in ten or twenty years, and would it still belong to his family? He'd lived here since the day he was born right upstairs, and he couldn't imagine living anywhere else on earth. But the financial problems wouldn't simply go away without some pain. The vote tonight had scared him. Two people had voted to sell land. It might start with a corner here or there, but once it started, the next piece would be easier and the next even easier. Where would it stop?

Legally, Colby owned 51 percent of the ranch; he'd inherited his father's stake, and Lynn owned the other 49 percent. His grandfather had considered himself progressive by giving Lynn that much. But Colby had always been more than happy to split the big decisions among the family members who lived and worked here. Not only did it seem fair, but he didn't always trust his own judgment. After the losses of the past winter, he didn't think he deserved anyone else's trust. If the family vote went against him, he could step in and exert his legal rights, so he hoped it didn't come to that. They still needed money, no matter what the final decision would be.

The only solution now would be to make sure that investor was interested enough to plunk down a whole lot of money. As much as the idea of more paying guests annoyed the hell out of Colby, it was the only way to save the ranch he loved.

He'd do whatever he needed to rope in that investor and get him to save the Z.

Anything.

With that resolution, Colby got up and left the room, pausing in the doorway to look back at the desk, picturing himself on his father's lap. Up in his bedroom, he had a photo of himself and his dad sitting at this desk. It was taken a few days before his parents had died, and it was one of his most precious possessions.

Heart heavy and eyes stinging more than he liked to admit, Colby made his way to the third floor and slid the note under his bedroom door.

Chapter Eight

ON THURSDAY Riley woke to roosters crowing directly in his ear. At least it sounded that loud. In fact there was only one rooster in a pen under the window, but he was a loud mofo. Riley stretched and yawned, more refreshed than he'd ever felt in the morning. All the fresh air and sunshine already had a soothing effect on him.

A little too soothing. After a life in big cities, the peace and quiet out here at the Rocking Z was hard to get used to. There was plenty of hustle and bustle, if you counted cowboys and cattle, and the herd of staff that needed to be fed. A little action wouldn't be unwelcome. Colby's face appeared in his imagination and had an effect on his body as well.

If Riley had to fantasize about Colby, that would do for the time being. He slid a hand under the sheets and, reminded he'd gone to bed au natural, wrapped a hand around his morning hard-on. Not the worst way to start the day, though he much preferred having someone else's hand on his cock. A few quick minutes and he splashed his release all over his chest.

He wrapped himself in his robe and had his hand on the doorknob when he spotted the blue notepaper three inches inside the door. He leaned down, letting his robe billow open, and picked it up. He unfolded the note and read:

It's a full moon tonight, would you join me for a moonlight trail ride?

It wasn't signed, but it had to be from Colby. Or was it from that tall, sexy wrangler who had given Riley the look and made a point to introduce himself as Riley served him chicken at dinner? Stan? Stang? That was it: Stang. Short for Mustang. Like a bucking bronco, he'd told Riley with a wink. He was a few years younger than Riley, but that never stopped him before, especially given Stang's bold move. Riley shook away the thought. No, the note was from Colby. Wrangler Stang didn't know Riley was sleeping in the house.

Now Riley couldn't get to the kitchen fast enough. He was ready to forgo the shower when he remembered he had spunk all over himself. He dashed into the bathroom for the fastest shower in the West and got dressed in his checked chef's pants and white jacket. He had a few other colored jackets, and it made life simple not to stress over what to wear. He'd save real clothes for later, when he dressed for his romantic trail ride with Colby.

Riley was the first in the kitchen and had the coffee brewing when Willa and Katrina arrived, far too cheerful for six in the freaking morning. A glance at the clock made Riley wonder if he'd made the right decision. Back in Paris, more often than not he was just coming home this time of day.

Chuck shuffled in two minutes later, apologizing with fear-filled eyes. Riley wondered what prompted that response, then realized he had that big chef's knife in his hand as he chopped herbs for the egg dish.

They'd finished prep work and Riley and Willa were making omelets when the screen door squeaked open and Colby came in, hair damp from an early-morning shower. His boots were clean and shiny and his jeans were deliciously well fitting. Riley forgot to breathe.

"Morning. Is it too early to grab a cup of coffee?" Colby asked, eyes on Riley as he spoke.

"Not too early at all!" Katrina dropped the knife she had been using to chop fruit and turned toward the coffee machine.

"Katrina, let me show you how to make an omelet," Willa said, stopping Katrina in her tracks.

Katrina glanced at Colby, then at Riley, eyes begging him to let her get the coffee. Riley grinned at Willa's accurate perception of the situation.

"Katrina, I'll get the coffee. Watch Willa and learn a new technique."

"Okay," she replied, but her smile had washed away like footprints on the beach.

Colby's grin brightened the room as he nodded to Riley when Riley handed him a steaming mug of black coffee. "Milk, sugar?"

"No, sugar, I take it black." Colby sipped at the hot liquid with a completely straight face, but Riley had to stifle a laugh. Wouldn't do to be seen flirting with the boss while his staff were watching.

"Let's go sit in the dining hall?" Riley suggested as he put lots of milk in his coffee. He craved a real cafe au lait but didn't have time to steam milk for himself. When the guests arrived, they'd start preparing a limited range of coffee drinks. Guests might want an "authentic" ranch experience, but it had to start with the right coffee in the morning, Lynn had warned him. Riley understood completely.

"What time is moonlight?" Riley asked, unable to restrain himself. There were a thousand other things to talk about, a hundred things Riley wanted to say, to explain. Why had his brain gone right there?

Colby gave him a blank stare and Riley's heart stopped. "Moonlight?"

Shit, it hadn't been from Colby. Riley sipped coffee and scalded his tongue. "Uh. Ah. Ow."

"Nine o'clock work for you?" Colby asked, raising an eyebrow.

"You tease!" Riley lightly slapped Colby's arm. "When did you stop by?"

Colby put his mug down and leaned back in his seat. "Nine fifteen maybe."

"I was dead asleep by then. I think I'm out of practice getting up so early."

Colby nodded. "I hope you can stay awake tonight. Maybe you should try to fit in an afternoon nap between lunch and dinner."

"Fat chance. We'll be busy all afternoon."

"Do you need another person in here to help? I can talk to Rachel."

"Thanks, but we'll be fine after everyone settles in to the routine. Me included. These three are good workers, and once they know what they're supposed to do, they'll get faster and it won't take so long. We'll be working like a well-oiled machine by the time the first guests arrive next week."

"Fine. Just let me know."

"My hero. Again."

Colby touched the brim of his hat and grinned.

Riley forgot to breathe again. How nice to have someone interested in him after Denny's betrayal made him doubt himself. But did Colby want anything more than a "riding partner"? It didn't matter, at least not yet. Why couldn't Riley simply enjoy whatever there was between them? He deserved amazing sex from a sizzling hot cowboy, didn't he?

This was going to be a wonderful summer.

THE DAY dragged for Colby after he finished breakfast and headed for the barn to get Twenty-four. The wranglers had groomed and saddled her so she was ready and waiting. Colby was used to doing this himself, so he checked over the tack to make sure she had the correct gear.

"Looks like they took good care of you," he said, running his fingers across the smooth line of her shoulder. Her golden coat gleamed in the early morning light, making it clear how she got her name. "I could sure get used to someone getting you ready every morning."

The horse nickered and bobbed her head. Even if she didn't understand the words, she liked the soothing tone of his voice.

"Don't you worry, I won't stop taking care of you." He would make sure to clean her up at the end of the day and give her a treat.

He went to the barn office for the morning meeting with the hands to discuss the day's tasks. The four men who worked on the ranching side of the business—reporting to Colby—were already waiting, still sipping mugs of coffee.

"Mornin', boys. Any disasters yet?"

A chorus of replies echoed around the small room.

"We need to worm the stock this week. We'll rotate in the stock from each paddock. Two teams. One to round up the cattle into Corral One the other to dose them and transfer them into Corral Two." He would take Tommo and Daisy for the round up, while Marcus, Kit, and Texas handled the worming procedure.

"Marcus, you and your team will help round up until we have the first fifty corralled, then you'll stay and work on those as my team brings them in and takes them back out again."

"Sure thing."

He had a system of rotating cattle among the several pastures, always leaving some areas unused so the grass would grow back. He'd take stock from one pasture and return them to a different location. That also assured no cattle would get missed or get two doses of the worming medicine.

Colby and his team shuttled cattle into the corral all morning. They only took thirty to forty head on each round to avoid overcrowding in the corrals, so it was a drawn-out process. By eleven it felt like he'd made a hundred trips, and the sun was hitting its strength. He was sweaty and nearly out of water.

"Break for lunch, men," he said once the corral gate had been closed after the last cow in this bunch.

"All right!" No arguments from his team. They quickly tethered their horses in the shade, loosened the girths, and left them with feed and water.

Marcus also gave his crew a break and they took turns washing up in the bunkhouse bathroom before shuffling over to the dining hall in a dusty pack.

Outside the hall Colby waited, letting his crew enter first. He wanted to calm his nerves. Why did the prospect of seeing Riley get him going like a teenaged girl? All Riley had to do was smile, and Colby's engine was racing. That wasn't a good thing. Well, it was, only not when he was around his crew.

He opened the door and his mouth watered at the amazing smells mingling inside. Platters piled high with quesadillas made with colored tortillas sat on the table at one end of the room, and the aroma of grilled burgers and toasted buns filled the air. Riley had made some thin-cut french fries, sprinkled with a bunch of herbs and spices so tasty no one slathered them in ketchup. For dessert, two kinds of cobbler, with crispy pastry atop fresh, sweet fruit. Riley and his staff sat at a table nearby, ready to refill anything. Lunch was always buffet style, even when the guests were here.

Riley's back was to Colby, but he turned as Colby neared the buffet, gifting him with a bright, wide smile. Colby smiled back and nodded. It wouldn't do to be too friendly in front of the staff, at least not yet. He and Riley needed to discuss how to handle things. They'd get a chance to talk that night. For the time being, they could be friendly to each other in public, with just enough heat in their gazes to warm Colby's mood and make him wish it was tonight already.

Lunch break raced by like a Derby winner, and Colby had to be content with a few quick sexy glances from Riley. He gathered his crew, mounted his horse, and headed back to work, counting down the hours until dinnertime, when he'd share another secret smile with Riley. Funny little butterflies in his stomach kept him company all afternoon, and he wondered why Riley affected him this way.

Whoa, he told himself. Don't get ahead of yourself here. He'd spent a couple of hours all told with the guy, not counting the time they were asleep. But those were good hours.

Strains from that song from *Grease* ran through his head the rest of the afternoon. "Summer Lovin'…."

Who was he kidding? A summer fling was all he could expect. Not that he'd had one before, but he sure looked forward to it just the same.

AFTER DINNER, Riley couldn't finish cleaning up in the kitchen fast enough. Thankfully, some of the housekeeping staff rotated through dish duty for each meal, so Riley and his crew didn't have to clean up as well as prepare the meals. But Riley wouldn't leave while anyone was working in his kitchen. Instead, he supervised and started prep work on breakfast until the last dish was clean.

Eight fifteen. He still had more than an hour until he was to meet Colby. Plenty of time to get ready. First a shower to wash away any lingering odors of lunch or dinner. As he soaped up, he wondered if Colby was doing the same thing at that moment. Funny that Riley was in Colby's shower just then. Images of naked Colby danced around Riley's brain and his body told him that was a good thing.

He lowered the water temperature when his imagination—not to mention his cock—got a little too active. Was he really looking forward to some casual sex with a hunky cowboy? Damn right. Two weeks ago he never thought he'd be looking to hop in the sack with a near stranger, but after Denny's behavior, this seemed tame. At least Riley wasn't cheating on anyone.

Unless Colby had a lover somewhere else. Maybe he had a girlfriend, and that's why he didn't want to make a big thing about starting up with Riley. He frowned. He really didn't have enough information about what Colby was thinking. Tonight they'd have plenty of time to talk about all of those things.

He turned the shower off and slipped into a nice warm fluffy robe to walk to his room. Colby's room.

He put on his second best pair of underwear, short boxer briefs made of pale blue whisper-thin cotton that didn't leave too much to the imagination about what they covered. It was why he'd bought them in the first place and he was glad to have someone to appreciate them.

Then he slid into dark denim jeans, a turquoise-and-white striped shirt, and the shiny boots he'd bought for Cowboi night in Aspen. Turning around in front of the mirror, he smiled, pleased with his outfit.

It wasn't quite dark outside, but the moon hovered large and ghostly in the late-evening sky. Nearly full, it cast a lovely pale light on everything. As he walked alone, the atmosphere bordered on eerie, until a peal of laughter bubbled up from the direction of the staff quarters.

On his way to meet Colby, Riley stopped in the kitchen, looking for something to bring along on their ride, then changed his mind. Would Colby think he was taking food purchased for the staff and guests for personal use? Not a good way to start this job. Next time he ordered supplies, he'd add a small order for himself, since he didn't know when he'd get into town to do any of his own shopping. His car was still out of commission.

Back on the path toward the barn, Riley passed several horses penned in a large corral with a six-foot fence—taller than Riley. A dark one watched as he walked by, and out of nowhere another horse trotted up and poked his head through the posts, nuzzling Riley's arm. He jumped three feet in the air, then put a hand to his chest as he caught his breath.

"Just Bandit introducing himself." Colby's voice further startled Riley. "Hey."

"Hey. Bandit?" Riley put out a hand to stroke the horse's velvety muzzle.

"That's not his original name, but he has a knack for sniffing out treats in your pocket or taking a bite of anything you've got in your hand."

Riley yanked his hand off the horse's nose.

"He hasn't taken a whole hand yet, so I think you're okay."

Riley let out a relieved chuckle. "Hi, Bandit." The horse nickered and Colby handed Riley a piece of carrot.

"Go ahead and give that to him."

Riley took the carrot. He had a vague memory that he was supposed to hold it out on a flat palm.

"You spend much time around horses?"

"I had some riding lessons when I was a kid." He recalled the immaculate stable and the snobbery of both the staff and other students. Back home, riding had little to do with horses and more to do with appearances. And winning competitions.

"Looks like you remembered something of how to act around them."

Riley turned to Colby, whose smile stood out brightly despite being partially obscured in murky shadow. That smile warmed Riley's heart and the heat kept going south. For the first time this evening, he took a good long look at Colby, letting himself respond to Colby's proximity, his scent, and the sparks he felt rekindling after their all-too-brief kiss two nights earlier.

"Hey," Riley said, sure he had a gooey look on his face and not caring. Colby made him all melty inside.

"Hey." Colby closed the distance and slid an arm around Riley's waist while moving in for a soft kiss.

Riley's knees threatened to give way and he leaned into Colby. They deepened the kiss and Riley gripped Colby's arm for balance because the world was spinning in the best way.

"Wow."

"We haven't even started yet," Colby said. "You ready for a ride?"

"You've got me a little off balance." Riley bit his lip. Why had he said that? God, he was ruining this already.

"The sentiment's mutual." Colby glanced at the ground. "I like that. You okay to ride?"

"I'm really out of practice. I wasn't sure if you really meant a ride on a horse or just...."

Colby shrugged, a charming little gesture that made him even more adorable. "What other kind of...?" He laughed. "Ah. Well, you showed up. Should I take that as a good sign?"

Now Riley felt embarrassed. "I'm not sure how to answer that."

"Let's just take this one step at a time."

"Sounds good to me."

"I've got an idea. Just a little change of plans." Colby took Riley's hand and led him into the barn. The scent of animals was only slightly countered by the grassy aroma of fresh hay. The barn had high ceilings with a row of stalls along one side, a fenced-in pen at one end, and some rooms—probably offices—at the other end. A few weak bulbs made a feeble attempt to illuminate the space, but the gloom prevailed. Once Riley's eyes got used to the low level of light, he saw horses moving around the stalls.

Colby went into the third one and Riley waited outside while he unsaddled that horse and the one in the next stall. "We'll take Granite instead. He's down at the other end."

Riley peered into the stall as Colby entered and put the bridle on the horse and led him into the aisle. He was big and stocky, and a pretty dark dappled gray. "He's part draft horse, so he's real sturdy." Colby saddled him, checking the girth twice. "Hop up."

"Uh, he's really big."

"Trust me." He pulled out the stirrup while Riley stabbed at it with his left boot, finally getting it in with some help from Colby.

As Riley hoisted himself up, Colby pushed from below, one hand firm on Riley's ass with the right amount of leverage to get him into the saddle without flying off the other side. Damn, he was really far from the ground on this horse. Not that Riley was afraid of heights, but he estimated the chance of falling off as extremely high until he had some practice. Maybe this wasn't such a good idea. Was getting laid worth cracking his head open? Or worse, embarrassing himself?

Riley glanced down at Colby, his sexy plaid cowboy, and decided it was. And it would be so much better than last time because he wouldn't be half-drunk.

"Now, kick your feet out of the stirrups."

Riley followed directions, and Colby swung himself up behind Riley, settling against his back and reaching around to take the reins.

He felt warm and strong and very, very good as he practically cradled Riley and got Granite walking.

EVERY TIME Colby shifted the reins, his arm brushed against Riley's side, and Colby's breath was warm against Riley's right ear. It was perfect. They made their way through the little stand of trees beyond the barn, leaves ghostly in the pale moonlight.

"Where're we going?" Riley asked, though he really didn't care.

"Not too far. Just up to that rise. Can you see it?" Colby pointed but it was too dark to make out anything. "Lovely view."

Riley refrained from mentioning it was dark and there wasn't a view of much.

From the dark a cow mooed suddenly, and Riley gave a start. Colby's arms tightened around him, pulling him close, steadying him against a firm chest and abs. "I guess we're not really alone," Riley said.

"Never alone on a ranch, just out of sight of everyone else."

Riley nodded, swaying with Colby to the horse's slight rocking motion as Granite walked along an invisible trail. He heard only the soft clopping of hooves, Colby's breath, and the buzz of a million insects. The saddle creaked occasionally. Colby didn't speak, and though Riley felt the need to break the silence, he restrained himself. It was nice not talking, just listening, aware of everything around him for the first time since he'd come to the Rocking Z.

"You ready for me to pick up the pace?" Colby's voice was a soft whisper.

"Fine with me."

By some invisible communication, Granite broke into a slow trot. A bouncy trot, but Colby held Riley firmly enough to keep him from bobbing on the smooth, hard surface of the saddle. Another signal encouraged Granite into an easy canter, rocking his passengers.

The wind whistled in Riley's ears and fluttered his hair. He and Colby moved back and forth in an easy rhythm with each stride. Kind of like sex, but intimate in a whole different way. Riley loved it. He felt safe and comfortable in Colby's saddle.

The trail curled uphill and Granite slowed his pace, to Riley's disappointment. He was slightly out of breath from the sheer excitement of the short ride.

"We're almost there. Another few minutes." Colby reined the horse upward toward a rock formation that had been impossible to see from below. As they came around a bend, Riley spotted a campfire.

"Looks like we've got company?"

"Not if I can help it." Colby stopped Granite and slid off. "You can bring your leg around the front and slide down, or put your foot in the stirrup and swing down from there."

"Maybe I'll just slide this time." Riley found it harder than he expected to bring his leg over the pommel and thought he looked like a cheerleader practicing the splits. Finally, he got his legs into the right position and slid down as Colby caught him.

Once he was on the ground, Riley realized the campfire had been set into a fire ring next to a blanket and pillows and a little table. He spotted a bottle of wine and some cupcakes left over from lunch. His heart swelled so much he thought it might burst.

"You set this all up? When?"

"After dinner. I came out here a while ago, set up the fire and everything. I hope it's okay. Not much privacy, and it's too far to go into town for a proper date on a weeknight."

"It's wonderful. Perfect."

Colby smiled, the firelight catching his eyes and making them gold and brown and a little blurry. Maybe it was the smoke, and maybe it was something else.

"Come sit down and have some wine."

"Wow. This was not what I expected at all." Riley sat and let Colby pour him a glass of wine. It was a plastic wine glass, but that didn't matter. Safety first.

"I'm afraid to ask what you were expecting."

Riley sipped wine while he composed a reply.

Colby beat him to it. "I wasn't sure myself, but I decided we should talk first, before, uh… anything else."

So Colby was expecting some action tonight. Riley wasn't sure if he was glad or a little insulted that Colby thought he was that easy. Then he remembered what he was doing when Colby first saw him and figured it was a vast improvement to get a glass of wine and a blanket and not just get bent over a fence—or a cow.

"Talking is good."

"It's a little tricky since you work for my aunt. I don't really know how to handle that."

"Right, I work for your aunt, not the ranch, and not you. That's good."

"Yes, but I don't want anyone to think you're getting special treatment."

"You could sleep with all of them, then I wouldn't be." Riley ventured a laugh.

"I hadn't considered that option." Colby pressed his lips together in thought for a moment. "Naw. I'm not interested in the rest of them."

"I understand. We should just look like friends to everyone else. I'm fine with that." Riley saw Colby's concern about fairness. It was another nice aspect to his character.

"For the time being anyway." Colby sipped at his wine.

"I'll follow your lead on that."

Colby nodded. His gaze bore into Riley, under his skin, examining him in a way he wasn't sure he liked. "How did a pastry chef from Paris end up throwing biscuits on a ranch in Colorado? Seems like most people head in the opposite direction. It's not like you're here for the horses."

Ignoring the little dig about his riding ability, Riley took a deep breath. How should he answer that one? The truth was a good start. If he and Denny had had more truth between them, Riley wouldn't be here on top of a hill in Colorado with the sexiest cowboy he'd seen since the Marlboro man.

"I had a restaurant job lined up in Aspen, but I found out my boyfriend hadn't been missing me that much while I was finishing up my studies in Paris. Walked in on something I'd prefer never to see again." He pursed his lips and focused on controlling his breathing. He didn't want Denny back, but it didn't stop the pain. He drained his glass and put it down on the table.

Colby refilled the glass, and Riley glanced down at the wine shimmering in the moonlight and shivered.

Chapter Nine

A SORT of stricken look came over Riley's face, and Colby had to say something. "That explains a lot. How long were you two together?" That was probably the worst topic to discuss and he cursed himself.

"Couple of years. After it's over, it seems like a lot longer, you know."

"I don't know. Never had an ex-boyfriend. Never had a boyfriend. I'm sorry to hear that happened." Too many dangerous tools within easy reach out here on a ranch. Not that he would resort to violence, but part of him thought Riley's ex could use a good scare.

"I was sorry too, at first, but it's a good thing I found out what he was really like. You know, before I spent another few years with him."

Good for Colby, too, he realized. It wouldn't do to say that. "Still, it must have been nice to have a real relationship, even if it didn't work out in the end."

Riley took a sip of wine. "I am done with relationships in general. Too much effort for too much disappointment. Not again." He raised his glass to Colby. "To the end of relationships!" He took a big gulp of wine and set the glass back on the table, shivering in his shirtsleeves.

"Wind's picked up a bit. You look cold. Lemme put more wood on the fire." Before Colby could get up, Riley was in his lap and kissing him, tasting of wine.

That was one way to change the topic of conversation. Colby pulled Riley in, easing Riley's legs around his waist, their bodies fitting together well, mouths coming together again. Riley pressed in close, already hard, and a shiver went through Colby, but not from the cold.

They wasted no time getting each other out of their clothes, then lay down side by side on the thick blankets Colby was glad he'd put out in advance. Riley clung to him tightly, cock poking up against Colby's abs. Before he had a chance to reach for him, Riley rolled Colby back and knelt between his knees, the tip of his generous cock glistening in the moonlight. Riley leaned down to kiss and suck at Colby's nipples, dripping cock trailing along Colby's leg and abs.

Every touch set Colby's skin on fire, and he could barely get enough air into his straining lungs.

Then Riley moved lower and took Colby's cock into his hot mouth. Sooo good. Riley's tongue soon found all his trigger points, and he was so hard he thought his cock would break off. "Slow down, you're killing me."

Not that Colby was complaining, but he didn't get Riley. A few minutes ago he was all shy smiles and misty-eyed when he'd seen how Colby had put some effort into their date, and now he couldn't wait to get down to business. For Colby, getting here was part of the fun. He liked a little making out, more foreplay, even if the goal was some good, clean fucking.

When Riley said he was done with relationships, he hadn't been kidding. Colby just needed some time to switch gears from moonlight date to fuck first, ask questions later.

He sat up and pulled Riley in close, getting two good handfuls of firm, curvy ass as he licked at Riley's enormous cock. It was as big as he had remembered it, and now he had plenty of time to get to know it better. All summer, in fact.

What a long, hard summer it could be.

He sucked the firm flesh, enjoying Riley's shudders and moans while he raked his fingers through Colby's hair. He played with Riley's balls, enjoying Riley's reactions.

"Now you're killing me."

"You want to come now?"

"Not yet. After. Or with you inside."

"Okay." Colby looked up at Riley, then went back for a few more licks. "I really like sucking you. I want to get you off like this."

"After you."

Colby nodded, mouth too full to speak. Then Riley pushed him away, gently, but Colby got the message. He got up and reached for the backpack he'd brought with the blankets and fished out everything they'd need. Riley took the vial of lube.

"How about using some of this while you're down there?" He grinned and held his cock out for Colby to suck again.

Colby took the lube and knelt down, using one hand to slick Riley's ass while he used the other and his mouth on Riley's cock. As he pushed his fingers in deeper, tremors went through Riley's body all the way to the tip of his cock. Colby was tempted to finish him off like this, but he would wait and do what Riley requested.

When Riley was slick and ready, Colby stood up and let Riley put the condom on him. Their gazes met and Colby wondered whether this was all some kind of dream. He'd never had sex at the ranch. If anyone else here was gay, he didn't know.

"Time for my ride?" Riley asked.

"Oh yeah." Colby sat down on the blankets and expected Riley to settle into his lap. Instead, Riley slid his feet into his boots, those ridiculous shiny black boots that no real cowboy would be caught dead in.

But as Riley walked over, naked and hard, wearing nothing but those boots, Colby didn't think he'd seen anything hotter. He was wrong. Riley walked toward Colby, taking high steps so the boots flashed in the firelight and Riley's dick bounced and swayed. Maybe he would have made a good cowboi at Club Rawhide after all.

The smile on Riley's face told Colby he was enjoying himself, enjoying the way he teased. Then Riley came close and planted his feet outside Colby's thighs. He took one more step so the tip of his cock was just brushing Colby's lips. Pre-come dripped, glistening in the moonlight.

Colby opened his mouth and sucked in the tip, swirling his tongue around as Riley grabbed at the back of Colby's head. He tasted so good and Colby's body shouted that it'd had enough playing around. His cock ached.

Riley stepped back and looked down into Colby's eyes.

"Riders up?"

"'bout time." Colby put his hands on Riley's hips and pulled him down into his lap. It took a bit of shifting around, but once Riley slid down onto Colby's cock, it was all worth it. Riley's tight heat overwhelmed Colby's senses. He thrust up as Riley moved up and down and they found a good rhythm.

Riley had sturdy thighs and good balance. And his ass fit perfectly into Colby's hands as he held on, moving Riley into just the right spot so that all he could think about was his cock sliding in and out of Riley's ass and the little moans Riley made each time he took Colby inside.

Riley wrapped his hands behind Colby's neck for balance and his cock slid up and down Colby's abs. He could barely breathe from excitement and exertion. When everything rose to a crescendo, he pulled Riley's head close and held him still for a deep kiss. He needed to have Riley's mouth on his as he thrust up one final time and let go.

As Colby came, Riley shifted his hips to keep the stimulus going until Colby was pumped dry. Riley kept the kiss going too until Colby had to pull away to breathe.

Riley pressed close against Colby's chest. "I love the way you kiss me. Your mouth drives me crazy." Riley's voice was husky, wanton.

Colby smiled. Riley leaned down so their foreheads touched, both out of breath, panting, sharing the same air. When Colby could speak again, he leaned back so he could see Riley still in his lap, still tight around him.

"Let's see if you're right about that. Stand up." Colby helped him up with both hands under his ass, till Riley again stood straddling Colby's lap, cock still hard. Colby reached for it and took it into his mouth again.

If Riley's groans, or the way he held onto Colby's head, or the intensity of his orgasm were anything to go by, Colby had succeeded.

AFTERWARD, THEY lay on their backs.

Riley watched the stars twinkling above them. "I can't remember the last time I saw so many stars. The city's too bright. I used to know the names of the constellations when I was a kid. We had a place on an island that was so dark at night I was afraid at first. My dad bought me a telescope so I'd be able to see the stars and know where I was."

"Did that help?"

Riley inhaled, trying to recall. "Maybe. At least I had something else to think about. That's my dad for you, into distraction and bait and switch."

"You don't get along?"

"I didn't turn out like he expected."

"You mean gay?"

Riley glanced toward Colby, then back at the sky. "He doesn't care about that. He wanted someone to follow in his footsteps, same college, family business, tradition. His world never interested me." Riley swallowed. He'd sugar coated the situation. "What about your family? Parents, siblings?"

"I'm an only child." There was something heavy in Colby's pause before he continued. "Born and raised on this ranch. Haven't been all that far from home, except when I went away to college. But that was in Fort Collins, a ways north of Denver. Yeah, I guess I am the traditional type." Colby's voice got soft and low.

Riley couldn't imagine staying in one place his whole life. He got bored, needed to try new things, have new adventures. "Your parents got tired of this place?"

"No." The word was a raspy whisper. "They died when I was seven. They were on—" He stopped. "There was a car accident. I wasn't with them."

Sharp pain skewered Riley's heart. Shit. He'd come across like a real bastard, bad-mouthing his father when Colby didn't have a dad around anymore. "I'm really sorry to bring that up."

"It's okay. I don't remember much about them anymore. Except my dad showed me the constellations too. We'd do overnight trail rides and...." He stopped talking, voice creaky around the edges.

Riley rolled onto his side and traced a fingertip along Colby's arm. "Are we staying here overnight?"

"Wouldn't you rather be back in a nice warm bed?"

"Your nice warm bed."

Colby nodded. "I forgot about that. Wouldn't you rather be in my bed?"

"I like how that sounds, but only if you're there too." Riley played with strands of Colby's hair. "It might be warm, but it wouldn't be as nice as this." He leaned forward and kissed the corner of Colby's mouth.

Colby pulled Riley into his arms and they kissed for a while, slow deep kisses that got Riley dizzy again. When they parted, Colby touched a fingertip to one of Riley's peaked nipples.

"Cold? You've got goose bumps too."

"I think those are from you. I like how you kiss, Colby."

"I like how you do everything." Colby wrapped his arms around Riley again.

"Let's stay out a while longer. I'm sure you know how to keep me warm."

"I've got another blanket."

"Not what I had in mind."

Colby grinned and slid his hand along the curve of Riley's ass.

DAWN WAS brightening the sky with golden fingers when Riley woke, tangled with Colby next to the burnt-out campfire. A cool breeze ruffled his hair, and he pulled the blankets around their bodies. The movement woke Colby, who stirred and murmured against Riley's shoulder.

"Morning."

"Morning." Riley rubbed at his eyes and yawned. "Oh, shit, what time is it?"

"Five or so."

"I've got to be in the kitchen by six." Riley threw off the blanket and scrambled to his feet. His cock was half-hard and he noticed Colby's was too. He tried not to stare or think the thoughts that went through his mind. No time for any morning fun.

"It's a quick ride. I'll clean up everything later on. No one comes up here except guests, and only when we bring them."

"I'll help. Come get me at the kitchen?" Riley pulled his boxer briefs on, but his cock still pushed out the thin cotton. He moved to the other side of the flat area and peed over the edge, his back to Colby.

Colby did the same, giving Riley some space, then got dressed and saddled Granite.

"Thanks, Colby. This was really nice." Riley put a hand on Colby's shoulder before he swung himself into the saddle.

"Yeah. It was." Colby slid a hand along Riley's boot, smiling. "Riley, just one thing. These boots are sexy as fuck on you, especially last night. I get dizzy thinking about it. But these aren't the kind you need for riding. They're made for dancing and looking good."

"They're not all that good for dancing. Or walking. They really only seem to be good for fucking." Riley felt his cheeks warming. What had gotten into him? All this fresh air and beautiful mountain scenery seemed to have turned him into a sort of sex maniac. Or maybe it was just Colby.

"Yeah. Well, you hang on to them for that. But I'll find you some good sturdy riding boots, okay?"

"I'd like that."

"Just promise me you'll wear these again?"

Riley liked the lusty way Colby asked. "Promise."

Colby pulled himself up behind Riley and took Granite's reins. They rode in silence for a while, Granite picking his own path home.

"Hey, Colby?" Riley turned around slightly.

His heartbeat accelerated. "Yeah?"

"Could I drive? I'd like to learn how to ride better. I know you're not a wrangler, but...."

He smiled. "Sure. Take the reins and let me see how well you can control him."

Riley took one rein in each hand. He'd been taught English. "We're heading home. It's pretty easy."

"Can you get him to trot?"

Riley clucked to Granite and kicked his sides softly. The horse broke into a trot and Colby held on to Riley so he wouldn't bounce much. It took some thigh muscles to stay in the saddle, not post up and down like riders using an English saddle with shorter stirrups.

Granite slowed to a walk and Riley couldn't get him moving again, so Colby took the reins. "It'll be faster if I 'drive,' but we'll arrange for you to have some instruction. It might have to be with the guest wranglers if I'm really busy."

"That's okay. I don't want to waste your time."

"You couldn't waste my time." Colby planted a kiss on Riley's ear. "I just never know when an emergency will crop up. I wouldn't want to stand you up, or waste *your* time. But speaking of time." He coaxed Granite into a canter and they made it back to the barn in short order, before the sun was fully up. A crowing rooster and the dairy cows greeted them, but all the humans still seemed to be inside.

"The coast is clear. You can get back to the house without anyone knowing you were out."

"Thanks, Colby." Riley turned and kissed Colby, mostly lips with a little flash of tongue. He swung a leg over the horn and slid to the ground. "Hey, I forgot to tell you. The flat over the kitchen should be ready today. I'll be staying there tonight."

Colby nodded.

"How about a housewarming tonight? You'll be my first guest. Unless you'd rather get back to your own bed."

Colby nodded and his eyes had that sexy glint that turned Riley's insides to jelly. "What time?"

Chapter Ten

THE NEXT week flew by at the Z as Riley fine-tuned his menus and coached his staff, who were really starting to shape up.

Riley and Colby fell into their own comfortable routine of Colby coming upstairs to Riley's flat over the kitchen once the barn chores were finished. A few days after their moonlight trail ride, Colby brought a box with him and handed it to Riley.

"What is it?"

"The usual method is to open the box. I'm kind of a traditionalist. Go on. It won't bite."

Riley picked up the box and shook it. "Not a pony, is it?"

"Did you want a pony?"

"Not really." As a kid Riley hadn't, only because he knew his parents bought it for all the wrong reasons. It was only now he understood how someone might become attached to their horse. He knew Colby had a soft spot for Hickory and Twenty-four. "Pierce Brosnan?"

"Did you want Pierce Brosnan?"

Riley raised an eyebrow.

"Okay, dumb question. If I had Pierce Brosnan, I wouldn't be sharing." Colby shook his head. "Just open the damn box!"

Inside was a pair of boots. They weren't new. Riley glanced up.

"If I got you a new pair you wouldn't have them broken in by the end of the summer. These are ready to go. Perfectly broken in."

Riley picked one up. The dark brown leather was soft and supple, smooth beneath his fingertips. It didn't have fancy stitching or a long pointy toe. They looked just like the boots Colby and his ranch hands wore.

"They're an old pair of mine. Might be a bit big. Go on and try 'em on, if you want 'em. I won't be offended if you say no."

Riley had never had a hand-me-down or a used anything in his life, except the crappy car he bought in Aspen. His mother would have palpitations if she knew how excited he was to receive these.

"Of course I want them. Thank you!" He wrapped himself around Colby and kissed him thanks. It was a little while before they got back to the boots.

Riley's feet almost swam in them.

"Try with two pairs of socks. That might be good enough."

It was.

"Will I still be sexy if I'm wearing only these boots?" Riley asked.

Colby leaned back against the couch. "Why don't we find out?"

Riley threw him a roguish look and shed his clothes in nothing flat. Then he stepped into the boots again.

"Oh, yeah. That works for me." Colby got up and put Riley over his shoulder—just like that night they met—then carried him into the bedroom.

Later, as they got dressed Riley asked, "So how can I pay you back for these?"

"I thought that's what you just finished doin'." Colby grinned.

"No. Something else. Maybe I can make some of your favorite dishes?"

Colby looked at Riley for a moment. "You know how to make those peanut butter cookies with the chocolate kisses?"

Riley let out a snort. "Sure. That's not what I meant. Pick something really special."

Colby's lips were pressed thin. "They are special—to me. My mom used to make them."

Riley felt like he'd been speared with a red-hot poker straight through his chest, then stabbed through the eyes with it a few times for good measure. "I can make those for you, sure."

"Thanks. You can fancy 'em up if you want. I'm sure you'd come up with something you think is special."

How could he respond to that? Riley just reached out and held Colby's hand.

"I have to get back to work."

As Riley watched him leave, he knew he wouldn't alter the recipe at all when he made the cookies for Colby.

RILEY WORE his new boots every time he went in the barn or the corrals. Consequently he got in lots of riding with Colby, both kinds.

The first guests were due on Sunday, so everyone got Friday night off. Colby and Riley went into Aspen to spend the night. They didn't stay at the Marriott, but they did go to Club Rawhide after dinner for some dancing and a couple of beers each. Just past midnight Riley thought he saw Denny enter the club, and he fought the urge to plaster himself against Colby and show off his new cowboy. That was immature and not very respectful of Colby. But they did make out on the dance floor during the slow songs.

A little later, when Riley and Colby were leaving, he spotted the guy again. It *was* Denny, and he was with Phillip. They were holding hands, but Riley noticed the way Denny was staring at a tall guy with short blond hair and not paying any attention to Phillip. Now instead of hating Phillip, Riley felt a little sorry for him, and hoped Denny wouldn't just toss him away for the next guy.

He didn't mention the incident to Colby as they walked down the street to their hotel. Once they were in their room, Riley forgot all about Denny and Phillip. Wrapped in Colby's strong arms, he forgot his own name and how to breathe, and that was as close to perfect as he could imagine.

EXCITEMENT BUZZED on Sunday morning as everyone waited for the first guests to arrive that afternoon. Some rented cars at the Denver or Colorado Springs airports and drove themselves, while Lynn sent Marcus in a ranch van to collect another group of guests from a resort in Aspen.

Riley knew Colby had only reluctantly allowed Marcus to make the run to Aspen, even though it should have been his afternoon off. Colby suspected Marcus had another reason for the trip, and he didn't make waves with Lynn.

The first week of summer season was something of a dry run, with only half the usual number of guests, allowing the seasonal staff to get up to speed before welcoming a full house the following week. Riley was glad for the shakedown, akin to the soft opening common with restaurants. He was able to start cooking some more complicated menus and get a sense for what the clientele expected.

By now, Chuck had settled into his kitchen duties, and a mutual respect grew between him and Riley. Willa took on a mentoring role with Katrina and helped keep Chuck in line.

And most evenings, after a long and tiring day, Riley fell into bed, exhausted, only managing to stay awake because Colby was there waiting for him. They chose to keep their nighttime rendezvous from becoming public knowledge. Willa had easily guessed there was more to their relationship than Colby getting a few extra pastries in the morning when she spotted him already sipping coffee in the kitchen as she reported for her shift on three consecutive days.

"She knows how much I love your buns," Colby teased that night, trying to smooth away Riley's concerns. "I don't think it matters if it's just her. She likes you. There's no agenda for her."

"She's too good at everything. I think she's a ringer. Secretly infiltrating my kitchen and looking for ways to do me in so she can have my job."

"Paranoid much?"

"What about Wrangler Stang? I see him making eyes at you when he's shoveling manure in the corral."

Colby shook his head and made a snorting sound. "Yes, very romantic. But you have nothing to worry about. I am not interested in him."

"Just make sure you tell him that."

THE FIRST week went smoothly enough. The few hiccups were taken care of quickly, and the guests seemed to be having a great time. Riley didn't have as much free time for Colby, but they spent what time together they could.

The wranglers kept the guests out of Colby's hair and caused very little strain, yet Colby seemed oddly distracted as the week wore down. Riley wasn't sure if he'd be prying to ask, but he took the chance one night before they went to sleep.

"We're having a big family meeting on Friday night. You know the prospective investor is coming next weekend. We have a lot of things to discuss before he arrives."

"I didn't mean to pry."

"You're not. I'm just not ready to discuss it yet."

"I understand." Riley held Colby's head against his chest and smoothed his hair back. Riley had heard about the money problems, and he'd seen for himself all the things that they kept repairing instead of replacing. It was one of the reasons the ranch hands were so busy. Even in his flat and the kitchen he saw how old and worn some of the equipment and furniture was. A fresh coat of paint and new curtains could only hide so much.

He hoped this investor would solve their problems. He hated to see Colby stressed out.

"MR. WELLINGTON should be arriving on June first, next Sunday." Rachel stood at one end of the dining room and addressed the family at the Friday night meeting.

"Does he have a first name, or are we supposed to call him Mr. Wellington the whole time?" Colby tried to keep the annoyance out of his voice. He reminded himself how important Wellington's visit was.

"I don't actually know his first name," Rachel said. "He signs everything 'B. Fitzgerald Wellington.'"

"What the—" Colby stopped himself just in time.

"He's from Boston or thereabouts. I guess it's some kind of family name. Kind of like yours, Colby."

Colby couldn't argue with that. Colby had been his mother's maiden name. She didn't have any siblings, so he might be the last Colby, just as he was the last Zane. That had never occurred to him until just that moment.

"Mom, I'd like to meet with Riley to go over some ideas I have for menus during Wellington's visit."

"I've already given him a heads up, and he's got everything under control. We're meeting Sunday morning after brunch to finalize the menus and orders, just to make sure we have plenty of time to make changes if we can't get an important ingredient. You should sit in with us."

Colby wondered what Riley planned. He'd ask about it later.

"Is his visit going to mean any extra work for our side of the operations?" Uncle Jake asked, glancing from Rachel to Colby and back again.

"I'll handle whatever it is, just let me know," Colby interjected. He remembered that Uncle Jake's swing vote was, well, still swinging. He'd do what he could to take any extra work off his uncle's plate.

Everyone stared at him.

"What?" he almost bellowed.

"I thought you were against this whole guest ranch thing, and now you're offering to help?"

"I'd rather have a bunch of city slickers running around than watch as the Z is sold off piece by piece to the highest bidder."

"Relax, Colby, we're not selling pieces off." Lynn reached across Alicia to pat Colby's hand. He fought the urge to pull away. He still suspected she was one of the people who voted to sell a parcel to fund the guest ranch expansion.

"That's not entirely clear, based on the last meeting." He made a conscious effort not to growl or sulk, but his emotions were shredded and raw over this topic. Why did no one else feel this way? They'd all grown up here, except for Uncle Jake.

"I think we're all going into Wellington's meeting with an open mind," Uncle Jake said.

"But it's going to depend on him as well. Whether he likes the place, the layout, the family." Rachel added. "Colby, I'm glad to see you're on board for this. I will let you know what you can do."

"Anything you need." Colby was ready to bend over backwards for Wellington's visit.

"See, hon, the sky's not falling." Lynn raised her eyebrows. "You always get upset in advance, and nothing's ever as bad as you think it's gonna be."

Colby decided not to respond.

"Take Riley, for example," Lynn continued. "You complained till you were blue in the face on that issue, but I haven't heard a single word against him since he arrived."

"That's right, Colby," Alicia finally chimed in. "I see you and Riley seem to be getting along just fine."

"What?" Colby calmed himself just in time. What did Alicia know?

"Willa says Riley lets you have samples before they set up breakfast." Alicia winked.

"Sometimes I have to get started before breakfast and…."

"Or Riley's sweet on you." Lynn teased.

Colby was caught between a rock and a hard-on—a hard place. His brain was overloading, and there was no good way out of this. "I admit I was wrong about hiring him. He's a good cook and runs the kitchen just fine. Not that you didn't do a great job, Lynn."

"You don't have to spare my feelings, Colby. I'm thrilled he's here. He's a much better cook than I am, and it frees me up to handle more of the guest ranch duties, so Rachel can focus on the books and on the marketing." Lynn paused. "I'm sorry I mentioned anything about Riley. It was out of place. I'm not sure but I think he's gay, so I—"

Colby was trapped again. "Enough about the chef. Are we done talking about Wellington's visit? Because that's what we came here to discuss, right?"

"That's right," Rachel said. "I'm done."

"Me too," Lynn said. "I'm sorry I mentioned Riley. Even if he's gay, your personal life is none of my business. But I know it's hard for you to meet people out here and—"

"Lynn!" Colby got up and left the room before he said or did anything he couldn't take back.

He kept going until he was outside in the back garden, then stopped before heading to Riley's. He needed a minute to think. Too many things were piling on at once. The pressure of Wellington's visit, hoping he'd offer to invest on favorable enough terms to keep Uncle Jake from voting to sell, then Alicia's big mouth about him and Riley.

Why did he care if his family saw them together? Apparently they'd all be thrilled if he and Riley hooked up.

Only they didn't know what Colby knew about Riley. What was more and more difficult to accept every day: Riley had said he wasn't into relationships, that he just wanted a summer fling. Lynn and Rachel wouldn't get that. They were probably already pairing the two of them up, with the expectations that straight women had: picket fences and happily ever after.

Problem was, Colby was starting to think he might want something like that. He'd never met anyone he could even imagine any kind of future with, but he and Riley fit together in so many different ways. Then again, Riley had traveled the world and lived in Paris and New York. Life on a ranch would soon bore him and he'd move on to his next adventure. Riley had no interest in Colby except to warm his bedroll. Well, there was nothing wrong in Colby enjoying plenty of awesome sex and not even considering more.

If only Colby could make himself accept that.

AN HOUR later, Riley heard Colby's footsteps outside his door and he opened it before Colby even had a chance to knock.

"I take it you're glad to see me?" Colby asked with a lopsided grin.

"Good guess." Riley was wearing sweats and no shirt. He'd gotten out of the shower fifteen minutes earlier and his hair was still dripping onto his shoulders. "Want to see how much?"

"Do I."

Riley pulled Colby in by his collar and started kissing him before the door was shut. Colby kicked at the door and it slammed, but Riley didn't care. No one else was in the kitchen building this late. He'd sent Willa home forty-five minutes earlier when he had finished for the evening.

Colby slipped one hand down the front of Riley's sweats while the other went down the back, squeezing his ass. When Colby leaned down to get the sweats off, Riley grabbed his hat and put it on. Colby backed him into the bedroom, and he stumbled on the sweats still wrapped around one ankle. Colby held him tight, then got him on the bed and yanked the sweats completely off.

"You are glad to see me," Riley said.

Colby replied with a kiss so powerful it would have knocked Riley off his feet if he hadn't been on his back. He helped Colby get his pants down his thighs, then rolled a condom onto him as Colby pushed a slippery finger inside Riley's ass. The urgency of Colby's desire ignited Riley's even more.

"Ready?" Colby asked as he settled Riley's ankles onto his shoulders.

"Oh, yeah."

The words were barely out of Riley's mouth when Colby plunged in, sending ripples of pleasure throughout Riley's body. Above him, Colby kept up a furious pace, fingers digging into the flesh on Riley's hips as he went deeper and harder.

Each thrust rocked Riley's body. He'd never seen Colby like this before. He slowed just enough to shift Riley's legs so he was on his side, plunging in at a new and pleasurable angle. Colby moved Riley easily, kind of like the way he flopped the calves onto their sides out in the corral. Then Riley was on his knees as Colby pounded into him from behind. This felt even better, though Colby's belt buckle kept swinging up and smacking against Riley's thigh. Colby's grunts and gasps only heightened Riley's enjoyment.

A few minutes later Colby came with the intensity of an avalanche. He panted against Riley's back before falling onto the bed. Riley lay on his side facing Colby, who was still wearing his shirt and had his pants somewhere around his thighs.

"God, I needed that," Colby said.

Riley reached out toward the top button on Colby's shirt. "Are you leaving?"

"Not yet."

It wasn't quite the answer Riley wanted, but he finished the rest of the buttons and peeled the shirt off. Colby's chest was still heaving from his exertions. "Let me get your pants off."

"That can wait." Colby wrapped a hand around Riley's cock and gave him a slow, satisfying hand job. Riley shot his load all over his throat and Colby licked it off. "I like your taste," he said. Then he got up, dealt with the condom, and finished undressing.

Riley watched him. His body still hummed from the intensity of their… well, if he had to describe it, it had been fucking. Simply the satisfying of physical urges. There hadn't been anything intimate about the experience. Despite Colby lying next to him, Riley felt a chill sink deep into his bones.

Had something changed? Or had he just imagined that Colby had been more tender and caring before tonight? It would be a mistake to ask. Maybe it was just a result of the meeting Colby had been dreading.

"How was the meeting?" Riley asked. "If you want to talk about it?"

"Not as bad as I expected. The guy's coming June first. I guess you've got plans for something special to wow him?"

Riley nodded. "I've been working on adapting some recipes for outdoor cooking, and on making some of your aunt's recipes a little more elegant. I think it's going to be a good mix of traditional and experimental."

"Experimental?" Colby frowned. "I don't see why you have to mess with something that already works."

They'd had this discussion before, and Riley knew he'd never change Colby's opinion with words. "You can decide after you taste it. Food is better in reality than in theory."

"I suppose."

"What's really worrying you?"

"I told you. This guy. All these changes."

"Rachel and Lynn make it sound like the investor's a good thing. Why don't you agree?"

"Thing is, I do now."

"Why'd you change your mind?"

When Colby didn't reply, Riley dropped the subject, but the silence hurt. Why didn't Colby want to talk about it? Maybe there was some trouble he wouldn't discuss with an employee. He reminded himself he wasn't Colby's friend, or boyfriend, and he couldn't expect special treatment. Colby had been clear from that very first night.

Stupid, Riley told himself. How could he let himself get attached so easily to a sweet smile, some cowboy charm, and a really good lay? He'd told himself he didn't want another relationship, but he found himself falling for Colby, wanting more from Colby than what they'd done tonight. Good sex wasn't enough to build a relationship on. It was how he'd ended up with Denny, and by now Riley should know better. It took more than surface attraction and a few things in common, and he and Colby didn't have anything in common.

Bad idea. Time to step back and not push for anything more from Colby. Just enjoy whatever he was willing to spare, even if it was only a few nights in his arms.

Riley snuggled up to Colby's heat and pressed himself close. He loved the strong, muscular arms around him, and the way his heartbeat synced itself to Colby's so they were like one, bound by one heart. He allowed himself a contented sigh and kissed the soft pale underside of Colby's throat.

"Can't stay over tonight." Colby unwrapped Riley's arms and legs and got out of bed with no explanation in the break from their routine.

In the starlight Riley watched him step into his boxer briefs and pull on his jeans and shirt. The temperature dipped twenty degrees as Colby shut the door behind him and descended the steps silently in his socks.

Riley's heart raced, blood pounding in his ears, a familiar panic taking over. It reminded him of that day in Aspen when he'd arrived at Denny's apartment. Riley got up, tugged a T-shirt and thick sweater over his head, and yanked on a pair of sweats too ugly to wear in front of Colby. Then he got back in bed and pulled the blankets around him, trying to get warm again.

Nothing calmed him. He got up and sat in a chair near the window, arms hugging his knees to chest. He gazed out, and even with the moonlight, the stars were bright in the crystal clear night sky.

He took a deep breath and searched for the familiar patterns he'd sought out as a kid. Out west everything was in a slightly different place but he soon found a few. Andromeda. Pegasus—how appropriate, he thought. Corona Borealis. Pisces. He whispered the names over and over until a weary peace settled over him.

IN HIS own bed, Colby tossed and turned. He didn't get a lick of sleep, and when the rooster started crowing, he pulled his achy body out of bed and under a cool shower to wake up enough to go about his day.

He felt like a real heel for the way he'd treated Riley. Sweet, sexy, caring Riley, who seemed genuinely concerned about Colby's problems. It was hard not to fall for the guy, but Colby wouldn't open up and leave himself vulnerable. He didn't go in for literature, but he thought it was Shakespeare—no, it was some other guy whose name escaped him—who said better to have loved and lost. But Colby didn't see how that could be true. He better stay firmly in the "never loved at all" camp. Much safer there.

He dressed quickly and went downstairs to the kitchen before anyone else in the main house was up. He packed up some bread and cheese and grabbed some fruit from a jade-green glass bowl on the kitchen table. He made sure to take enough to last for breakfast and lunch so he wouldn't need to come back until dinner.

If he could get through another twelve hours without seeing Riley, he might be able to wean himself away from the warmth and affection and that gorgeous smile. It wasn't even the way Riley smelled or tasted or the things he could do with his mouth and hands or that enormous cock of his that had Colby hooked. It was Riley's crooked smile and the way his eyes crinkled when he laughed and that pretty, pale blue ring around the bluest irises he'd ever seen.

Suddenly Colby's appetite was gone, and the last thing he wanted was food. He felt a little sick as he trod the path from house to barn. He saw someone coming out of the dining hall wearing a white apron. From the distance it looked like Riley. Colby stopped dead in his tracks and waited until he realized it was Chuck, and then he continued along the path instead of skulking around the back.

He made it to the barn without seeing Riley and counted it as a win. His crew would arrive after breakfast, so he settled himself at his desk and drew up a list of work assignments as he nibbled on an apple.

Marcus and Tommo arrived twenty minutes later, along with two of the wranglers, who shouted greetings as they headed to the paddock to bring in the horses the guests would ride in the morning session.

"Missed you at breakfast," Marcus said. "Brought you these." He put a small wicker basket covered in a checked napkin on Colby's desk. Daisy got up from the corner and wagged her tail as she sniffed in the direction of the basket.

"I got up early and came to work, then lost track of time." He looked at the basket and then at Marcus.

"Homemade cro-saints." Marcus grinned. He hadn't said the word right but Colby wouldn't correct him.

"Thanks, but no."

"Riley sent them special. Got cheese and bits of bacon in 'em. I had about five of 'em. Delicious."

Shit. Colby had made fun of all the work Riley did making croissants, staying late to roll out the layers of dough and butter, then getting up early to let them rise again before baking. "All for some puffy bready things? Now if they were more substantial, like a whole meal, maybe they'd be worth all that effort," he'd said a few nights earlier.

Goddamn Riley had listened to him, adding in bacon and cheese. He lifted a corner of the napkin and the buttery, bacony aroma filled the small office. Colby's mouth watered, but he held firm to his resolve and put the napkin back without taking one.

"They're still warm. Eat 'em before they cool off."

Colby looked up at Marcus and shot him a deadly stare. "We got work to be doing, not gabbing about muffins."

"Cro-saints."

"Forget the fucking pastry. You got three paddocks to ride the fences. Take Tommo. Here's a list of places I spotted yesterday that need reinforcing." He thrust the sheet of paper at Marcus with all the pent-up anger, fear, and frustration he'd stewed in overnight, then got up and stomped out of the office.

He went out to the sick pens, the area where they kept injured animals until they were healthy enough to put back on the pasture. He examined each one, four head of cattle and two horses, and made notes so he could call the vet with a status update. By the time he was finished, Marcus and Tommo had left to tend fences: their horses were gone.

Kit and Texas were sitting in the office when he got back, waiting for their orders for the day. He gave them assignments and they left.

He called the vet, who would stop in to see the one cow that wasn't healing, and started in on some paperwork. The little basket was still sitting at the end of his desk, and he picked it up and placed it on a file cabinet out of sight. Half an hour later his stomach growled, and he glanced toward the basket.

"Who would it hurt to try one?" he said out loud, the sound of his voice startling him.

Daisy's tail thumped against the floor. She was all for eating them.

"No. I'm stronger than that." Why deny himself? It made no difference in the scheme of things. Riley wouldn't sense Colby's weakness if he didn't see him eat it, right? Colby stood up and grabbed the damned basket and pulled out a pastry. It wasn't warm but the layers were so crisp and flaky a few peeled away as he lifted it out of the basket. He bit off half of it and savored the smoky bacon and sharp cheddar tang. "Oh, yeah. This was the right decision."

"Thought I heard you talkin' to someone." Uncle Jake walked into the room as Colby was finishing off the second croissant.

"Humm? No, just Daisy." Colby wiped flaky evidence off his face with the back of his hand and tried to chew faster. "Nope. All alone here, doing some paperwork and ordering feed for next week." He felt guilty and tossed the last bite to Daisy.

"I had that on my to-do list."

"All done. I got an early start today, and I'm about to head out to check on the calves in Lookout Pasture. The ones we're scheduled to brand next week."

Uncle Jake nodded. "That'll be quite a treat for the guests. Rachel's booked a full house, and charged 'em all extra for the event."

Colby shook his head and counted to three silently so he wouldn't be tempted to complain. The guests were allowed to participate in the easy and safe activities. That extra money was financing more than a few repairs they'd been putting off for far too long. "What'll she think of next? Selling tickets to watch the bulls cover the cows?"

The look on Uncle Jake's face told Colby she might already be planning to do that.

"Well shit fire and save the matches. What's that crazy filly of mine gonna think of next?"

Colby nearly collapsed in a fit of violent laughter.

RILEY DIDN'T catch a glimpse of Colby until dinner, when he arrived in a group with the other ranch hands. Marcus waved at Riley, but Colby's attention was always somewhere else when Riley glanced over at the cowboys' table. He was too busy working to do anything about it, and it wouldn't have been exactly subtle to wander over there just to speak with Colby.

When Riley finally had a free moment, he noticed Colby and his group had already left the dining area. Suddenly he was transported back to junior high. Who liked who, and who was going to tell the object of their affection? Riley was always on the outside of that dilemma because never in a million years would he tell Billy O'Neill he wanted to kiss him behind the bleachers. He ended up having his own first kiss with Pauline Russell, who dragged him back there. If he'd had any doubts, Pushy Pauline convinced him he was gay.

None of that helped with the Colby situation. As he lay alone in bed, staring out the window at the twinkling constellations, Riley realized it was for the best. It was too soon to start something new after Denny, and fooling around with your boss's nephew only complicated the issue.

Sleep wasn't far away that night, after another long, busy day. Riley was thankful this job tired him out so much, or he'd be awake counting cracks in the ceiling the rest of the summer.

The following day was busier than usual. He left the supervision of breakfast and lunch in Willa's capable hands as he focused on dinner. Tonight was the first chuck wagon dinner. The Z had a gorgeous old horse-drawn chuck wagon and he would prepare several dishes out in the open. The guests were treated to a late afternoon trail ride to the dinner spot and then a twilight ride home afterward.

While most of the guests were still enjoying lunch, Riley packed up the chuck wagon, which Marcus had parked outside the kitchen for him. He'd prepared salads and beans in advance and would grill the meat and cook the biscuits and dessert outside. He'd done a few trial runs with traditional dishes from Lynn's family cookbook, and they'd done a staff dinner cooked out of the wagon before the guests arrived.

Willa and two of the housekeeping staff would stay and offer leftovers from previous meals to any guests who didn't want to participate in the chuck wagon dinner. Katrina and Chuck would drive out in a ranch pickup to help Riley with the range dinner.

Once everything was packed up, Riley waited for Jake to hitch up the horses and drive him out to the designated spot.

AT THREE-THIRTY, Colby was rinsing his head off under the sprinkler at the side of the barn when Marcus shouted his name.

"What's up, Marc?"

"You busy?"

Colby used his hands to squeegee water off his head and stood up. Cool rivulets trickled under his shirt. Nice and refreshing. "Just got back from bringing in a few runty calves. What do you need?"

"Jake's not back from town yet, so he asked me to cover his jobs this afternoon, but I'm still checking in the feed shipment. Can you spare an hour or two?"

"Sure thing. What do you need?"

"It's the range dinner tonight, so—"

Colby's brain tuned out the rest of the sentence. Range dinner?

"Colby?"

"Sorry, what?"

"All you need to do is hitch Granite and Greco up to the wagon and drive Riley out to the spot."

Riley? Colby had planned nearly every minute of the past two days to avoid even seeing Riley, and now he was the only one available to drive the chuck wagon out for him?

"I wasn't planning to go."

"Colby, you okay? You don't have to stay out there. Bring Hickory along and you can come right back."

"I don't have time for that. Riley should drive the wagon himself."

"Well, Riley doesn't know how to drive the wagon yet. Might be a good idea to teach him while you're out there." Marcus cocked his head and stared at Colby. "I thought you two were friends, so I didn't think you'd mind."

Best not to draw any more attention to the situation by arguing. "Yeah, just I'm busy too."

"Fine. I'll take him if you finish counting in the feed for me." Marcus handed him a clipboard with a mess of scribbled words and figures. He couldn't read Marcus's handwriting or figure out what he had or hadn't counted. He'd have to start from scratch. Colby looked around and realized he'd assigned everyone else to jobs out on the land.

Colby handed the clipboard back to Marcus. "Fine. You finish this and I'll deal with the chuck wagon. See you later." Colby turned the spigot back on and stuck his head under again to cool off, otherwise his brain might catch fire. He was wet and dirty and probably smelled like a pile of dung.

That should keep Riley away but good.

Chapter Eleven

RILEY CHECKED his watch again, wondering where Jake was. He had everything timed out, and he needed to get the meat started by four thirty or it wouldn't be ready when everyone arrived at six. He hoped Rachel had something planned to entertain the guests until dinner was finished. He paced back and forth by the wagon, staring at the thing yet again.

It was built in 1870, according to Jake, made from heavy painted wood and tin and covered with canvas. It was a sturdy box set on wagon wheels, and inside it held a modern propane-powered refrigerator, a set of grilling equipment, and various pots, pans, and utensils. Chuck and Katrina would bring the plates and flatware and all the beverages in one of the pickups, and set the picnic tables up while he cooked.

He was just pulling his cell phone out of his pocket to call Jake when he spotted a familiar shape turning the corner of the dining hall and coming toward him. Colby's hat was low over his eyes, so Riley couldn't see the expression on his face, but the hunched shoulders and hands balled into fists were enough to guess.

"You ready to go?" Colby tugged at the door rather than looking at Riley. "Got everything locked up tight inside and out?"

"Uh, yeah. Locked up tight."

Colby tested everything anyway. "You got the outfit in there?"

"Oh, crap. The outfit. It's inside." He glanced at Colby. "Do I have to wear it?"

For the first time, Colby threatened to smile, but seemed to catch himself in time. "Yeah. Lynn likes it. Go up and get it while I bring the horses around."

"Okay." Riley went back inside and collected the chuck wagon costume: a vintage jacket, pants, and wide-brimmed hat so battered it looked like an elephant had sat on it. It was too big, and he could barely see with it on. He'd figure something out later. It was hot outside, so he exchanged the chef's pants for cotton shorts. He'd change into the outfit when the guests arrived. When he got back to the wagon, Colby already had the two horses positioned on either side of the center shaft and was hooking up the first one.

"Is that Granite?" Riley asked. It was a gray horse; beyond that Riley couldn't tell the horses apart. The other was big and stocky but pale brown with a cream-colored mane and tail.

"Yeah, it is." Colby's tone was enigmatic. "The other one is Greco."

"Like the artist?"

"Artist? Don't know."

"El Greco? He was Greek, but he had a Spanish name and...." Riley stopped babbling. "You need some help?"

"Yeah. Can you adjust those straps on Granite like I'm doing on Greco?" Colby indicated which ones and Riley copied his motions.

When the horses were secured, Colby climbed up on top of the front of the wagon. Riley looked up at him. It was a long first step, and Colby was much taller than Riley. He put a foot on the step and reached for the seat, several feet higher, to hoist himself up, but with the clothes over one arm he couldn't manage.

"Give me your hand," Colby said as enthusiastically as if offering to cut off his own testicle. He quickly helped Riley into the seat beside him and picked up the reins. The horses set off before Riley had settled in and he tumbled into Colby's lap, face first.

"Jesus, Riley."

He'd been in that position before but never in public. "You could have waited till I was ready."

Instead of replying, Colby grabbed Riley's belt, pulled him up, and put him down on the bench. "Hold on. Once we get out of the Home Paddock it's going to get bumpy. Where're we headed?"

"What?"

"Where's the dinner spot?"

Riley hadn't paid any attention, but he recalled Jake giving Katrina and Chuck a map. "Uh, North something."

"North Paddock?"

"Yeah. Sounds right."

"There's over a hundred head of cattle in that pasture."

"Does that matter?"

"Of course it matters. Either a guest or the stock is going to come to grief if you try and mix them. And they don't take to fire at all." Colby shook his head and stopped the horses. "Could it be North Point?"

"How many cows are over there?"

"They're not cows. Stock or cattle." Colby practically spat the words. "But, none. It's got a good view of the next valley and it's nice and flat."

"Well that sounds like a winner, doesn't it?"

Colby let out an unpleasant grunt. "It'll take an hour to get there."

"Thanks for the warning."

Colby's frown sucked all the energy out of Riley, so for the next twenty minutes they rode along in uncompanionable silence.

"Sh-shortcake!" Colby slapped his thigh.

"What?" Riley cringed wishing he hadn't said anything. Colby was in the kind of mood that frightened him.

"I forgot Hickory."

"We got two horses. How many more do we need?"

"To ride back. I'm not staying for dinner."

"Oh." Riley kept himself from saying "good." Was it only two nights earlier they'd been in each other's arms? What the hell had happened? Why had Colby turned into this monster? Riley had no clue what he'd done to effect this change in Colby. Out here he finally had a chance to be alone with Colby, but he was afraid—literally—to ask.

Twenty minutes later they passed the spot where they'd spent the night on their first date. First and last. Riley bit his lip and pretended his heart wasn't aching. He couldn't forget how sweet Colby had been that night, riding behind him on Granite, holding him close, and how they'd started out fucking, but ended up much more intimate and tender.

The spot was still on the horizon behind them when the wagon hit a rut and the whole thing shifted sending Riley into Colby's lap again. Worse, something inside shifted and crashed as the wagon righted itself.

"What the—?" Colby stopped the horses and hopped down. He hooked the reins on a prong. "You better get down here too."

Riley carefully climbed down, but tumbled the last step and landed at Colby's feet. Colby helped him up ungraciously.

"Something's busted in there." He unlatched the door and opened it cautiously. Nothing came flying out, but when Riley peered in he saw one cabinet had come undone and tubs of marinating meat had come free. An upper cabinet door had also popped open.

"I'll take care of it." Riley pushed Colby out of the way and climbed inside, bending so his head wouldn't hit the low ceiling. Luckily none of the tubs had opened up or broken or there would be a tidal wave of marinade sloshing around on the floor. Colby climbed in behind Riley and together they stowed the tubs of meat, hands and arms and legs bumping as they worked to secure everything in the cramped quarters.

Riley didn't know about Colby, but every time their hands came into contact, the temperature in the little wagon spiked. He couldn't breathe in the cramped, almost airless space. Colby was so close, not exactly smelling like he'd just showered, but arousing all the same. It was torture being so near him again and knowing the body snatchers had turned Colby into a bastard almost overnight.

There was one cabinet still open, and Riley stood up to reach it. He moved too quickly and overbalanced, flailing around for something to stop his fall and taking down a container of flour. It scattered like white rain, all over the counter, the floor, Riley, and Colby, making the smooth surface of the floor slippery. Riley went down again, knocking Colby on his back. He broke Riley's fall perfectly, and now they were face-to-face, Riley spread out over Colby.

Colby stared up and Riley reached for anything to help him get up. He thought Colby might punch him.

He never expected for Colby to put a hand behind his head and pull him down for a deep, hungry kiss.

COLBY WASN'T sure what came over him when he crushed Riley close and took that kiss he'd been fantasizing about practically since he'd seen Riley that afternoon, especially after he'd changed into shorts that showed off his shapely calves. Damn Riley and damn Marcus all to hell for breaking Colby's two days of staying away. One smile from Riley, the way his pretty blue eyes widened when he saw Colby, and Colby was doomed. He wondered how long he could keep up the bastard routine because it hurt like hell to see fear in Riley's eyes.

Colby almost lost it right then and there when Riley landed face down in his lap. It would have been so easy and so enjoyable to thread his fingers through Riley's soft hair and let him unzip Colby and—

Now, Riley lay sprawled on top of Colby, their mouths still pressed together, pouring passion and loneliness into a kiss as mind-blowing as the first one they'd shared up on the ridge not five minutes back on this same trail.

"Colby," Riley gasped the word as he sucked in air. "What...?"

"Later. Later." The last thing Colby wanted was to stop and talk—or think. He wanted Riley bad. Not for himself, but to apologize. "Right now, let me make it up to you." He rolled over so they were facing each other on their sides, still on the flour-covered floor of the old chuck wagon. He pushed Riley's shirt up and kissed his smooth, flat abs. Any doubts about whether Riley was into this flew out the window when Riley shuddered and moaned.

"Mmm. Yeah."

Colby unzipped Riley's shorts, then slid them and his boxers down so he could get some of Riley's cock into his mouth. He liked the way Riley clutched at his hair and lay back, letting Colby do what he wanted. Using hands and mouth, Colby had Riley hard as a rock in no time. Colby's cock was painfully stiff too, had been practically since they'd both come in to the wagon. Ignoring his own desire, he did everything he knew Riley liked, flicking his tongue across the slit, sucking his balls one at a time, and gripping the shaft of his cock tight while taking him in deep so he pressed against the back of Colby's throat.

"Good, Colby. Slow down. Gonna come real soon."

"Okay," Colby said around Riley's huge dick, then he started humming, the way he learned from a guy he'd met at Rawhide, and rubbing the spot just behind Riley's balls.

It worked like magic and Riley made a sweet little whimper and shot his load down Colby's throat, leaving him choking and nearly gagging. He had to concentrate to keep breathing and not embarrass himself.

"God, that was quick and dirty. Really dirty." Riley wiped Colby's face and his hand came away with a fine dusting of flour. "You look good enough to eat. Get your pants down."

"We don't have time. You have the dinner."

"I wish I could just say forget the dinner and do something filthy to you. I missed you so much. What time is it?"

"Almost four thirty."

Riley frowned. "I can take care of you fast."

Colby shook his head. He didn't want it to be like that. Riley deserved more. "Later. Tonight. Can I come by after the dinner's over?" Colby helped Riley get his pants back up. "I owe you an apology and an explanation. A lot's been happening and—"

"Yes. That's fine. Come over later and tell me everything." Riley kissed the top of Colby's head, so forgiving Colby felt like even more of a cad. A quick blowjob was no way to make up for the kind of dick-headed behavior he'd been guilty of the past few days. It wasn't Riley's fault that Colby was a coward and would rather run from a wonderful guy than get his feelings hurt.

"Let's clean up in here and get over to North Point."

"Maybe it was North Paddock after all."

Colby messed Riley's hair up, sending clouds of flour floating around them. "You."

"You sure you can't stay for the dinner?"

Colby had forgotten he'd done everything to avoid the chuck wagon dinner and Riley. "Well—"

"Cause I have a nice piece of meat with your name on it." Riley winked.

"How could I turn that down?"

"You better not or you'll owe me more than a quickie in a chuck wagon."

"I already do."

"Damned right. And I'm going to make sure you pay up."

Colby knew he had a dumb grin on his face. Why did Riley make him so happy one minute and so freaking scared the next?

BY THE time they got to North Point, Katrina and Chuck had arrived in the pickup and had set up the tables and benches and laid out dishes and cutlery on the buffet table. The four of them set up the grills, and Colby helped Riley shape biscuits out of premade dough. It was lucky Riley had brought the dough, because there wasn't enough flour left in the wagon to mix up another batch.

Riley plopped pieces of dough into a variety of containers and let them rise. He would set them onto the grills and hot coals after the meat had grilled, so he could serve piping hot, fresh-baked biscuits. The meat was almost finished when the first riders appeared on the horizon. Daisy raced ahead of them and directly toward Riley and the food.

"You're a smart little thing," Riley said and put out a bowl of fresh, cool water for her.

Rachel and Lynn had ridden out with the guests, but Riley wouldn't let them help. "You hired me so you wouldn't have to do so much work. Take this chance to enjoy dinner for a change."

"Riley, I haven't enjoyed so many dinners in a row until you started working here. I can't believe it took us this long to decide to hire a professional chef." Lynn sipped a Z Cooler, a low-alcohol cocktail Riley had created with a mix of fruit juices, shredded ginger, and some crisp white wine. He had brought a limited supply; Rachel had warned him not to let the guests get drunk because it was dangerous for them and the horses.

When Lynn spotted Colby tending the grills and helping Riley and his crew, she said, "Riley, I don't know how you succeeded in getting Colby anywhere near the guests. Care to share your secret?"

Riley glanced at Colby who gave him a *"Please* don't tell her" look even as he smiled. And Riley didn't, even though he suspected Lynn and Rachel would be pleased to see something develop between them.

Going by the scarcity of leftovers, Riley considered the trail dinner to be a success. Several guests asked for his recipes, and he promised to share them at the end of the visit. He'd suggest to Lynn that they consider compiling a ranch cookbook after the summer. They could give guests a complimentary copy and sell it off the ranch web site or other book distributors to people who couldn't get to the ranch.

After the riders departed, Riley stared at the mess left behind.

"It's going to take hours to clean this up," Colby said.

"Look, why don't you drive the wagon back, and I'll stay here with Katrina and Chuck. We'll collect all the trash and dishes in the truck, then come back in the morning for anything that doesn't fit in tonight." Under his breath he added, "Let yourself in and wait for me if you get back first."

"Hey, Riley?" Katrina jogged up to him. "The truck's kind of a tight fit. You should go with Colby and the wagon. Chuck and I can take back everything we brought out."

"Okay, then." With everyone helping, they loaded the truck and the wagon in no time, then Colby poured all the remaining water and ice on the grills and charcoal pits to make sure there was no chance of fire before he and Riley climbed aboard the wagon.

Katrina and Chuck waved good-bye.

It was dark now, with only the stars and the waning moon to see by.

"Your crew's really shaped up over the past couple of weeks," Colby said.

"They surprised me a little. Katrina didn't know a bulb of garlic from a bulb of fennel and now—"

"I'm not sure I know the difference."

"You didn't get hired to work in the kitchen."

"Good point. But you must be a good teacher."

"Thanks. Willa helped too. She's really sharp. I'm watching my back around her. She may be after my job." Riley chuckled, though there was a grain of truth to it. "With a little training she could run the kitchen. The Z really

doesn't need a Cordon-Bleu-trained chef. Not that I'm not grateful for the job."
Plenty of truth to that. He'd needed the break after Denny, so whatever this thing with Colby turned out to be was a bonus.

"Actually, we just might."

"What do you mean?"

"That's part of what I wanted to tell you about. Now seems as good a time as any. Best to get it all out now."

Riley's stomach did a few warning flips. Colby's comments worried him. He hated mixed signals. Something bad was hanging over them, yet the ranch needed him? He waited for Colby to continue, but the air suddenly had a sharper chill to it and he shivered a little.

"You know I grew up here and this ranch is the only thing I've ever really known. It's everything to me. Everything I ever had or wanted."

"Yes."

"A lot of things happened over the past few years and the ranch is struggling financially. The economics of our kind of ranching just can't compete against the spreads that use ATVs instead of horses, or the ones that feed their stock grain rather than grass. At the moment beef prices are good, but it never lasts long, and costs are constantly rising. We're squeezed so tight we can barely breathe. Rachel's guest ranch has been mopping up the red ink on the ranching side for a few years now."

"What's changed?"

Colby turned and looked at Riley, one eyebrow raised, as if surprised at the question. "This year is one of the worst. We lost almost a quarter of the herd over the winter. It's my fault." His voice faltered and Riley put a hand on his arm but didn't interrupt. "I found a new feed supplier that had lower prices and it turned out he was selling recalled feed lots. Some chemical contamination at the factory, and by the time the vet figured it out, we'd lost quite a few cows and some of the ones who survived lost their calves." Colby's voice got high and tight in his throat and Riley felt the pain in each word of the admission.

"That's rough."

"Not much of a bargain in the end. Well, we'll take a big hit at the sales because we've got fewer to sell, and we've lost the breeding stock as well as the calves. The only way to build up the herd again to a self-sustaining level is to get a capital infusion. Rachel wants to expand the guest ranch and fancy it up. That's why she and Lynn were thrilled to find you."

Riley nodded, wishing Colby would let on that he was a little bit happy about it too.

"There're two ways to get an infusion of capital. Sell off some land or bring in an investor to buy into the business." Colby's tone implied it was like choosing which arm to cut off. Neither was a good option. Riley had learned enough about running a business from his father to understand where Colby's concerns came from.

"I see what you've been dealing with lately. Can I help at all?"

"That guy Wellington is coming next week. It's so important he likes the place and thinks it's a good investment. I can barely think about anything else."

"I'm sure he's not the only potential investor."

"It's not just that. We had a family vote the other day, and it was a tie between selling and bringing in an investor. I can't believe it was that close. I never expected anyone to want to sell off as much as an acre of our land."

Riley couldn't understand it either. He thought this was a solid family business. "Who voted to sell?"

"It was anonymous, but I have an idea. Uncle Jake is the tiebreaker and the land's not in his blood. He's just an in-law here."

"He seems committed to keeping the place running."

"He's older and tired of always making do. I saw brochures for Fiji and Tahiti in the living room. You can't afford vacations in those kind of places when you run a cattle ranch unless you take a lot of shortcuts."

"You think he's going to vote to sell? You mean sell the whole thing?"

"I think someone wants to cash out, unless we can rope in this East Coast moneybags Wellington—or someone like him." Colby shook his head and clicked his tongue to get the horses moving a little more quickly. "The girls and I have equal stakes in the ranch, but majority vote can sell. You don't usually sell a quarter or half of a spread like this. I'd never be able to manage my part on my own. How would we even divide up the land? It would be a disaster."

"I've got lots of tricks up my sleeve to impress Wellington. Don't worry about that. How can I help *you*?" Riley softened his tone and edged closer to Colby. "Will you let me help you forget the stress, even for a few hours?"

"I'd like that. Not sure I deserve that after I pushed you away like that."

"I've only been here a few weeks, but I can see what you love about this place."

"I'm willing to do anything in my power to keep the Z going, intact." Colby paused and inhaled deeply. "Anything."

Riley didn't doubt Colby's determination and wished he knew the right thing to say or do, but he was lost. There was nothing Riley cared about the way Colby loved the Z. Riley had spent his whole life running away from family and tradition. He'd rather sleep on a park bench than go home and do what his father expected.

Not knowing where things stood with Colby only complicated the matter. If Riley was merely a friend with benefits, did he have any right to poke his nose into family business, or to presume Colby even wanted his opinion? Better to play it safe and not say anything unless Colby specifically asked. Colby would resent his meddling if Riley overstepped the boundary. Assuming Colby let Riley know where that boundary lay, and Colby wasn't much of a talker.

As the lights of home came into view, the horses had a little more spring in their step and cold dread filled Riley's gut. He didn't want this reconciliation with Colby to end. He liked having Colby to himself, proof in some small way he mattered. There would be time enough to sort out the past few days.

They rounded the last bend and came through the trees. It looked like every single light was on in the house and back garden, exactly like the night Riley had arrived.

"Was there another party scheduled tonight?" Riley asked. "I don't remember Lynn asking me for anything after the range dinner."

"Not that I know, but I stay out of guest-ranch events as best I can."

"Like tonight?" Riley couldn't keep the smile off his face.

"That was special." Colby's tone softened.

"Yeah, it was." Riley couldn't wait to reciprocate. "You'll come up after you put the horses away? I'll just bring the food into the kitchen."

"Sounds good." Colby stopped the horses behind the kitchen, and he and Riley dismounted from the driver's seat. "I want to see what's going over there. C'mon."

Riley followed Colby along the path that led to the back garden. The whole family was seated at the picnic tables with a bucket of ice and beer bottles and a bottle of wine.

"Oh, Colby, glad you're back!" Rachel stood up and headed for him.

Riley stepped back a pace, into the shadows. "What's this?"

"Colby, we have a surprise! Mr. Wellington's here. He came a few days early."

A tall, slim, and very good-looking man in his midthirties stood up from a picnic bench. He had an immaculately trimmed dark goatee and wore dark jeans and new cowboy boots, and when he saw Colby, he looked like he'd broken the bank in Monte Carlo.

"Good to meet you, Mr. Wellington." Colby put out his hand.

"Hi there, Colby. None of that Mr. Wellington. You call me B.F., or Fitz. Whichever you like." He took Colby's hand and held on while his gaze roved up and down Colby's body like he was breakfast, lunch, and dinner rolled up in one.

Even Riley felt uncomfortable watching him. "My, my, Colby. Rachel never mentioned her hunky cowboy cousin. Shame on her. Lucky day for me."

Mr. B.F. Wellington was as queer as a three-dollar bill.

Chapter Twelve

THE FAMILY and Wellington had little more than perfunctory greetings for Riley, so he wasn't about to stick around. Colby glanced back and smiled as Wellington steered him with a firm grip toward a bench.

After unpacking the chuck wagon, Riley headed upstairs and into the shower. He'd clean up the spilled flour and other mess in the morning, when he could see well enough to do a good job. His hair smelled like smoke, obscuring the scent of Colby after their little encounter before dinner. He went over what Colby had told him on the ride back about the ranch's finances and his fears of the ranch being sold out from under him.

Now Colby was putting all his hopes on Wellington's investment. Lesser of two evils, Riley supposed. For Colby anything was preferable to losing the land he loved. Again, Riley wondered how it felt to love something that fiercely. He'd never loved Denny with a fraction of that intensity. Once, he might have loved Josh Golden like that, but Josh had never let anyone get close to him. Now Riley understood why: Micah Solomon. He was glad Josh and Micah had found each other again.

Could Riley ever have a love that strong?

He rinsed and shut off the water. After towel drying his hair, he wrapped his favorite plush terry robe around himself and went to his fridge. He had a couple of bottles of sparkling water in there and not much else. Lynn had made it clear he was free to take whatever he wanted from the kitchen, but he was down there most of his waking hours and rarely hungry outside mealtimes. But now he wanted something. He just wasn't sure what.

It was past ten. Colby usually arrived by now, knowing he had to wake around five, but he must not be able to get away from the Wellington welcome party. Riley didn't begrudge Colby's priorities. A seasonal chef was pretty low on the totem pole compared to the guy who would save the ranch, no matter how much Colby enjoyed being in Riley's bed. He was glad they'd gotten over their recent problems, and Riley could be patient. He had no claim on Colby.

The reminder made him melancholy, and he opened a bottle of wine and poured a glass. A decent midpriced zin, perfect complement to grilled meats, but he barely tasted it. He only wanted the slight buzz that would relax him and let him get to sleep. He took the glass into the bedroom and peeled off the robe before sliding between the warm handmade quilts.

He woke up with a chill on his back that was soon replaced by warm, naked flesh. Colby. Riley turned his head as Colby spooned up behind him.

"I didn't want to wake you, but I couldn't stay away either." Colby kissed the back of Riley's neck.

"Mmm. That's nice. Keep going."

"Keep talking or keep kissing?"

"Dealer's choice." Riley rolled over and let Colby kiss him into a state of pure desire. It was a little frightening how one kiss or caress could turn him to jelly. So much for talking. Riley welcomed Colby inside and they communicated in an entirely different way until they reached a mutually satisfying conclusion. Not too quick, not too dirty, but just what Riley wanted and needed. They were good together in bed, having learned what the other liked. No more awkward moments or fear of doing the wrong thing at the wrong time.

"Thank you," Colby whispered against Riley's throat before he got out of bed to get a damp cloth. He always thanked Riley, a sweet, unnecessary gesture that never failed to touch Riley's heart no matter how often he heard it.

As they lay together afterward Riley let himself daydream about how easy it would be to get used to this.

Far too easy.

WHEN THE alarm went off at five the next morning, Colby smacked the snooze button and snuggled closer to Riley. He'd missed waking up with Riley the past few days. It was more than the way Riley fit perfectly into his arms and tasted so good, even first thing in the morning. It didn't hurt that Riley was the best lover Colby had ever had, but that wasn't enough. Riley seemed to appreciate Colby for who he was, never tried to change anything or make comments that held a hidden insult like most people with more education and more money. Maybe it was easier to get along when it was temporary. No desire to change the other person when you could simply move on when they stopped giving you what you needed.

Colby hoped Riley wouldn't move on too quickly. He leaned over and kissed Riley, as if that might postpone the inevitable.

The alarm intervened.

"Can you reach the snooze button?" Colby asked. He was under the covers on his way to check out Riley's cock.

Riley shifted and the buzzing stopped. "Colby, I have to get going."

"We have time."

"No, we don't."

Colby sucked the head of Riley's cock into his mouth.

"Oh. Mmm. No. I really don't have time. Please stop."

Colby ignored Riley's request. Riley's hard-on didn't give any indication of wanting Colby to stop.

"I have to redo all the menus now that Wellington showed up early."

"Wewindon?" Hard to pronounce with a fat dick in your mouth.

"Yes...." Riley trembled slightly as Colby slipped a finger into his ass. "You're evil."

Colby pulled off of Riley. "We could finish this in the shower. Save some time?"

"Good thinking."

Under the warm spray, Colby knelt and finished what he'd started, then soaped Riley up one way and down the other. Riley repaid the favor with a soapy hand job until the hot water started to run out.

When they were dry and dressed, Colby grabbed his hat and turned toward the door. He leaned down for a sweet good-bye kiss.

"Don't worry, Colby, I'll do what I can to impress Wellington."

That hadn't been foremost on Colby's mind at that particular moment, but he appreciated Riley's concern. "Sorry your plans got all messed up. But thanks."

"No problem. I know how important this visit is. I won't let you down."

"I never thought you would." Colby went down the steps and took the back exit out of the kitchen so he wouldn't run into Willa.

He couldn't get Riley's worried tone or furrowed brow out of his thoughts as he went to his office to change clothes and check on the animals in the barn and corral before coming back for breakfast.

RILEY WAS a certified culinary genius. If Colby hadn't already seen—and eaten—evidence of this, he would have been shocked and impressed when he arrived for breakfast. In the ninety minutes Colby had been gone, Riley had concocted a feast.

Colby recognized the familiar breakfast components, but it still impressed him that Riley had mixed, matched, and bumped everything up by an order of magnitude. Mini breakfast quiches with croissant crusts, filled with three different mixtures, eggs Benedict made with flaky biscuits rather than muffins, blueberry cinnamon waffles, and tiny breakfast burritos filled with smoked salmon, capers and a lemony sauce. Not that Colby knew a caper from a capon, but Riley had placed little cards in front of each item.

The ranch hands frowned and passed up the fancier items, but the first guests were exclaiming over the newest creations when Lynn and Rachel arrived with Wellington in tow.

"Colby, come and join us for breakfast?" Lynn called as he made his way through the buffet line with a loaded plate of goodies. He looked around but didn't see Riley. Poor guy was probably exhausted already and it wasn't even seven.

"Sure." He plopped another biscuit on his plate and approached the table Rachel had marked "Reserved." She really was going a bit too far. He expected a candlelit dinner—or maybe even lunch.

"Morning, Colby," Wellington said with smile far too bright for this early.

"Settled in okay?" Colby sat down and started in on a fancy quiche with huge chunks of bacon poking through the surface.

"Not exactly."

"Fitz, you sit down. I'll grab a few platters for the table, okay?" Rachel was all smiles.

"Perfect." Wellington chose the seat next to Colby. "Let me just steal one of those?" He reached for a berry-filled pancake-looking thing Colby couldn't name, brushing his hand across Colby's arm as he did so. Wellington popped the morsel into his mouth and made a sound and expression he should have been embarrassed to display at breakfast.

"Guess you're on East Coast time?" Colby fought for small talk topics and silently begged Lynn and Rachel to hurry up with Wellington's food.

"That's only part of it. My neighbors were quite *active* last night." He raised his eyebrows. "Kept me up far too late."

"Sorry to hear that." Good thing he wasn't staying near the dining hall. Riley could really make some noise. Colby smiled at the memory of that morning's shower.

Rachel arrived and set down plates of food, then described each item according to the handwritten signs Riley had placed on the buffet line.

Lynn joined then a moment later with mugs of coffee. "Colby, Fitz found the guest room a little bit distracting. I thought we could put him in your bedroom until the cottage we reserved for him opens up on Saturday?"

Served Fitz right for showing up early without warning. He'd thrown the whole ranch into a tizzy and he'd been here less than eight hours. What havoc could he wreak over the next ten days?

"Yeah, I—"

"Oh that's great. You don't stay there much anyway. And the bunkhouse has extra space…."

How did she know he wasn't in his room? Maybe his visits to Riley hadn't been as discreet as he thought.

"Hmmm, the bunkhouse sounds like fun…," Fitz said as he nibbled at something else off of Colby's plate.

"It's not. It's just what you'd expect from a bunkhouse. A bunk."

"Rows of *delicious* cowboys." Fitz laughed as if he he'd never heard anything so funny in his entire life. Lynn and Rachel joined in with nervous titters and exchanged glances. Colby wanted to crawl under the table and bite Fitz's leg, but the guy might find that a turn-on. Instead, Colby reminded himself he needed to make Fitz happy.

"Oh, there's Riley!" Rachel waved him over. "You need to meet our chef. He's Cordon-Bleu trained in both pastry *and* the general culinary course. He can cook just about anything."

"I should think he *would* be able to cook anything." The barb wasn't lost on Colby but Rachel kept smiling as Riley approached.

Colby flashed a "help me" look.

"I'm Riley Emerson. Nice to meet you." He wiped his hands on his apron and shook Wellington's hand.

"B.F. Wellington." He gave Riley an appraising glance that brought out a little curl of jealousy in Colby's midsection.

"You let me know if I can fix anything special for you."

Wellington sat down and pulled another pastry off Colby's plate. "I'm just fine for now, but I will have some special requests."

Riley nodded and touched his hat, then took his leave. Colby knew him well enough to notice the tension in his shoulders. Guilt washed over him for asking Riley to help cater to Wellington. He'd make it up to Riley as soon as possible. Maybe a romantic dinner and night in Aspen or Denver after Wellington had gone.

"What're your plans today, Colby?" Rachel asked.

"Work."

Wellington stared at him intently.

"Uh, check some fences and put out salt in a few of the paddocks. Why?"

"Fitz was hoping to ride, and he really wants to see how the whole ranch operates." She glanced at Fitz, who was still staring unabashedly at Colby. "If it's not too much trouble, we'd like to tag along and watch you at work."

"Nonsense, my dear Rachel. I can't take up all your time squiring me around. I can watch Colby just fine on my own."

He was already doing a dandy job.

"It's no trouble, Fitz—" Rachel started.

"You can show me around after lunch, Rachel."

"That's a deal. Thanks, Colby." She said, even though he hadn't agreed to anything. He had no choice now. She leaned over, winked, and kissed his cheek. He could feel the lipstick rub off and fought the urge to wipe it away, knowing it would leave a big smear.

COLBY'S MORNING was slow as a creek of molasses. He had so much work to do, and not only did babysitting Fitz Wellington slow him down, but every minute with him felt like an hour. After that excruciating breakfast, Colby couldn't wait to get out on the trail. Wellington wouldn't be able to touch him if they were on separate horses.

As he and Fitz made their way to the barn, Colby tried to get Riley's shocked expression out of his brain. Riley had to realize Colby wasn't reciprocating Fitz's interest? They'd just spent the night together, and before that all those hours with the chuck wagon for the trail dinner. Riley must understand. Colby was being nice to Fitz as a means to an end. He wasn't enjoying the attention.

In fact, Colby wished Riley would pay him as much attention. Then he remembered Riley wasn't into relationships and presumably wouldn't want Colby to get the wrong impression. Or maybe he wanted to spare Colby some pain by keeping it casual and private.

Either way, Colby shouldn't have to worry about Riley.

The trouble started—or continued—in the barn. Fitz didn't like the horse Colby picked out for him to ride, a pretty bay mare called Allspice, with more sass than the average guest-ranch horse. She wasn't an easy horse to ride, so an experienced rider, as Fitz had billed himself, should find her an enjoyable mount.

"She's a bit *plain*, isn't she?"

"Her looks have nothing to do with how she rides."

"What are my other choices?"

Colby counted to five in his head. "Calico Charlie's real pretty. Black and white paint." Colby led Fitz outside to the corral where the wranglers had tethered the horses for the guests in the covered saddling area.

Most of the horses rested on one hind leg and flicked flies away with their tails, half dozing until a rider chose them.

"They all look so bored, Colby. Let me take one of the working horses?" Fitz nodded in the direction of the smaller corral where Marcus and Kit were bringing the last of the ranch hands' mounts out.

"My staff ride those."

"There are still five horses in the corral. How about that pretty palomino?"

"That's Twenty-four. She's my horse and I rode her pretty hard yesterday cutting cattle. I'm resting her today."

"Oh." Fitz made some movement with his eyes that Colby hoped wasn't meant to change his mind. Did guys actually bat their eyelashes? Colby shuddered. Give him a no-nonsense cowboy—or easy-to-please Riley—any day of the week.

He finally got Fitz settled on Azura, a blue roan quarter horse. Marcus had handled Colby's morning meeting to assign tasks to the rest of the men, and he noticed them watching as he gave Fitz unprecedented special attention. But Colby wouldn't let Fitz keep him from doing his job.

"Let's do a warm-up in the paddock before we hit the trail." Colby needed to see how well Fitz could ride before he'd feel comfortable bringing him out on the open range. He didn't have time to go chasing after Azura to rescue the guy.

"You don't trust me yet, do you?"

"Humor me?" Colby tested one of his own smiles out and Fitz nodded. Colby said a silent prayer of thanks.

Fitz rode as well as advertised. He bonded quickly with Azura and controlled her expertly with hand, voice, and legs. He put her through a series of movements as Colby watched from atop Hickory outside the ring. Fitz rode up to the fence. "Did I pass your test?"

"With flying colors."

Fitz smiled, teeth sparkling in the morning light, reminding Colby of the Big Bad Wolf. "That's what I like to hear."

Now thirty minutes behind schedule, they headed out for Colby's chores, with Fitz keeping up nonstop questions about the ranch and the stock. He even helped as Colby made simple repairs to fences and didn't snap a single photo— unlike 99 percent of the other guests at the ranch.

They took a break with snacks Colby had packed up from breakfast, and Fitz's questions turned to the family and most of all about Colby. He did his best to fend off questions as they became increasingly personal.

"I don't quite understand why you keep moving the cows from place to place."

Colby liked answering this kind of question. "Cattle prefer new shoots, so if you keep them too long in one paddock, it will never grow back. They'll keep eating the newest grass and let the older grass get high and inedible." He paused. "We have three times as much pasture land as we need because it takes twice as long to grow the grass back as it takes the cattle to eat it. We move the stock between paddocks every week or so."

"I see." Fitz gazed at Colby as if this was the most exciting thing he'd ever heard in his life. Maybe he really was interested in learning about the ranching side of the business.

When Fitz asked, "You have a boyfriend?" Colby reevaluated his opinion.

"Enough. My personal life is off limits."

"Well, you'd say yes if you had one. So you're still on the market. And don't even try to deny you're gay, though you hide it well."

"Not that it's your business, but I don't try to hide it. Just no need to announce it around here."

"Your family knows?"

"Of course they do. It's just not a factor here on the Z."

"Sorry to hear that. Sounds lonely. I can already tell the ranch is everything to you. But you don't have anyone to share that part of your life with."

Colby didn't reply. Truth of it, Fitz was right. Colby had been lonely till Riley arrived, but a sophisticated big-city guy like Riley would never want to live on a ranch for more than a summer. "Let's get back to work."

RILEY AVOIDED going back into the dining room for the rest of breakfast. He had changes to make to the lunch menu anyway, he told himself. It didn't have anything to do with the way Wellington was hanging off of Colby.

"Nothing to worry about," Riley said out loud, as if that made any difference. Colby had spent the night with Riley, and he'd looked uncomfortable at Wellington's attentions. And Riley understood if Colby didn't push him away. The future of the ranch was at stake. He didn't have to watch it happen, though.

Lunch went off without a hitch. Without Riley's years of restaurant experience, he probably couldn't have pulled it off, but he'd dealt with missing main ingredients, last-minute warnings of food allergies, and worse over the years. B. Fitzgerald Wellington was nothing. As long as he liked the dishes.

Carrying out another tray of pulled pork empanadas, Riley scanned the dining area. Most of the guests were smiling as they ate, and a few came up to tell him how much they enjoyed the food. It was a nice change from the restaurant business, where he only heard from a guest when there was a problem. Pastry chefs never got to interact with customers.

Lynn, Rachel, Alicia, and Jake sat at a table in one corner of the room, but Colby and Wellington were nowhere in sight. Rachel spotted Riley and came up to the buffet as he was swapping out a platter of grilled beef with spicy orange compote.

"It's fantastic, Riley. I'm amazed you've been able to adapt to the change in menus. Thank you so much. Mom would never have been able to deal with this situation. I'm getting lots of compliments from guests."

"What about Wellington?"

"Fitz hasn't actually said anything yet."

"I guess it's a good sign. People like him complain when they're dissatisfied." Riley stopped before he said anything else. He couldn't insult Rachel or her plans.

"He seems quite satisfied. I think he's got a little crush on Colby." She gave a girlish giggle that belied her usual business-like mien. "That's the only thing that seems to put a smile on his face. I'll be honest, I thought Fitz would be more enthusiastic about the ranch. It's in tip-top condition right now. But Colby turned Fitz's mood around."

Riley nodded. He wouldn't have been able to speak around the knot in his throat anyway.

At that moment, Wellington and Colby came through the door, and Riley made an excuse to flee to the kitchen. He watched from behind the door as Colby and Wellington greeted the family before heading to the buffet together. They seemed to be getting along fine. Colby wasn't much for openly flirting, but he didn't seem stricken at the prospect of spending another meal with Wellington.

He wasn't sure which hurt more, knowing Wellington's interest in Colby might be reciprocated, or that Rachel had no clue Colby and Riley had a relationship.

What relationship? They'd fucked. It was that simple. They'd given each other pleasure and enjoyed each other's company before and after sex. That wasn't really a relationship. Colby had wanted to keep it private and now the only ones who had a clue were the two of them and maybe Willa.

"Riley, watch out." It was Katrina trying to get through the door with a platter of grilled vegetables. "Can you hold the door for me?"

He scooted out of her way and glanced at Colby again, hoping to catch his eye, but Colby never even looked in the direction of the kitchen.

Katrina came back. "Riley, Lynn wanted to talk to you for a minute."

"Sure." He felt faint and decided to splash some cold water on his face first. He took a few deep breaths in the staff bathroom and made sure his hair wasn't all messy looking before he went back. Waste of effort. Colby and Wellington had already left. "Lynn, what can I do for you?"

"Hi, Riley, lovely lovely lunch. I adored those pork things you served. I hope it won't be much trouble, but Fitz has given me a few requests for dishes he'd like you to prepare during his visit. Can you spare a few minutes now to look at them?"

"Yes." He sat down at the table. Rachel and Jake sat across from him, chatting about activities planned for the rest of the day. Lynn handed him a few pieces of paper and he scanned Wellington's requests. Mention of Colby's name caught his attention.

"I'll just have someone from housekeeping move Fitz's bags into Colby's bedroom," Rachel said.

"I can handle that for you. I know you're running the fishing trip this afternoon. Leave Fitz's things to me," Jake replied.

Fitz's bags…. Colby's bedroom? Riley couldn't concentrate on the recipes, and he felt his stomach flip-flopping so much he thought he'd vomit.

"Riley?" Lynn reached out for his arm. "You okay? You're shaking like a leaf. Are you coming down with something?"

Fitz's list fluttered in his hand and he pulled himself together. "No. I'm okay. Just felt a little dizzy. It passed. Sorry about that."

"You look exhausted. After the trail dinner and Fitz's arrival, I'm worried you're overextending yourself. Bring in a few extra people from housekeeping to help in the kitchen. I don't want you working yourself so hard."

"Thanks. I'll do that. Some of these dishes are a little too complicated, and I'll need to handle them myself. Did you want me to prepare enough for all the guests, or is this a special menu?"

"Can you make enough for everyone?"

"It would be difficult. But I could arrange a smaller party for the family and serve it in the house."

"That's a great idea. Could you manage it for tomorrow night?"

Friday dinner was usually something special, the final dinner for the guests who would be leaving Saturday after brunch and they tried to make it memorable. Fitz's request would mean two separate menus. Twice as much work. What was some extra time in the kitchen if it would impress B. Fitzgerald Wellington and secure the investment Colby wanted so badly? Maybe once Colby knew the Z was safe, he might relax enough to consider the possibility of a real relationship.

"No problem at all."

Chapter Thirteen

DURING THURSDAY'S dinner, Colby wasn't able to talk with Riley at all. He had been looking forward all day to seeing him, especially after that uncomfortable breakfast with Fitz Wellington hanging all over him. Over the course of the day, however, Colby had decided Fitz wasn't as bad as he'd seemed at first, at least if he kept his hands to himself.

As part of his due diligence, Fitz wanted to talk with the guests and spent dinner flitting between different tables, giving Colby some time to himself.

"He's probably asking their impressions of the ranch and inquiring after their satisfaction with their visit," Rachel suggested.

"I hope he doesn't make the guests feel uncomfortable," Lynn glanced from Rachel to Jake. "They've still got another whole day here."

"No one's had any complaints besides the minor things like a lizard in the bathroom or not catching any fish in the river." Rachel spoke with her mouth full of pork ribs served with a peach dressing. "Damn, these ribs are yummy. Another scrumptious effort on Riley's part."

"No argument from me on that." Colby felt a swelling of pride that the guests, staff, and family had been thrilled with Riley's meals. Return guests made special note of the improved menus, and Lynn's feelings might have been hurt if she wasn't such a gracious, good-natured person. But since Fitz had arrived, Riley had taken everything to a new level. "I may need to start jogging or something." Colby patted his stomach. "Or get some bigger jeans."

Alicia, sitting next to Colby, nudged his leg under the table and whispered, "I'll bet it's not just Riley's food that's doing that." In a louder voice she added, "Lots of ways to get *exercise* besides jogging."

The rest of the family laughed and Colby felt heat in his face.

"Okay, I need to go mingle," Rachel said. She stopped at the buffet to snag another dessert and headed to one of the guest tables to chat. They invited her to sit.

"We should too," Lynn said, tugging at Jake's sleeve. "We've had too much family time this week. Let's make sure Fitz doesn't find out about any of the guest problems before we do."

Alicia and Colby were alone, sipping coffee.

"You're in a pickle, ain't ya?" She offered him a wink.

"Meaning?"

"Don't play coy with me, dude. I see Fitz making puppy-dog eyes at you from across the room."

"What?" Colby fought the urge to look at Fitz.

"Well, he would if he thought you were looking. He's not very subtle. Do you like that?"

This was new territory for their conversations, and Colby didn't know how to respond. "It's... I don't know. I'm not used to any attention."

"Or you like the silent martyr type, like Riley."

"Huh?"

"There is something with you and Riley, isn't there? I hope so. He's so sweet."

"I thought you were into Riley. You called him dishy."

"It was a chef joke. God, you can be so clueless sometimes. Sure, he *is* hot. But not for me."

Colby sipped coffee and discovered his cup was empty. He pretended to drink anyway, so he wouldn't have to reply. Alicia kept staring at him until he was even more uncomfortable. "What do you mean martyr?"

"You can see a cow fart from sixty feet, but you can't tell when a guy two feet away is upset? Start paying attention to *people*, Colby. Riley was crushed when he saw Fitz all over you at breakfast."

This was news. "But I didn't do anything back."

"Yeah." She turned the word into three judgmental syllables. "You didn't. You also didn't look like you minded."

"I didn't want to offend Fitz!" Didn't Alicia get how important his approval was for the future of the Z?

"Jesus, Colby. The result was that you offended Riley. He's practically been hiding in the kitchen when you and Fitz are in the dining room. Didn't you notice that?"

It did explain a few things. "Why is anyone offended about anything?"

"Because they're human, Colby. They're not cow-herding robots."

He sipped coffee, forgetting the empty cup, then slammed it down on the table. "Alicia, I'm not a robot."

"Then make sure Riley knows he's more important to you than some dirt and some cows." She stood up and collected her plate and cup, dumping them in the bus bins near the kitchen door before she left.

Colby sat on his own for a while, thinking about her comments. He'd just met Riley a few weeks ago. Sure, they got on fine and Colby enjoyed his company. But Riley wasn't part of Colby's future. He didn't stack up against the ranch. Riley should be able to figure out that Colby was only being nice to Fitz to secure the investment.

From across the room Fitz gave him a warm smile and a fluttery wave. Colby squinted to see if he was also making puppy-dog eyes. What the hell were puppy-dog eyes anyway?

But Alicia wouldn't have said all that to Colby unless it was important. Had he upset Riley? Colby better make sure to talk to him about it sooner or later. He didn't want another rift between them. There would be time for that discussion tonight.

Fitz convinced Colby to stay up later than usual and attend the Thursday night activities: a short hike and ghost stories by the campfire. The location turned out to be the little rise where Colby had brought Riley for their first date, the moonlight trail ride. Colby thought about that night, and about Riley, the whole evening. He couldn't wait to get back and see him that night. With Fitz staying in his room, no one would notice if he stayed with Riley instead of the bunkhouse.

On the way back home, Fitz caught up with Colby. "I'm just a big inconvenience tonight, aren't I? Putting you out of your bed." Fitz gave a breathy whisper on the word "bed."

Fitz was wrangling for Colby to disagree, but he didn't give in. "Bunkhouse is fine."

"Look, it's a big bed. Room for both of us...." Fitz reached for Colby's hand and tangled their fingers together.

Colby was speechless. He stopped short.

"I'm being a little too forward, aren't I, Colby? I just can't help myself."

Colby swallowed and stared at Fitz. He was a good-looking guy, and in good shape. If he'd come up to Colby at Rawhide, Colby might have considered fooling around with him. "It's uh...." He closed his eyes. "It's not that. I...."

"Oh, right. Your family and all. I wasn't thinking. Not smart to do anything right in your house." Fitz nodded. "I'll be in my own cottage Saturday night."

"That's sounds better."

"Saturday night it is. I can't wait!" Fitz let go of Colby's hand and started walking again.

Colby stood there as guests and staff filed past him.

He had been afraid to say no outright, but he hadn't actually said yes to the invitation, had he? The way his gut rumbled told him that's how Fitz had interpreted Colby's response. He had three days to figure out how to get out of it.

COLBY PUT Saturday night out of his thoughts. He went to the bunkhouse after the hike and had another shower so he wouldn't smell like smoke—or Fitz, in case any of his distinctive cologne lingered on or about Colby's hair and clothes. Rejuvenated, he made his way to the kitchen and let himself inside through the dining room.

Lights were still on in the kitchen and he peeked inside, expecting to see Willa, but not wanting to draw attention to himself. Instead, he saw Riley sitting on a stool at the counter and poring through a pile of cookbooks. He looked intent. Best not to disturb him. Colby shut the door silently and headed for the stairs. He pulled off his boots before ascending.

There was a six-pack of the beer he liked in the fridge, so he popped open a bottle and had a few sips. The window was open and the buzzing of crickets and other insects filled the room. Every once in a while a bug would hit the screen with a crunch and a rattle. Colby sat on the couch, glad to be off his feet and out of his boots after the long day. His shoulders ached, and he hadn't realized how exhausted he was until halfway through the beer. He let out a relaxed sigh and picked up a culinary magazine from the coffee table.

A clock chimed softly to let him know it was eleven. Usually Riley was back by now, and Colby had to be up by five. Well, six really, but when he stayed with Riley, they set the alarm for an hour early. He smiled at the thought of their little routine. He'd never had a routine with anyone before. God, he wished Riley would come up and come to bed soon. All Colby wanted was to hold Riley tight and tell him not to worry about Fitz. He didn't care if Riley was too tired to fool around. It would be nice to snuggle close and fall asleep together.

What if Riley didn't want that kind of bed partner? They hadn't gotten that far in their discussions. Maybe he only wanted the benefits and not so much with the friendship part of things.

Then it was important to set that straight. Colby would stay and find out for himself instead of wondering.

He finished the beer, tossed the bottle in recycling, and headed for the bedroom.

He'd never been here alone and he took a few minutes to look at the photos Riley had on the dresser. There were some from Paris—a few had one of the people clearly ripped out of the image—and several of Riley and a girl who looked enough like him to be his sister, Estelle. He knew Riley and Estelle were close, and it was obvious from the wide smiles in the photos. None of the photos had anyone who looked like parents. A chair in the corner was piled with clean laundry—who liked putting clothes away? The bed stand drawer had condoms and lube, right where they'd left things that morning. Only eighteen hours had passed, but it seemed like a week since they'd seen each other.

Colby slipped out of his pants and shirt, then out of his shorts as well before crawling under the quilts and settling himself into one side of the bed. He pulled the other pillow close and closed his eyes.

THE ALARM clock went off at five.

Colby woke to the shattered silence to find himself still alone. His clothes remained folded on the dresser. Nothing had changed. Riley hadn't come back last night.

Surprise turned almost instantly to dread. Was Riley okay? Maybe something had happened to him! The last Colby had seen, he'd been in the kitchen reading cookbooks. Nothing too dangerous there. The only explanation he could come up with was that Riley had spent the night with someone else.

Unexpected jealousy boiled up inside, and Colby sat up in bed.

By the time he was dressed, jealousy had morphed into anger. Just one day with Fitz around and it looked like Riley had already given up on Colby. Was he that thin-skinned? Or was he just getting back at Colby for having to spend time with Fitz? Colby had to get out of here before Riley came back. He didn't want to look a fool for having waited all night while Riley spent the night with someone else.

He sped down the stairs and stopped to retrieve his boots. The hallway was still dark, and light spilled out from under the kitchen door as he passed. He hated wasting electricity, and it was far too early for anyone to be working here. And too quiet. Colby opened the door in order to turn the lights off.

Standing in the doorway he stopped and stared for what might have been a full minute. Riley had fallen asleep on the stool, leaning over the counter. Next to him was the pasta rolling machine and several containers of handmade pasta that he must have spent all night preparing.

Colby had been a fool; he'd doubted Riley's motives and his commitment to his job, and to Colby. Worse, Colby remembered that Rachel asked for something special for Friday's dinner: the dishes Fitz had requested.

Riley had spent the night to make Fitz happy, because he knew how important that was to Colby.

Colby backed out of the room so he wouldn't disturb Riley. He felt like a total ass for doubting Riley's actions or motives.

He'd have to make this up to him as soon as possible.

On his way back to the bunkhouse, Colby realized how lucky he was to have met Riley, but now he wondered whether he deserved to have someone like Riley in his life.

"RILEY, RILEY?"

Riley blinked and found Willa shaking him awake as he lay across the counter. "Oh, crap, I fell asleep! I'm almost done. Then I'll get to bed."

"It's almost six. Don't tell me you been here all night?" Willa looked freshly showered and even more cheerful than usual.

"Six? No, no, no, no. It can't be. I'm not nearly finished prepping for dinner."

"Dinner's under control."

"I'm not talking about the guests' dinner. This is something for the family."

"You look terrible, Riley. I'll manage breakfast without you. Go and grab some sleep and a shower. Not necessarily in that order."

He must look and smell pretty bad if Willa commented. "I can't put that all on you."

"Don't you think I can handle it?"

"Of course you can." He nodded. "Get some extra help from housekeeping if you need it."

"I was planning to. Relax. I'll put all this pasta away. Can I help with anything while you're having a nap?"

"Only if you have time. I'm not nearly done filling the pasta." The strips he made the night before would have dried out. He started pulling up damp towels and pressing shaking fingers to the strips of pasta. They were okay! Thank God.

"I can roll the dough, but I'm not that good with the filling."

"There are more balls of fresh dough in the walk-in. Roll them out and—"

She started pushing him toward the door before he finished. "I can figure that part out. Get some rest first."

"Thank you!" He almost hugged her, but she wasn't the hugging kind. He'd hug her later anyway, after he'd showered.

Upstairs he tumbled into bed covered with a rumpled pile of quilts, wondering how he had left without making the bed the morning before. Hadn't Colby helped him?

He woke two hours later, more refreshed than he expected. A nice shower finished the process, and he was ready to get back into the kitchen and finish prepping Fitz's special dinner. It would be a good excuse to stay out of the dining room so he wouldn't have to see Fitz and Colby.

His cell phone buzzed as he was getting dressed. Stella. He hadn't spoken to her for a week. He picked up.

"Hey."

"Hey, yourself. I wondered if I was calling the wrong number." She chuckled. "How's the hunky cowboy?"

"This isn't a good time. Let me—"

"Two minutes."

He sat back down on the bed. "Okay. I'm watching the clock."

"Nothing changes. You sound a little down, Riles, what's shaking?"

"Is that why you called?" He preferred to discuss his sister's life and not his.

"Kind of. I'm coming out there. Just about to book my room and flights. Week after next."

"Can you make it sooner?"

"Next week's all booked up so I couldn't get a reservation…. Wait a minute. I expected you to ask me not to come. Talk to me."

"Later. Just get the earliest flight you can and stay with me. I can't wait to see you."

"At least give me the one-minute summary."

"I like the cowboy. He likes me, but he's more worried about keeping this place from getting sold. He's cozying up to some potential investor and…." He felt sick thinking about it.

"That's terrible!"

Riley yawned.

"Did I wake you up or something? Isn't it the middle of the morning?"

"I was up all night working on a fancy dinner to impress Mr. Moneybags."

"You stayed up even though the cowboy's thrown you over for the bank account?"

She didn't have to be that blunt. Riley nodded. He couldn't find his voice to respond.

"You don't need the job or the money. Just come home. Or go somewhere fun and I'll meet you in a day or two. Don't knock yourself out."

"I'm not doing this for Colby. Well, not just for him. His family hired me so they could charge more and to impress an investor. I can't leave them all in the lurch because a sexy cowboy broke my heart." He paused. "He's not even boyfriend material. I mean he is, but he doesn't want a boyfriend. Oh, I don't know why I let myself fall for him." But Riley did know. Because Colby was a genuine good guy. He'd helped Riley that night in Aspen, and even now he was trying to save his family heritage.

"Keep that in mind. You don't want to live on a cow farm the rest of your life, do you? That's what you'd have to look forward to, Riley. No hot guy is worth eternal boredom."

"Cattle, not cows. And it's not at all boring. You'll see when you get here."

"You haven't been there long enough to know. Everything's fun at the beginning, even matrix algebra. It never lasts." She giggled. She'd dropped out of MIT, and their father had blamed Riley. That was just another thing they'd bonded over. "I'll decide when I get there, assuming you're staying."

"I'm staying. But I can't wait to see you. You can sleep on my couch for a while, till your room is available."

"Okay, I'll let you know my schedule. Call me later to talk more. And just treat it as a job, nothing personal. You always do your best, but you have to separate yourself from the emotions."

"Thanks, Dear Abby."

Stella made kissy noises and hung up. Her conversation cheered him enough to get back downstairs and back to work.

Chapter Fourteen

COLBY HAD a quick shower in the bunkhouse, dressed, and raced back to the dining hall for breakfast. It was a little past six o'clock, and about a quarter of the guests were already there—the ones who liked watching the wranglers bring in the horses so they could help groom and saddle them. Some just liked watching the ranch hands go about their jobs in the home corrals.

Today there were more early risers than usual because Rachel had scheduled "Watch a Cowboy at Work," where guests could tag along and help with some easy tasks, like dropping salt and protein supplements.

Fitz was already seated at the family's usual table, all alone, wearing an eager smile. He stood as Colby arrived. Colby nodded and waved, then headed for the coffee. Fitz intercepted him at the coffee urns.

"Good morning, Colby."

"Hi, Fitz. You're up early." Colby gulped a few steaming mouthfuls, eager for the invigorating caffeine to kick in.

"I signed up for the Cowboy at Work ride." He gave Colby a charming smile. "You're part of that, right?"

"Marcus is leading the guests on that." Colby noticed Fitz's smile dwindle.

"Can I shadow *you*, then?" Fitz lifted an eyebrow.

"Actually, I've got some office things to handle, then I'll be out in the paddock. Paperwork is boring; that's why it's not part of the official event." Colby ventured a grin, trying to balance friendliness with leading the guy on too much.

Rachel came in and clapped her hands. "The Cowboy at Work ride is leaving in five minutes. Who's coming? Finish up and meet us at the little corral ASAP." She left as quickly as she had arrived. She was damn efficient.

"See you a little later, then?" Fitz asked.

"Yup. Gotta grab a bite here first." Colby watched Fitz stare at the door, then glance back to him. "Rachel won't wait."

"Okay." Fitz gave him a disappointed smile and left.

Colby waited until the door shut behind Fitz, then raced for the kitchen.

Inside, Willa, Katrina, and Chuck were chopping things at the center island. There seemed to be an unlimited supply of things needing to be chopped in a kitchen. Colby glanced around, expecting to see Riley.

"Hi, Colby, can we help you with something?" Willa put down her knife.

"I—uh—I...." He took a breath. What was he nervous about? "I was looking for Riley." He craned his neck in the direction of the walk-in and the little desk Riley used for paperwork.

Chuck and Katrina glanced at him quickly, then went back to concentrating on their tasks.

"He's not here."

Colby had already figured that out. Was she being obtuse on purpose? Fine. He'd get to the point. "I need to talk to him. When will he be back?" There weren't that many places he could be at this time of day. It wasn't like Riley to shirk his responsibilities in the kitchen or dining room.

"He's running a little late this morning."

"Okay, thanks." Colby glanced toward the back door that led to Riley's flat. Stuff it. He didn't care who saw him heading in that direction. No reason to hide. Colby strode past Riley's staff, went through the back door, and took the steps two at a time.

Outside Riley's door, he had second thoughts. Maybe Riley didn't want his crew to know he was spending time with Colby. They needed to discuss that too.

Colby had his hand raised to knock when the door opened.

Riley's hair was damp, and he had dark circles under his eyes. But Colby still felt a tremor of excitement go through his body at the sight.

"Hey," Colby said.

RILEY STARED at Colby for a full two or three seconds. He wore the crooked grin that made Riley a little dizzy. It had the usual effect on him, and he put a hand on the doorjamb.

"What's up?" Riley tried to sound cool and collected when he was anything but.

"I need to talk to you." He paused. "Want to talk to you."

"I'm heading to the kitchen. Can we talk there?" Riley forced himself not to give in to Colby's overwhelming physical presence. The strong shoulders, square jaw, and crinkly eyes were not going to get the better of him.

"It's personal."

Colby's body filled the doorframe. It would have been difficult to get around him, even if Riley wanted. He didn't want. He liked the determination in Colby's voice and the little hitch when he said "personal."

Riley stepped back a pace.

Colby moved forward and pulled Riley into his arms as he closed the door behind them.

Riley slid his arms around Colby's waist and leaned forward into a kiss. He wasn't prepared for the power, the raw need in Colby. The emotion was like a wave crashing over the bow of a ship, and Riley held on tight.

Colby kissed Riley hard, passionately, staying just this side of the line to losing control. Desire coursed through Riley's body, and his brain gave up trying to process thoughts. Instinct took over.

Riley stepped backward, bringing Colby into the bedroom, and they fell on the bed, side by side.

Colby's cock stiffened against Riley's leg, mirroring Riley's own arousal, but Colby didn't try to take things further than kissing. He gave Riley an open-mouthed kiss, but pulled away when Riley pushed with his tongue. The kiss continued, lips only, and Riley longed to taste Colby more deeply. Without warning, Colby plunged his tongue in, making a whole meal of the kiss. Finally, he pulled away, chest heaving from oxygen deprivation. Riley's senses were on high alert, his head dizzy from excitement and Colby's passion.

"So, what did you want to talk about?" Riley gasped between deep breaths.

"I forgot."

"Then kiss me some more." Riley's attraction to Colby was too strong to stop now. If this was all there was to their relationship, Riley could accept that. For now, he just loved the sensation of being in Colby's arms. Blood buzzed in his ears and everything tingled. His clothes were in the way. Luckily Colby was in the process of remedying that by unbuttoning Riley's shirt. He always knew just what to do.

Riley slid his hands under Colby's shirt, smoothing his palms against hard planes of muscle beneath the warm skin.

Once the clothing was gone, they covered each other with kisses, licks, nibbles, and nips. With Riley on his side, Colby lay behind him, prepping him and quickly donning a condom before plunging inside. Riley gasped at the immediate pleasure of Colby filling him, the heat and pressure combining perfectly.

The only sound in the room was the soft slap of skin on skin and their mingled moans and grunts. Colby timed slow deep thrusts with strokes to Riley's cock, letting Riley come first before he let go, rocking Riley's body with the power of his orgasm.

"I REALLY did come up here to talk to you." Colby propped his head on his hand as he lay next to Riley. "Honest."

"I believe you." Riley's grin belied the comment, and Colby felt self-conscious.

"I just couldn't help myself when I saw you. I missed you last night." He picked up one of Riley's hands and planted a kiss. "And I owe you an apology. More than one."

"Last night? Did we have plans?"

"I came over but you weren't here. I waited... fell asleep. Then this morning when I left, I noticed you were still in the kitchen."

Colby wasn't prepared for the expression of amazement on Riley's face. "You waited for me here last night? You weren't with...."

"With... who?"

Riley looked away. "I heard Jake say he was putting Wellington's luggage in your room and...."

"You thought I was spending the night with him?" Colby sat up in bed and stared. How could Riley think that? "Why?"

Riley moved to a sitting position. "Well, the luggage thing for one."

"Fitz wasn't happy with his room and they put him in mine. I was supposed to stay in the bunkhouse." Colby shook his head. Stupid misunderstandings. Thank God he hadn't waited to sort this one out. "Did you forget you stayed in my room when you first got here? Without me."

"But I wanted you to come up. Fitz sure looked like he wanted you too."

"That doesn't mean I want *him*. Why would you think that?" Colby put a hand on Riley's shoulder, easing him back onto the bed.

"Why wouldn't I? You told me how important he is to keep the Z in one piece."

"That's true, but one has nothing to do with the other." He lay down next to Riley again and traced a line down his throat that made it difficult for Riley to think and form words and sentences.

"Maybe you were just trying to keep him happy."

"It's never good to mix business with pleasure." Colby swooped down for a kiss.

"What do you call this?" Riley wrapped his hand around Colby's recovering erection.

"Well, there are always exceptions."

"DID YOU make these ravioli?" Fitz held his spoon toward Riley, who peered down to examine the piece of pasta.

"Yes." He stood in the family dining room after serving the special dinner Fitz had requested. It had been a treat to see Lynn and Jake's expressions of delight as he brought out each platter, carefully arranged and garnished. Best of all had been Colby's face, especially as he took a taste and gave Riley that special smile he'd so far only used in the bedroom.

"Hmm." Fitz turned to Rachel and said, "They're not the quality I expect from a graduate of Le Cordon Bleu. Unevenly cut."

Sweat dripped down Riley's spine. It wasn't only the heat and the heavy chef's jacket that Rachel had asked him to wear. "My assistant hasn't had as much practice as I have."

"So you *didn't* make them yourself?" Fitz blinked and let out a sigh. He turned a beseeching gaze on Rachel.

"I think they're marvelous. What's in 'em again, Riley, honey?" Lynn asked, spearing another with her fork.

"Braised short ribs in a red-wine reduction. That's beef raised right here on the Z." He noticed a well-deserved flash of pride on Colby's face. The beef here really was top-notch.

Lynn beamed. "Tastes and sounds like something you'd get in a big city like Denver." She closed her eyes as she chewed.

"As good as Paris or New York, Mom," Rachel said. "And far more elaborate than the usual fare here."

"You can charge guests twice as much if you can serve food like they'd get in New York, Rachel. Don't you see?" Fitz went on.

"Guests seem happy enough with Riley's twist on old-fashioned dishes and the chuck wagon classics," Jake said. He picked at his food and threw apologetic glances at Riley every time he was served a new item.

"We want to bring in a different *class* of guests." Fitz glanced to Rachel, clearly expecting her to back him up. "People who expect the absolute best, even at a ranch."

Riley saw Colby cringe at the words "even at a ranch." Jake and Lynn looked rather insulted too.

"I think there's a happy medium between the traditional dishes and haute cuisine," Riley said. "We can certainly elevate some of the—"

Fitz cleared his throat and smiled at Riley, but his glance threw daggers. "That's a discussion for a different time and place, I believe. This isn't a staff meeting."

"I think we're fine here, Riley. Thank you." Rachel gave him a warm smile, but her eyes looked tired.

It took a moment for it to sink in that he'd been dismissed like a servant. "Okay, then. I'll be in the dining hall supervising the guests' dinner." He gave a polite bow, with an extra glance at Colby, who barely met his gaze. Riley straightened and left through the kitchen.

He had taken only two steps when he unbuttoned the chef's coat and pulled it off. The cool evening air felt great, lowering both his body temperature and his emotional temperature. He'd held his tongue for Colby's sake, but Riley wasn't sure how much more Fitz he could take. Worse, he knew how awful Colby felt being stuck in the middle, afraid to rock the boat and risk losing even a corner of the ranch.

Riley vowed to keep biting his tongue. He shouldn't have mentioned that Willa helped with the ravioli. It wasn't fair to throw her under the bus like that. What he served was his responsibility, no matter who prepared it. He'd make sure no criticism came to her. She'd done a great job on a difficult dish.

He slipped into the kitchen through the back door, waving to the housekeeping staff, who were busy cleaning up the kitchen. He pulled on his chuck wagon shirt and a clean apron and sailed through the doors into the dining area.

COLBY WATCHED Riley leave, wishing he could go too. Poor Riley. He'd stayed up most of the night prepping these amazing dishes and Fitz had done nothing but criticize every single one. Everything was delicious. Colby had never eaten anything this fantastic in his whole life.

At least not food. He felt heat rising in his cheeks as he thought about Riley in a whole different way.

"I don't think I could manage another bite."

"But you haven't had dessert yet." Fitz put a hand on Colby's arm and let it stay long enough to send a message. "Have you ever had a dark chocolate hazelnut mousse before?"

Given that Fitz hadn't been satisfied with a single dish Riley had prepared for him, this was rich. "Well, no."

"I can't speak to the quality of this one, but please, stay."

"I reckon Jake and I should probably head over to the dining hall to see to the guests," Lynn said. "I'll have dessert later."

"What, you're leaving?" Fitz turned his charm up a few notches.

"It's the last night for the ones with Saturday departure, and it's not right to leave the staff to entertain them." Jake turned to Rachel and Alicia. "You two coming?"

"Fitz and I have more things to discuss," Rachel said. "Colby, would you please"—she dragged the word out twice as long as usual—"take my place in the dining hall for a little while?" She gave him a sweet smile, and he knew she was up to something. Something he had no intention of stopping.

Colby started to grumble. Only Rachel knew it was for show.

Rachel wiped her mouth with the fancy cloth napkins Lynn had set out in honor of Fitz. "Colby, I know you never enjoy hanging with the guests. But I'd *really* appreciate the favor."

"You're going to owe me." He tried not to smile. "Excuse me. Duty calls." He picked up his hat from the sideboard and put it on, nodded to Fitz, and left without another word. He kept himself from running down the path to the dining hall but still he left Jake and Lynn in his wake as he made his escape.

Inside the mood was festive, Taylor Swift playing in the background. Animated voices rose above the sound of clinking silverware. Riley and his staff moved from table to table, chatting with the guests. Wranglers and ranch hands were sprinkled at various tables, eating or chatting with guests they had gotten to know during the week, but it was really the family's responsibility to make sure guests had a great time, tonight of all nights.

Colby stopped at the first table, where a couple from Michigan were sitting with another couple from somewhere in California.

"May I join you?"

The guests nodded and assented.

"Have you all had a good visit?" Colby asked.

"Wonderful."

"Fantastic."

"We don't want to leave!"

He spent the next five minutes chatting with them and thanking them for coming before moving on to the next table.

Riley came by with a tray full of steaming hot apple fritters. "Who wants another?"

The aroma made Colby's mouth water. "I'll take one, please."

Riley set the plate down in front of Colby. It contained a spicy-smelling fritter and a creamy-looking sauce.

"What do y'all think of the food this past week?" Colby asked before taking a bite of the scrumptious-looking dessert.

Everyone praised Riley and his staff. Colby liked to see the color rising in Riley's cheeks at the voluminous compliments. He looked so damn sexy right now, like he had that morning after they'd kissed good-bye for the day. It was hard to keep his hands off. Good thing they were in public.

The door opened and Aunt Lynn, Jake, and Alicia came in and scattered to various tables to chat with guests. Colby moved on to another table, expecting Rachel and Fitz to show up any minute. But they didn't.

There would be a moonlight trail ride later—the last planned event of the weekend. Presumably Rachel would be there for that. And Fitz. Colby had promised Rachel that he and a few of the ranch hands would participate. He'd have to get his temper under control by then because right now he was furious with Fitz's insults about Riley's hard work.

"Thanks, so much, Colby. It's been a fantastic weekend. We're going to recommend all our friends try to get reservations this summer. If we had any more vacation time, we'd come back." The guests sitting with Colby got up to leave, the woman giving him a hug and the man shaking his hand.

Colby nodded and watched them stop to chat with Lynn and Jake before they left. Colby was alone at the table when Riley passed by.

"Riley, have you eaten yet?"

"Later. When dinner's over."

"Did you have lunch?"

"Probably. I can't remember."

"Sit yourself down right now. You look like you're going to fall over."

Riley shook his head, but his skin was pale and drawn, eyes dark with circles. "I'm fine. I'm too busy to take a break."

"Five minutes. There's some sort of law about taking breaks. I had to take a class. As your employer I'm ordering you to take your required break right now."

Riley's eyes crinkled when he smiled. "Well, if you put it like that...." He put the tray down and sat next to Colby.

"Stay right there." Colby hopped up and piled a plate with food from the buffet and brought it back for Riley.

Riley glanced around, watching Lynn, then scanning the other tables.

"Eat. Or you're fired."

With a nod, Riley picked up the fork and ate a few bites of food.

"The dinner you made for us was incredible. I can't even put it into words. I've never had anything like it. Are those the kind of dishes you learned in France?"

Riley nodded. "I spent a couple of years in culinary school and most of the past ten years working in top restaurants, learning from the best chefs in Europe. But someday soon I'd love to make something special just for you."

"I'd love that too. But I can't imagine anything better that what you prepared tonight."

"That meal was nothing. I can make those dishes in my sleep."

They both broke into laughter, their heads close together, hands almost touching.

The front door opened and Fitz Wellington strode into the room.

Chapter Fifteen

RILEY STARTED but Colby put a steadying hand on his arm.

"I need to talk to him. But you know why."

Riley nodded as Colby stood up. He wished he didn't have to do it this way.

Fitz came towards Colby and stopped, halfway between the table and the door. Colby knew power games when he saw them. Stubborn cattle and unbroken horses pulled the same maneuvers. Like the stock, Colby needed something from Fitz and he knew how to get it. He had to make it seem like Fitz's idea.

Fitz stared and Colby plastered on a smile he didn't feel. "Fitz, I didn't think I'd see you until later."

"Later?"

"On the ride. You are coming on the trail ride tonight, aren't you?" Colby cocked his head and smiled.

"Yes. Of course."

"Good. I need to help with the horses right now, but I'll see you later."

Colby turned and caught Riley's eye. He gave what he hoped was a reassuring smile before leaving for the barn. He met Marcus and Tommo there, and they helped the wranglers saddle enough horses for the guests before tacking up their own horses. Jake joined them.

"Tommo, can you get two more horses? For Riley and Willa. Granite and Bingo would be good choices," Jake said and Tommo headed into the barn.

Colby stared at Jake.

"I gave them the rest of the night off because they worked so many extra hours on that dinner tonight." Jake shook his head. "You really liked that fancy stuff?"

"Yeah, I did."

"You think we should be serving that to all the guests?"

"It's not up to me. That's up to Rachel and Lynn. I thought it was good, but I don't know I'd like to eat such rich food every day."

"I was hopin' you'd be on my side, boy."

"How so?"

"Lynn and Rachel think the sun shines out of Wellington's ass. I don't particularly like his manner."

Colby didn't respond. Far too dangerous territory.

"You want to ride with Fitz tonight?" Jake asked. "I know he's awfully sweet on you."

How the hell could he respond to that? Best to stay silent.

"I won't get into your business, Colby. Sorry. But Riley's still a timid rider, and I want someone to stick close to him. Who should I ask?"

"I'll handle it."

"Works for me." Jake gave Colby a knowing smile.

When the riders came out to the corral, Colby made sure Riley got paired with Granite, since he'd already ridden the horse and should feel more confident on him. He noticed Riley had changed into jeans and the boots Colby had given him. It gave him a little thrill every time he saw Riley wearing them in public. Tommo helped Riley mount, then Colby swung up onto Hickory.

Fitz rode toward Colby, cutting between Riley and Colby. Riley looked unsteady in the saddle.

Jake rode up. "Colby, I hate to ask, but can you take the sweep? We have some weaker riders and I need my most experienced man pulling up the rear."

"Sure, Jake." Colby threw a disappointed glance to Fitz. "You'll be bored to death if you ride along with me, Fitz. I have to make sure to pick up anyone who falls off."

"I don't mind."

"I'm working. I can't relax and have a fun ride. But you should. Stay up front with Jake and Rachel."

"It's such a beautiful night...."

"Every night's like this during the summer. Clear sky, a million stars, and crisp, fresh air. And next night ride I'm off duty." Colby pushed up an eyebrow, hoping he didn't look like a damn fool to anyone watching, but especially hoping Riley didn't see this. Even though it was a sham, it pained Colby to flirt with Fitz anywhere near him.

"And tomorrow?"

"Off duty." Colby nodded though his guts were in a knot. He hadn't figured out how to get out of his date with Fitz. If he wasn't so damn busy running the ranch, he'd consider falling and pretending to break a leg—even actually breaking a leg was preferable to a night with Fitz. But solicitous, possibly obsessed Fitz would probably want to stay at his bedside and keep him company. And then Colby wouldn't be able to get away.

"Heading out!" Jake called from the front of the group. "Tommo and Marcus, take the count." Two people counted the riders before they left and then again when they returned to make sure no one was left on the trail.

AFTER THE ride, Riley went up to his flat while Colby and the other hands put the horses away. An hour later he heard footsteps on the stairs and met Colby at the door wearing a smile and nothing else. Colby swept him into his arms. He smelled of horses and good, clean sweat, and his stubble rubbed Riley's cheeks delightfully raw.

"I need a shower. You're all clean smelling and I'm getting you dirty."

"I like that."

Colby made a sexy little growl deep in his throat and Riley was hard. Why did he have to be so irresistible?

"We can both shower. After."

"I like the way you think."

That wasn't all Colby liked. He let out another excited growl when he discovered Riley had slicked himself up and was ready and eager.

"Come here and have your way with me." Riley tugged Colby toward the couch.

"The bed's more comfortable."

"Let's do something different. Just fuck me on the couch."

Colby appeared taken aback. Should Riley have said "please"? It defeated the purpose. He wanted some hot and heavy sex, and Colby was being too much of a gentleman.

"I don't want to fuck you."

"Even if I ask you to?" Too much explanation ruined the mood. Riley sank to his knees and pulled Colby's cock into his mouth, feeling it harden and fill his throat. He spit-slicked a finger and pushed it inside. That always revved Colby into high gear.

"Oh, wow. Damn you." This time Colby got the message. He slid on a condom, then bent Riley over the back of the couch and plunged right in.

Riley let out a contented sigh and spread himself wider, enjoying the way Colby let himself go with each thrust. Riley came against the back of the couch even before Colby did.

Only then did Riley let Colby lead him into the bathroom for a shower.

Still damp they lay together in bed with the lights off, gazing out the window at the twinkling stars.

"Riley, I don't know what to do."

"About what?"

"About you, the ranch. Fitz." He let out a sigh that made Riley's heart ache.

"Let's take one at a time. You have to do what you need to for the ranch. I understand that."

"I hated watching Fitz treat you like garbage tonight after you worked so hard on that dinner. I wanted to hit him."

"You hid that pretty well."

"I didn't know what to do."

"I can handle the criticism; I've had worse from restaurant customers. I don't work for him. As long as Rachel and Lynn are happy with my performance, I'm okay."

"I'm really pleased with your performance." He traced a line down Riley's cock. Moonlight made Colby's teeth look like a row of pearls when he smiled.

"Glad to hear that."

"Couldn't you hear it before? You make me shout."

Riley felt all warm inside. He loved the noise Colby made with him. "Yeah."

"But that's part of the problem, too." Colby shook his head. "What's going to happen after the summer?"

It was the question Riley had been avoiding. What if he said the wrong thing? Why couldn't Colby have waited till Stella got here to give him some advice? "What do you mean?"

"If Fitz decides to invest, I think he's going to be around a lot."

Riley hadn't considered that.

"Can you handle working with him? I don't know how I'll deal with him once he's a part owner. I can't keep sucking up to him. And I can't ask you to tolerate his insults. It might be worse once he's knows I was never interested in him. That I've only ever wanted you."

Riley's heart started thumping like the bass line to an '80s disco song. He didn't know what to say.

"Riley, I hate to see you leave at the end of the summer. I know you only wanted something temporary, but...."

"You m—" Riley's voice cracked and he started again. "You talking about the job or something personal?"

"I don't know about the job. I'm talking about you and me. I know you wouldn't like living on a ranch after spending your life in big cities. I—I—oh, hell. I don't know what to say. I'll miss you like hell when you go back to the city where you really belong."

Riley waited to see if Colby would ask him directly to stay here, but he didn't. Where *did* he belong? Paris? New York? He'd easily find work there with his experience and connections. Even Denver or Aspen wouldn't be that hard. But if Colby didn't want him, then it would be too painful to stay nearby.

He threaded his fingers through Colby's hair. "I'll miss you like hell too."

Had they already broken up? Or was this simply planning ahead to make the process easier? Riley was at a loss. He thought he'd just told Colby he wanted more than a summer with him. What had Colby meant?

Colby rolled away and stared up at the ceiling. "I think I told Fitz I'd spend the night with him tomorrow. It happened so fast I didn't even realize until it was too late."

Riley nearly choked, but he held it back. It took a minute before could breathe again. "Because you like him, or for the ranch?" It was too late to take the question back. He closed his eyes and felt the room swaying.

Colby didn't respond. Or wouldn't.

Riley forced himself to sound calm. "You should do it."

COLBY COULDN'T have heard Riley correctly. "You *want* me to sleep with Fitz?" He rolled back over and stared at Riley.

"I think you should do what you need to, for the ranch."

"You're okay with that?" Colby hadn't expected his heart to ache this much. Was Riley giving him the boot? Or did he not care if Colby slept with someone else too?

"Does it matter?"

"It damn well does. Tell me the truth." He gripped Riley's arm and had to stop the urge to shake an answer out of him. "Don't you care?"

"I want you to be happy, Colby. I know losing even an acre would kill you. If that's what you need to do, then I won't try to stop you. I don't want you to worry about my feelings."

Colby just stared. Dear, sweet, thoughtful, deluded Riley, who thought Colby might actually want Fitz. "I don't want him at all. Riley, I want you."

"Wouldn't it be worth it? If you slept with him and guaranteed the Z would be safe, why not?"

Colby tried to see Riley's expression but a cloud had blocked the moonlight. Colby had only ever slept with guys he wanted. Sure, on more than one morning after, he'd realized he'd made a mistake, but the consequences were minor. Could he pimp himself out for the ranch? It would be easy enough to sleep with Fitz. He was good-looking, and even if the sex was awful, there was really no downside. Get him to sign the papers, then break things off. Why not? "I never even considered it before."

"It seems like an easy choice to me. Did you ever see the film *Indecent Proposal*?"

"No."

"Robert Redford offers a married woman a million dollars to spend the night with him. She and her husband agree that the money is worth one night. Their relationship is solid and they really need the money."

Colby's stomach shifted. "If it turned out okay, they wouldn't have made a film about it."

"For them, the money wasn't a good enough reason, and they ended up hating each other."

"I wish you hadn't mentioned this. It can't turn out good for me and you."

"But the ranch is more important to you than just money, right? And it's more important than I am. So, in this case, the prize is actually worth it. I would never hold that against you. The fact you're so worried about it only reinforces my opinion."

"You're kidding me."

"You have some time to think about it. You don't have to decide right this minute. I'll support whatever decision you make, and I won't take it personally if you do. It's got nothing to do with our relationship."

"Would you do it, if it was your ranch?"

This time Riley lay back and stared at the ceiling. "I never cared about anything the way you care about this ranch. I've spent my life running away from family tradition and responsibility. But if I did.... Then I probably would."

Colby stared out the window. The stars were visible again. He wanted Riley to hold him close and beg him not to sleep with Fitz. It took a while for everything to sink in. Riley cared so much for Colby that he was willing to let him do this to get the thing Colby wanted more than anything.

Was that love?

Colby expected his heart to burst through his chest. He spooned up behind Riley and held on for dear life.

Chapter Sixteen

RILEY'S ALARM went off at five and they made love again, slow, silent, bittersweet.

"You want to shower first, or together?" Riley asked.

"I'm off today. No hurry."

"I'm not." Riley's smile drooped. "But it's self-service breakfast, so I can probably be a little late."

Today was departure day and guests would trickle out until around noon. New guests would begin arriving at three, when Riley would have a welcome buffet ready, leading into a standard dinner service.

Together they took a leisurely shower, soaping and caressing each other, taking their time, as if this might be the last time they were together.

Riley wasn't happy about the decision they'd reached the night before, but they both knew it was a practical solution. He couldn't let Colby lose the ranch because of him. They'd really only just met, and no matter how much they felt for each other right now, Riley knew it would be difficult for their relationship to go very far. Colby would never leave the ranch and Riley couldn't stay. One or the other would be forced to break the tenuous thread of their growing affection.

Colby pulled Riley close for a kiss, deep and powerful, as he slid soapy hands along the curve of Riley's ass. As much as he loved the sensation, he couldn't get aroused. They'd tired each other out already that morning. Riley pushed Colby against the wall and slid down his soapy body, giving plenty of attention to washing his cock and heavy sac. Colby hardened slightly so Riley rinsed off the soap and started with his mouth. He first kissed the tip of Colby's cock, then flicked his tongue under his balls.

"Tickles. But I'm not gonna get hard again."

"We'll see about that." Riley was no quitter.

"Even if I do, it's just not gonna happen."

"You like this, don't you?"

Colby tugged Riley back to a standing position and pulled him in close. "You don't have to prove anything to me. Please don't try. I just want to hold you, to feel your body next to mine."

They kissed under the spray until they'd used up the hot water, then reluctantly separated. They took turns drying each other, then lay back in bed.

Riley rolled onto his side, leaning his head on his hand and took another long, slow look at Colby's nude body. Pale brown nipples, deep navel, sexy trail of hair leading to a messy shallow bush that couldn't hide his beautiful cock. There was an assortment of nicks and scars along his shoulders and torso, and a pale gash along his shin. How had Riley never spotted this before? He traced it with a fingertip.

"Broke my leg in the rodeo when I was eighteen. Bull threw me straight up, then stomped on me when I finally hit the dirt."

"Ow." Riley rubbed the raised skin. "Sounds like a crazy thing to do, riding one of those huge bulls."

Colby shook his head. "It was worse than that. They gave me the puniest one, seeing it was my first time. I was more embarrassed than hurt, at least till I got to the hospital. Uncle Jake was furious."

"He didn't want you in the rodeo?" What kind of parent or guardian would?

"No, because I was out of commission for two months and he had to pay another hand to do my work." Colby chuckled. "Said he was gonna take the guy's wages out of mine. Not that I got much, being family."

Substitute cooking for traveling for bull riding and it described Riley's family situation. His father hated to bring in outsiders when his flesh and blood should be taking responsibility for the business.

"Did you rodeo again?"

"Yup. Sat that same bull the next year, and set a state record on time."

Colby's satisfied expression warmed Riley's mood. He reached out to trail a fingertip down Colby's shoulder, circling one nipple. Tonight, Fitz would be doing this very same thing. Kissing the spots Riley loved, kissing and sucking Colby's pretty nipples until they got plump and hard. A knot formed in his throat when he thought about that.

Colby took Riley's hand in his and leaned up for a sweet kiss. "I'll still look and feel the same tomorrow. I'm still yours. But say the word and I won't do it."

"I'll support whatever you decide, Colby." They kissed again, for longer, needier. "But I know it's not going to just be tonight. He's going to expect you to stay with him until he leaves. All week."

Colby tilted his head. "All week?"

DOWN IN the dining hall, Colby grabbed a coffee and waved to the few guests who had come down at the crack of dawn. With a welcome dose of caffeine coursing through his veins, he headed for the main house. Before he rounded the last turn, he heard Fitz's voice.

"Be careful with those bags. They're Louis, you know. Worth more than you make in a year, probably."

Colby hovered behind the large oak tree, staying out of sight.

"Sorry, sir." It was Ricardo, one of the housekeeping staff. It was their busiest day, moving guests out, shuttling luggage, and cleaning in time for the new arrivals.

"Where are you taking those anyway? Is my room ready?"

"Not quite yet. But it's first on the list to be cleaned. I just want to make sure we have your bags available as soon as it's ready. Breakfast is being served all morning, and since you're staying over, Rachel or Alicia can arrange a morning ride for you."

"I'll sort that out myself. Now let me see where you're going to be leaving my bags."

A thank you would have been a nice gesture for putting the staff out, but Fitz didn't add one. Colby frowned.

Footsteps moved away from the house, toward the guest cottages. Colby glanced cautiously around to be sure Fitz was out of sight before making his way through the back garden to the kitchen door.

Rachel and Alicia were sitting at the big table nibbling on toast.

"Morning, Colby. Looks like you can have your room back," Rachel said.

"If you need it," Alicia added and winked.

"Oh? What's that?" Rachel glanced from Alicia to Colby.

"Rache, did you have any other prospective investors? Besides Wellington?" Colby was glad to change the subject. This would distract her for hours.

"I talked to a lot of people—referrals from my MBA classmates—who expressed interest. But quite honestly, not many wanted to follow up after I sent business plans and financials to them. Fitz was the only one interested enough to come out for a look. Why?"

"Do you think he's the right fit for us?"

"He's really interested, and if he's pleased with what he sees this next week, I'm certain he's ready to sign a contract and fork up the capital."

"I thought you liked him." Alicia looked Colby right in the eye. "Don't you?"

"He sure likes you, Colby." Rachel sipped at her coffee and checked her watch. "Still ten minutes before we should get to the dining room for good-byes, Leesh."

"I've got mixed emotions, Rache. I don't like how he treats our staff," Colby said.

"You mean Riley?" Alicia said.

"That's just another level of complication." Colby noticed Rachel staring at him. The time for secrets was past. "He's been pretty rude to the seasonal staff and my ranch hands. Will he be around much if he decides to invest?"

"Can't you just be nice to him this week, Colby? A little extra nice?" Rachel asked.

"I'm trying, but it's not fair to Riley."

"What's Riley got to do—" Rachel stopped as she was about to take a sip of coffee. "You and Riley? Really?"

"Really."

"That's great, Colby. Riley's fantastic," Rachel said.

Alicia nodded and grinned.

"Oh, forget what I said, then. I'll tell Fitz he's coming on too strong if you want." Rachel checked her watch again.

"I will be "extra nice" to Wellington if he's our only hope, Rachel. I can do just about anything to save this place. But if there's another option, please let me know. Sooner rather than later. Before tonight." He hoped it hadn't sounded as ominous as it felt to him.

Rachel put her hand on Colby's. "The numbers look really bad right now, and we're almost out of the line of credit at the bank. If we get any cancellations this summer, we'll really be hurting. We'll have to sell something: stock, land, cut staff. I just don't have enough surplus on the guest ranch side to cover any unforeseen problems on your side of the business. It's that thin margin that keeps the guest ranch from being more attractive to an outside investor."

"Then we should sell off some stock. I can bring fifty or a hundred head to the sale in Alamosa in two weeks."

"Colby, that's just stopping up one hole in a rusty old bucket. A capital infusion like Fitz is offering will get us a shiny new bucket that will keep bringing in revenue for years and years."

"We better go," Alicia said. She stood and ruffled Colby's hair. "We should talk more later, 'kay?"

He nodded and watched them leave.

Years and years of financial security.

There was no other choice.

BREAKFAST WENT smoothly for Riley. He only had to make a few appearances in the dining room to speak with departing guests, promise to send recipes and accept envelopes with tips for himself and the kitchen staff. That had been a surprise after years in the restaurant business. No one tipped the kitchen staff or chef. Here in the hospitality industry, guests offered monetary thanks to everyone who made their stay enjoyable.

He locked the cash in his desk, intending to distribute it to his crew the following day. Lynn or Rachel would have more to add to the pot. He wouldn't take a share for himself. He already was paid far more than the others, and the tips wouldn't make a dent in the pay differential from the Antelope Inn job.

How his world had changed in a month. He had a job he really enjoyed, a crew who grew more confident and competent every day, and a beautiful setting. Even a glance out the kitchen window afforded beautiful Rocky Mountain views. Nothing like Paris, but deeply satisfying in a whole new way.

And he had his own sexy Plaid Cowboy.

"Riley, the Platts are asking to see you," Katrina said as she barreled through the door from the dining room.

"Okay, thanks." He wiped biscuit dough from his hand on a damp cloth and pushed through the door.

There at the first table sat Colby and Fitz. Riley couldn't help staring.

Fitz had his hand on Colby's thigh and leaned close trying to give him a bite of ham and cheese tartlet.

Colby's back was to Riley, but Fitz gave him a gloating smile that stopped Riley in his tracks.

He'd accepted that Colby would be nice to Fitz and even sleep with Fitz. That had been fine when it was theoretical. But he hadn't expected to have to watch Fitz put his hands on Colby or act as if he'd "won." How on earth would he get through the day—and the night?

"Riley, we can't thank you enough for the fantastic food." Mrs. Platt took one of his hands and Riley had to forcibly turn his attention to her.

"It's a damn sight better than last year's food," her husband said.

She gave him a look.

"Well, not that last year was bad," Platt stammered. "But this was an incredible surprise. Hope you'll be here next year. We might stay two weeks."

"If all goes well…," Riley began, trying not to watch Fitz over Platt's shoulder. All was not going well at the moment. Could it be put right again?

He'd told Colby this wouldn't change anything between them, but Riley wasn't so sure.

Shades of Denny with Phillip flashed through his brain and his stomach churned. "Excuse me, please." He raced back inside the kitchen and into the bathroom, but he managed to keep everything down. Good thing he hadn't eaten yet. He splashed water on his face and gulped a few mouthfuls from the palm of his hand before smoothing his hair back and returning to the waiting biscuit dough as if nothing had happened.

Give it five minutes, he told himself. Work for five more minutes instead of running out there to tell Colby you don't want him to go through with it. Five excruciating minutes passed while he pounded the dough far beyond submission.

"Riley, didn't you say the secret to biscuits is not handling them much?" Chuck asked from across the counter.

"Huh?" Riley looked down at the misshapen dough in his hands. It was ruined. It might make some bread sticks or coffee dunkers. He pushed it aside and pulled another batch from the large plastic bin and set about making some proper biscuits.

Five more minutes.

He couldn't keep this up all day and night. How the hell could he handle this?

"Riley?"

The voice startled him and he knocked a mixing bowl and spoon onto the floor with a terrible clatter that had his nerves even more on edge. He turned to find Colby. Alone.

"Hi." Riley tried to smile.

"I volunteered to take guests into Aspen and pick up the next batch. I'll be gone all day."

"Okay." Riley wouldn't ask if Fitz was going too.

"I thought you might want to come along. You haven't had a day away from the ranch since you arrived."

Riley hadn't realized that. When he first arrived, he'd expected to be bored out here. As it happened, he hadn't even thought about leaving. There were so many things keeping him here—besides Colby. He'd enjoyed riding and hiking and even swimming in the river.

"I'd love to, but I've got a lot to do for the buffet." He shrugged and looked into Colby's eyes, unconsciously asking the question he wouldn't speak.

"He's out riding fences with Tommo." Colby smiled and reached out for Riley's hand. He gave it a warm, affectionate squeeze then brought it to his mouth for a kiss. Right in the middle of the kitchen. In front of Chuck and

Katrina! "I'll see you at the welcome buffet. Anything you want me to bring back from Aspen for you?"

Riley nodded. "A plaid cowboy," he whispered.

"All yours. I promise." Colby said in a low voice and touched the brim of his hat. Riley's heart stopped, then started up in double time when Colby gave Riley a quick hug before leaving.

Riley stared after him for a minute.

"So, Beef's out of our hair for the day?" Chuck asked as he cut a tray of biscuits and flopped them onto a baking sheet.

"Beef?"

"That's what the guys are calling Wellington. B. F. Wellington. Beef."

Riley couldn't stop laughing.

RILEY DIDN'T see Colby again until late afternoon. The guest ranch was full this week, and the two dozen guests chatted and nibbled and sipped like they hadn't been fed in weeks.

Rachel and Alicia appeared in deep discussion with Beef—Riley couldn't stop thinking of him that way now—while Lynn and Jake made the rounds greeting guests. Colby shuttled between host duties, stopping at the buffet table on a regular basis to give Riley a bright, reassuring smile. Fitz's gaze followed Colby and landed on Riley like a laser. He rubbed the spot, worried it had burned a hole in his skin.

Poor Colby. Riley stopped feeling sorry for himself to realize how much pressure Colby was under. Caught between personal desires and family duty, and his own sense of propriety. Under any other circumstances, Colby would never sleep with someone for personal gain; he had too high a standard of morality.

That first night together in Aspen, it had been Riley who'd initiated sex. The memory made Riley smile. Fitz's laser-beam gaze sharpened, and Riley tried to ignore it and focus on work.

Dinner went smoothly. Riley prayed for some culinary disaster to absorb his attention, but he and his crew had the routine down pat now and it went like clockwork. He fought the urge to light a tablecloth on fire or spill soup all over the floor.

Lynn came into the kitchen as they were cleaning up.

"I want you all to come to the square dance tonight. Alicia, Rachel, and I have the refreshments under control. Time for y'all to relax and have some fun. You'll be there, won't you, Riley?"

He smiled and gave a tiny nod even though he had no intention of attending.

"Thanks, Lynn!" Willa and Katrina chorused. Even Chuck looked interested.

"He's already spotted a girl he wants to dance with." Katrina poked Chuck in the ribs and he shrugged.

"Riley, you should ask Colby for a dance," Willa said.

"Totally," Katrina added. "Don't let Beef get all the attention."

Riley shook his head and went to his desk and pretended to concentrate on recipes.

Behind him, the others finished cleaning up.

"I'd fucking deck the guy for moving in like that," Chuck said. He kept his voice low, but Riley could still hear every word. He was amazed at Chuck's comment and strained to listen over the sound of clinking dishes.

"Deck who?" Katrina asked in a loud whisper.

"Beef. But I can see why Colby is being friendly to him," Chuck said.

"Why's that?" Willa asked.

"Beef's some rich investor who might buy into the guest ranch. I guess Colby doesn't want to risk rocking the Benjamin boat."

"Where'd you hear that?" Katrina asked.

Riley wanted to know too.

"You hear stuff if you listen. One of the housekeeping girls told me she overheard a whole conversation between the sisters. I just put the pieces together."

"I'm sure you're dead wrong," Willa said.

"Well, it all fits," Chuck replied.

They turned to other topics of gossip for the next fifteen minutes until they had finished their duties.

"Riley, we're done. Can we head out?" Chuck asked.

"Sure. See you tomorrow morning."

"Aren't you coming to the dance?" Katrina asked.

"No."

"Yes, you are." Willa said. "We'll meet you guys over there," she said to the others.

After they left Willa turned to Riley. "Come on. Just a few minutes. I'm sure Colby would like to see you there."

Riley hadn't considered that possibility. "Five minutes. And no dancing."

"Go upstairs and change. I'll wait for you here. I'll come up and get you if you're not back in ten minutes."

Riley couldn't decide whether to wear his best clothes or grab the first ones in the closet. The rest of tonight was already planned out. Showing up to impress Colby wouldn't change the outcome. Worse, he would look like more of a loser when Colby left with Beef. He compromised with a nice shirt and comfortable jeans. No boots. The fancy black boots stood in the closet mocking him. He'd met Colby the night he'd bought them. Only after near total humiliation. Then they'd spiced up more than a few evenings for them since. He kicked the boots to the back of the closet and put on some other dressy shoes he could dance in.

Not that he was planning to dance. He'd show up, let Colby know he wasn't crying into his pillow, then come home and cry into his pillow. *No, no crying.* There was no reason to cry. This was simply practical. If Colby didn't follow through, the results would be far worse than Riley's peace of mind.

He smoothed his hair in the mirror and let Willa take him to the dance.

The dance was held in the back garden of the main house. Picnic tables around the perimeter held an array of snacks and drinks. A three-piece band—fiddle, guitar, and tambourine—and a caller performed at one end of the garden. Most of the guests had already arrived, attired in their best Western wear, or their notion of Western wear. At least half of the assembled attendees were on the floor, clearly enjoying themselves.

Any other night and Riley would have found this charming and fun. Tonight it felt like the prom from hell.

Fitz was dressed to the nines in something the singers on *Hee Haw* might have worn back in the day. Colby, like Riley, had opted for a nice shirt, but hadn't made more effort on his appearance. He even wore his dusty Stetson, not some clean, fancy hat for appearances like some of the guests.

Riley was glad Colby hadn't tried to look his best for Wellington. He recalled their first date—the moonlight ride and the night that followed—with Colby wearing his best, looking and smelling clean and freshly washed. He couldn't watch if Colby danced with Beef. He busied himself at the refreshments, keeping his back to the dance floor—and Colby.

"Having trouble deciding which kind of punch to have?" Colby's voice startled Riley.

Colby came up behind him with a quick hand across Riley's back. The skin burned at the fleeting touch. Riley had to bite his lip, and he didn't trust his voice.

"I'm going to tell him it's just this one time. Just tonight. If that's not enough, then the deal's off." Colby stood next to Riley as he spoke, neither looking at the other.

"What if he wants more?"

"I'll cross that bridge later."

"Colby, you can't do that."

"I can't have it any other way. I can't do this to you—to us."

"Thought you might need some help carrying our drinks," Wellington came up to the table and moved between Colby and Riley. "Unless you want to call it a night now and turn in?" He glanced over at Riley as he asked the question.

Riley balled his hands into fists and wished he'd learned how to meditate. Maybe he should retreat to a Zen monastery right now and swear off relationships and happiness.

"Not yet. I'm enjoying the music."

"You can hear it from my cottage." Beef put an arm around Colby's waist and moved him back toward the dance floor.

Colby glanced at Riley and gave a tense smile.

Riley fled back to the kitchen.

Chapter Seventeen

THE MOMENT Colby couldn't avoid any longer finally arrived. The band was packing up, and Fitz's grip on his arm was getting progressively tighter. In the distance he saw a flash of lightning and heard thunder rumbling a moment later. It was as if even Mother Nature disapproved of what Colby had agreed to. So far tonight, he'd managed to avoid dancing more than once with Fitz by agreeing to partner single guests, mostly female, but when a male guest asked him to dance he gladly accepted. He even danced with Wrangler Stang.

"We must be getting close to your bedtime, Colby. I know you rise bright and early to get to work." Fitz had toned down the possessiveness after that staring match with Riley, and he'd been attentive and good company. He was even nice to the staff for a change. It was like Dr. Jekyll and Mr. Hyde. Once Fitz had a clear path to Colby, he'd almost become a pleasure to spend time with, unless Riley was around.

Yet, Colby hadn't wanted to dance more than once. It wasn't fair to Riley, even if he wasn't there to see it. But the rest of the staff would have seen, and it put Colby and Riley in a bad light because they had no idea why Colby was spending so much time with Fitz.

"Ready to go?" Fitz asked again and Colby nodded. He didn't trust himself to speak.

They waved to the lingering guests and staff and took the path to Fitz's guest cottage. It was one of three, all placed far enough from the other buildings for complete privacy. Colby hadn't been in one since they'd been built. He never cared much for the guest side of the business until recently, after he'd discovered how vital it was to the financial health of the whole ranch. And after Riley had arrived.

Another flash of lightning lit up the night sky as Fitz unlocked the door, then waved Colby in ahead of him.

There was a fire crackling in the fireplace and a champagne bucket near the refrigerator located by the front door. The glossy wooden walls and thick carpet added a mix of elegance and rusticity, and the room was spotlessly clean.

"You like champagne, Colby?"

"S-sure." Colby barely uttered the word. Now he was here and his throat tightened again and his lungs refused to accept oxygen. Maybe he would pass out and wake up later with no memory of the event. Had anyone ever roofied themselves?

Fitz popped the cork and poured champagne into two flutes, then handed one to Colby and urged him towards the couch. He picked up a remote control and turned on some music—soft jazz. The sound did nothing to ease his jangled nerves.

"You're awfully nervous, Colby. What's the matter?" Fitz sipped some champagne.

Colby took a small sip. He needed to keep his head. Or would this be easier if he was drunk? He remembered the night he met Riley. Drunk and out of control, Riley barely noticed what was happening to him. It would be an improvement over being stone cold sober and completely aware. He took another, larger gulp of champagne.

"I've never done this before."

Fitz's eyebrows shot up. "You haven't? I suppose you lead a sheltered existence here on the ranch. Such a shame."

Colby was content to let Fitz think he was a virgin. He drank more champagne.

"But you like men, right?"

"Yes." Oh, God, would it have been as easy as saying no?

Fitz put a hand on his arm, warm and firm, then started tracing patterns with his fingertips. "I thought so. My gaydar's almost foolproof. I'll say I've imagined being with you since the moment I first set eyes on you. If Rachel had mentioned you, I would have been here much sooner." Fitz took his hand and squeezed it, then looked into his eyes.

Colby looked away, unable to bear such a direct gaze. Fitz reached up to trace the curve of Colby's jaw. The touch was gentle, more of a caress than Colby had expected.

"You have such beautiful lips." Fitz ran his thumb over the lower lip. "Soft and beautiful. I'd like to kiss you."

Colby closed his eyes and nodded. When he opened them, Fitz was moving closer. Their lips touched so softly he barely felt it, then Fitz slid his arms around Colby's waist, pulling him in. The first kiss was a tender brush of lips as Fitz's fingers stroked the back of Colby's neck.

The contact last a few seconds before Fitz pulled back.

It hadn't been bad. But it hadn't been Riley.

Fitz leaned in again, this time parting his lips and letting his tongue brush against Colby's. Colby let his mouth open slightly as Fitz's tongue tangled around his own, but he didn't kiss back. The kiss was rich and a little sweet, like the champagne.

The tenderness in Fitz's touch surprised Colby. He'd expected Fitz to get right to business and take what he wanted from Colby, but instead he was taking every step so slowly, so considerately. Was this better or worse than just pulling each other's clothes off and doing the deed?

Worse. This was far worse. This was too close to what Colby had with Riley. Sweet, caring touches. He wanted this night with Fitz to be quick and impersonal and ugly. Just a couple of guys getting each other off, like he'd done plenty of times before at Rawhide. Better to speed this up.

Colby finished his champagne and pulled Fitz in for another kiss, this time deep and aggressive. Fitz returned as good as he got and started on Colby's buttons. When they broke for air, Fitz's chest was heaving.

"You're a quick learner. I like that. I want to make you feel so good you won't want to get out of bed for a week. Call in sick—"

Colby took another kiss so he wouldn't have to listen.

Now Fitz had Colby's shirt half off and was playing with his nipples. The kissing and the champagne had his head spinning. The nipple play got him hard, and he felt a deep shame wash over him as his pants grew unbearably tight. Fitz palmed him through the denim and it felt better than Colby wanted to admit. He was already in high gear. Fitz was an excellent kisser and he quickly found Colby's hot spots with his hands.

"Let's get you out of those boots and jeans, cowboy." Fitz slid onto the floor between Colby's knees and pushed his face into Colby's crotch, lips tracing the outline of his erection through his jeans for a moment before he turned his attention to Colby's boots. When those were off he went for the belt, then unzipped Colby's jeans.

"Oh, yes. We are both going to enjoy this." Fitz was practically salivating as he reached down into Colby's shorts.

Then Colby's cell phone rang. He retrieved it from the floor and pulled Fitz's hand out of his pants so he could talk.

"Yeah?" he tried not to pant into the phone. He hadn't checked the caller ID and had no clue what this would be about.

"Colby, I am so damned sorry to call on your night off." Marcus spoke quickly, excitedly. "But McLean just phoned. The lightning hit a tree near the fence line, and he thinks at least a few animals may be in danger. They're trapped between the fence and a stand of burning trees."

"Where are you?"

"Driving over right now in the SUV. I already called the fire department and I've got most of the hands with me. I left a message with Doc Madison's answering service."

"Good work, Marcus. I'll wait at the barn for the vet and gather more supplies. Let me know when you get to the fire."

"Fire?" Fitz asked.

"There's a fire and some of the stock are in danger. I have to go." Colby was already heading for the door, stopping only to pick up his boots and do up his pants. He hopped around on one foot before taking a moment to sit down and get the boots on before he started moving through the door. He was halfway to the barn before he realized his shirt wasn't buttoned.

RILEY RETREATED to the kitchen after leaving the dance. The only sure distraction was cooking. He gathered butter and flour to make puff pastry, a tedious process involving rolling the dough out then chilling it, then rolling, repeated over and over. He made a few batches with a sprinkle of sugar for desserts, and as an experiment, added a touch of cumin and chili powder to another batch. It would be a nice base for a savory dish. The endless rolling was mind-numbingly boring and left him too much time to think, but he'd have at least a month's worth of dough to freeze when he was finished.

At one point he thought he heard Colby making his way upstairs, but Riley's mood plummeted when he realized it was just thunder rolling past. He expected to hear rain, but it didn't come, just more ominous thunderclaps.

Time moved at a glacial pace. Riley was gathering materials for another baking project to work on while the pastry dough chilled when the piercing shriek of sirens caught his attention. He raced outside and spotted Colby running for the barn, shirt flapping in the breeze. Riley fought the urge to run after him, despite his concern over the sirens. He couldn't bear to face Colby fresh out of Beef's bed.

The sirens grew louder and Riley gave in to curiosity. Two fire trucks stopped in front of the house and Colby and Jake were talking to the firefighters.

Lynn came up to him, pulling a robe tightly around herself against the nighttime chill. "Fire up at the border with McLean's, our neighbor to the west. Luckily it's near the road, otherwise they'd need helicopters."

"Fire? How?"

"Didn't you see the lightning? It can easily start a fire when it's been dry too long. First time we've had one on our property."

"Is anyone hurt?"

"No. But McLean says some stock are trapped by burning trees. They're not particularly smart and they're liable to hurt themselves trying to run away. They get caught on fences, barbed wire. It's sad."

"What can we do?"

She looked down at Riley's floury hands and kitchen apron. "Don't tell me you were cooking, at this hour?"

He shrugged. "Couldn't sleep. Cooking helps. Sometimes."

"Why don't you help me prepare food and water for the fire crews and our hands? Most of them are up at the fire right now."

Riley looked around and noticed Colby was gone along with the fire trucks. Jake ambled back toward Lynn and Riley.

"Colby's gone up to take care of the stock. The vet's meeting them all up there."

"We're going to make sandwiches and drinks," Lynn said.

Guests had begun wandering toward the barn and driveway. Riley spotted Beef Wellington too, wearing a cushy robe. He tried not to take any pleasure knowing Fitz didn't get a whole night with Colby. He'd give anything for Colby not to be facing a fire and risking his life to save land and stock. He'd even give him another night with Beef to spare him this kind of pain.

Jake explained to the guests what was going on while Riley and Lynn headed for the kitchen. Alicia and Rachel soon followed to help in the kitchen. They wouldn't need to call in Riley's crew.

Colby and Marcus phoned in reports every hour or two. The sun was barely peeking over the horizon when the fire trucks pulled into the driveway. The crews filtered into the dining hall for hot coffee, cold water, and lots of food. They looked exhausted and made only occasional small talk, though they all made a huge effort to thank everyone for the food.

It was another hour before Colby came back. His face was sooty and he wore a fireman's pants and jacket. He came into the dining hall and clapped a few of the fire crew on the back, shaking his head as they spoke.

"What happened?" Riley asked Alicia.

"Not sure, but I'm guessing we lost some stock. Colby never gets that look on his face over a downed fence." She took the platter of sandwiches from Riley. "Go sit with him. I've got things under control here."

"My crew will be arriving soon."

"And they can function for half an hour without you."

"Okay." Riley collected a plate of sandwiches and cookies to bring to Colby. He was three feet from the table when Fitz walked in through the door and headed for Colby.

Colby raised his head and spotted Riley just as he was about to turn away.

"Fitz, let's talk later. I'm beat and I'm hungry."

Fitz looked at Riley and twisted up his mouth before moving back to the door.

"Riley, sit down."

"Colby, are you okay?" Now Riley couldn't hide his concern as he saw Colby's face up close and noticed a bandage on his left hand. "Are you hurt?"

"Burned my hand a little. Par for the course. I can't get a grip on the stock with those fireproof gloves."

"Do you want to talk about it?"

"Not really, but thanks for asking." He grabbed a sandwich and ate it in two huge bites. As he chewed he put his good hand across the table to hold Riley's.

"How about the cows?"

Colby gave a weak smile. He tried to get Riley to stop calling them cows. "We lost a few in the fire. The vet's working on a few more who probably won't make it. But we saved more than half. There's this little calf whose mother… died." The look on his face told Riley it hadn't been an easy death. "We'll put the little guy with a cow who lost her own calf during the night. If we get them paired up he should survive." Colby smiled for the first time since he'd come in this morning.

Riley sat there holding hands while Colby finished his food. Firefighters drifted out of the hall and kitchen crew drifted in, but Riley didn't give them any attention. He wished he could help Colby, and he'd stay as long as Colby wanted him to.

When the first guests started looking for breakfast, Colby squeezed Riley's hand. "I should let you get to work. I'm sorry for keeping you. Thanks, Riley."

Riley nodded and watched Colby stand up. He was proud of himself for not mentioning Fitz, but it took all of his willpower.

Then Colby came around behind him and leaned down for a hug and to plant a kiss on Riley's cheek. He smelled like smoke and sweat. "Nothing happened. And nothing will." He squeezed Riley's shoulder and left.

Colby went up to the main house and took a long, hot shower to wash away the night and the stench of smoke. The schedule was all fucked up today, and he really should be in the barn managing the situation. He'd allow himself an hour or two for a nap and then get to work. With a towel wrapped around his waist he headed for his room.

He couldn't remember the last time he'd slept in his bed. Housekeeping or Aunt Lynn had kindly changed the sheets after Fitz had departed, and Colby didn't even remember crawling under the blanket.

The sun was high when he woke up, and he covered his eyes against the glare. The face of the clock was obstructed—a note card was propped up, with Lynn's handwriting.

> *I turned off your alarm. You need your sleep and the rest of*
> *the day off. Jake's handling everything.*

He tossed the card aside and let his anger ebb away into thankfulness for his family. For a change he would listen to Lynn, let her look after him and give himself a little break. After shaving and dressing he headed into the barn.

The vet had treated all the injured animals, Jake had gotten the cow to accept and nurse the orphan calf, and everything was back to running the way it should. Even without Colby.

He was feeding Hickory some carrots when Jake came out of the office.

"You catch up on your sleep?"

"I'll never catch up, but I feel like I'm back with the living."

"Good. All the tasks have been assigned. I gave the men half shifts today. The ones who worked the fire have the morning off, and the others have the afternoon off."

"What's my assignment?"

"It's chuck wagon dinner tonight. Just help out with the trail ride there and back."

"I can help drive the wagon." He remembered the week before when he and Riley had reconnected. Then he remembered Fitz Wellington. He groaned.

"No need. Riley's going to drive out with Willa. You're on Fitz duty this evening…."

Colby nodded. He had to sort that out once and for all. During a chuck wagon dinner wasn't the best choice. He'd talk to Fitz before the ride and let him know there would be no rain check on last night.

Then Tommo called, needing Colby's help with some stock in West Paddock. By the time he got back to the barn, the guests were saddling up for the trail ride. Fitz rode up on Hickory.

"I hope you don't mind me riding your mare. She moves beautifully. A pleasure to ride." He gave Colby a look that promised other riding pleasures and Colby simply nodded.

"No problem at all." Fitz was an excellent rider, but Colby didn't like Fitz's presumption that he could do as he pleased here. But if Fitz riding Hickory was the worst thing this evening, he'd be happy with that result.

Jake tossed Colby an apologetic expression. "Got Twenty-four ready for you. Wrangler Steve is on sweep, so just enjoy the ride. I'll catch up to y'all before dinner is served."

THE RIDE out to the spot for the chuck wagon dinner with Willa was relatively uneventful given that there had been a fire on the ranch the night before. Riley was building skill and confidence driving the horses, and they only got out of control once, heading off the trail and bouncing the wagon over a fallen branch that made everything inside crash together when they landed. It was no worse than the time with Colby. And now Riley had learned his lesson about how to pack and secure everything in the wagon.

Katrina, Chuck, and Alicia met them in the pickup and together they set up the grills and picnic tables and set out the spread while Riley and Willa finished grilling the meat and got the bread, biscuits, and pies ready to cook once the guests arrived. Everything would be piping hot and freshly baked.

They greeted the riders as they arrived, and Riley served trays of refreshing low-alcohol cocktails, dreading the moment Colby and Beef would arrive. When he spotted the sun glinting off Colby's palomino mare it was time for Riley to focus on finishing dinner. He retrieved the first tub of biscuit dough and popped the lid off.

Only it wasn't biscuit dough. It was puff pastry. He pulled lids off of every tub and found nothing but puff pastry. Not at all interchangeable with the thick, flaky biscuits that went with the barbecue and bourbon beans. He'd been so preoccupied with his troubles, he'd put the wrong labels on the tubs while he was making dough the previous night.

Time to improvise. He could layer everything in pie plates and pass it off as cowboy potpie, but he didn't have the right dough for that either. Nope, best to admit to the error and bake up some flaky squares along with the loaves of bread.

Willa set the bread and pastry squares onto the charcoal pit and waited.

A sudden gust of wind came up from the south, sending charcoal dust whirling over the whole prep table. And Riley had left the lids off some of the tubs while frantically searching for the biscuits. Now the bread, pastry and the dessert pies were covered in a fine mist of gray ash that was impossible to remove without damaging the carefully risen dough.

"Shit, shit, shit!" Riley said under his breath.

"Oh, no. What do we do?" Willa asked, ineffectually trying to brush charcoal ash off raw dough. "Oh, God, it's all ruined."

"I think it will be easier to brush off when it's cooked and the dough firms up. Maybe no one will even notice."

People noticed. Most of them just brushed the dust off and kept eating.

"You can barely taste it," Rachel said.

"This is so authentic," one of the guests remarked. "So rustic."

"This is the worst bread I've ever tasted. And what in God's name are these flaky squares supposed to be?"

Riley counted to ten and then walked in the opposite direction of Beef Wellington.

COLBY'S HEART ached when Riley explained to the guests about the dough mix-up. Most of them shrugged it off, having dulled the edge of their hunger with delicious finger foods and unique cocktails with clever Western names. The aroma of roasting meat put most of them at ease and they sat eagerly at the picnic tables awaiting whatever Riley had prepared for them.

Everything tasted delicious and there wasn't a single complaint until Fitz bit into a dusty, gray piece of pastry instead of the plump flaky buttermilk biscuit Lynn had been going on about during the ride out.

"This is the worst bread I've ever tasted. And what in God's name are these flaky squares supposed to be?"

"That's just how they'd come out on the real chuck wagons," Lynn said, patting Fitz's arm.

"Where's that damn cook?"

"He's more than a cook—" Lynn glanced at Colby.

"No, Lynn. He's far less than a cook." Fitz's voice was cold, uncompromising.

Guests were staring.

"Fitz, taste the meat." Colby touched Fitz's plate to distract him. "This pork is amazing. What do you think?"

"Any fool with a watch can barbecue meat. That doesn't take much talent. But baking, that's where you can take the true measure of a cook. Even a chuck wagon cook. They were judged by their biscuits."

Guests were murmuring and taking bites of everything, comparing opinions. A few who had been pleased moments before started frowning.

Spaghetti *Western* • 163

"Fitz, let's go for a walk. Please?" Colby hoped Riley wouldn't see them walk away from the table but he couldn't let Fitz go on complaining and upsetting the guests.

"Fine." Fitz followed Colby out of hearing range of the guests.

"Look, dinner tonight isn't up to the standard you expect. Things go wrong. It's a cookout. It's not a Michelin three-star restaurant. Cut us some slack. Please. Rachel and Lynn can work with Riley and—"

"And what? Something else will go wrong next time. The man can't run a kitchen properly and his skills are highly dubious. Did you verify his Cordon Bleu credential? This is unacceptable. I'm sorry but Lynn and Rachel aren't qualified to run the food program of a high-level guest ranch operation. I'll have to take control over that aspect. They do quite well with housekeeping and events, but I do have some—"

"We're getting the cart before the horse, Fitz. Let's wait till tomorrow when you can meet with them to discuss your concerns. I'm not even part of the guest ranch side of things."

"That's right, Colby. You're pretty and when you kiss me I can't think straight. But you don't know anything about running a restaurant or a hotel. Leave all that to me." He put a hand on Colby's upper arm and gave a squeeze. "It won't be difficult to replace Riley and then you'll see the…."

Colby's brain stopped processing words. His whole body felt like it was on fire. Replace Riley? A buzzing filled his ears and he stepped away from Fitz. Everything was spinning out of control. Even if Colby spent the night with Fitz, it wouldn't save Riley's job if Fitz took over the kitchen.

He glanced back to the chuck wagon and spotted Riley and Willa pulling pans out of the coals. Colby couldn't remember when Riley had taken even half a day off since he'd arrived here. He was up before dawn and stayed up into the wee hours on a regular basis to accommodate guests, or help in the case of an emergency like the night before.

Fitz was still ranting. Colby reached out and took his arm. "You're right. It's Riley. And there's an easy solution to that. But now I'm going to finish my dinner. You can join me or you can keep complaining."

"I'll join you. And later, Colby? Are you free after dinner to join me again?"

"Yes. I am. Should I go to your cabin?"

"Sounds perfect."

RILEY DIDN'T expect to find Colby waiting for him when he finally got the chuck wagon back to the spot behind the kitchen.

"Riley, I need to talk to you."

"Let me unload first."

"I'll help."

With Colby's assistance unloading and tending to the horses was quick and painless. Riley barely had a chance to thank his crew before Colby ushered him upstairs.

"What's going on, Colby?" Riley was exhausted and angry at himself for so many failures at dinner. He hadn't even driven the team well. "The whole dinner was a disaster. I'm sorry."

"You have nothing to be sorry about. You're human. You made a mistake, and you can't control the elements. End of discussion. The guests loved it, even with a little ash."

Riley ran a hand through his hair and frowned. "I really messed things up with Fitz."

"No, you didn't. You actually fixed them."

"What?"

"He wants to replace you."

"Colby, how can that be fixed?" And why was Colby smiling as he told Riley? "That's terrible."

"But it's not. Because now we know we can't do business with him, we—"

"But you can't keep going without him!"

Colby shook his head. "No. We don't want him to invest. He wants to run the food stuff and make lots of changes and—"

"Look, let me just make this easier for you. I quit. I'll pack up and be out of here before you even know it." The words tumbled out before Riley's brain had a chance to approve them. Riley didn't want to leave. It was the last thing he wanted, but it was the only way. "I can't let you give up this opportunity because of me." Tears welled up in his eyes and his throat closed up. He had to get out of here before he lost control. It was all he could do for Colby.

"It's not because of you. It's for you. I can't give you up. And I won't let Beef Wellington force me into something I don't want."

Riley barely heard Colby. He was already in the bedroom, throwing clothes into his suitcase. It only took a few minutes. He hadn't brought all that much with him.

"Let me get out of here now, before I think too hard about this and—"

Colby kissed him hard or he might have finished that sentence. Several minutes later, Colby let Riley breathe again. "You're not going anywhere. I won't lose you."

"Colby, you can't risk the ranch over me. You're not thinking clearly. You were born here, you grew up here, you want to die and be buried here...." He stopped, recalling that Colby's parents were buried on the property.

"I don't know if I want that. What do you imagine? Me, all alone when I'm eighty, riding the fences and going to bed alone every night? No family, but plenty of land and cattle?"

It was a pretty accurate picture of Riley's thoughts about Colby's future. "Isn't that what you want?"

"No. Maybe a younger generation will take over. What makes this place special is family. If Fitz comes into the picture, he'll throw all our family traditions and values out the window. We'll be numbers in a spreadsheet to him and we'll lose touch with why we want to keep the ranch in the first place. Because it's a place we're proud of, with a history and a way of running things that we're proud of. Otherwise, we might as well take our name off the ranch, because it wouldn't represent us and our values anymore."

Riley started to wheel the suitcase toward the door.

"I wouldn't have figured this out without you, Riley. You brought out the worst behavior in Fitz, and then we could see who he really was. And none of the family want him to be part of our ranch."

"Great." Riley the Useful. With a moniker like that, maybe he had a future at Ren faires.

"That's not all I figured out." Colby took hold of Riley's arm and stopped him from going through the door. "The moment he said you could be replaced, it hit me. You can't be replaced. There is no replacement for you."

"As much as I'd like to protest, he's right. Another chef could do as good a job."

"I don't mean as a chef. I mean here." Colby touched his heart. "Riley Winthrop Emerson, I love you."

COLBY TOOK a deep breath and rapped on Fitz's cottage door.

Fitz opened it, wearing a robe and probably nothing else. He gave Colby a warm smile that melted right off his face when Lynn, Jake, Rachel, and Alicia filed in after Colby.

"What's this?"

"I imagine it's not quite what you were expecting, Wellington," Jake said with as much gruffness as Colby had ever heard.

Fitz pulled his robe tightly closed and put his knees together as he sat on the couch. "Colby?"

"We had a little family conference after dinner," Lynn said. "We talked to Riley. Well, Colby did. Riley quit tonight. He even packed up his belongings, and he'd be off the premises by now, but—"

"Is that so?" Fitz's smile returned. "See how easy that was?"

"We like Riley," Alicia said. "The guests liked him, and his staff adore him. Hiring him was the best thing Mom's done in a long time."

"You can't run a top-notch restaurant or hotel based on who you *like*." Fitz shook his head. He glanced up at Colby again. "Colby understands, don't you? Even you said Riley was the problem."

Colby sat next to Fitz, on the couch where they'd kissed twenty-four hours earlier. "That wasn't quite what I said. I *don't* like Riley. Truth is, I love him." He watched Fitz's eyes widen and felt like saying it again and again. He glanced at his family and they nodded, smiling. "Riley was willing to give up his job here, even encouraged me to spend the night with you, just to get you to invest in us and save this ranch. He doesn't look for problems, he looks for solutions, even if they're unpleasant. And I almost listened to him. I almost put the ranch above what really matters: family and being able to live with myself."

Colby turned to Alicia. "You said I had to decide if Riley was more important than some dirt and some cows. Well, he is. And we all are. I know what makes our guest ranch special is that we treat our guests like they're part of our family when they come here. That matters more than fancy wine and perfect raviolis."

Jake stepped forward. "We can't change the way we do business here, Wellington. Because it's not a business to us. It's a lot bigger and a lot more important than numbers on a spreadsheet or in a bank account. If you can understand any of that, then we might still be able to come to some agreement. If not, then we'd appreciate if you'd be ready to leave by checkout tomorrow."

Everyone stared at Fitz for a moment, and then they filed out of the cottage, leaving only Colby.

"Thanks, Fitz."

"Thanks? For what?"

"For opening my eyes. Now I have to go make sure Riley doesn't drive off. He still thinks he can fix this by leaving. That's how crazy, kind, and self-sacrificing he is. There's no piece of dirt that's worth losing a man like that." Colby stood up.

"Hang on. What did you mean when you said, 'It's Riley and there's an easy solution'?"

Colby nodded. "After all your criticism of him and his cooking, I realized I was in love with him. And that the solution to the Riley problem was to get rid of *you*, even if it meant we don't get an investor. You were the only person who had any issue with Riley."

Fitz huffed. "I sent you running into his arms?" He shook his head. "And you're willing to lose the ranch, for *him*?" His tone was sardonic.

Colby put his hat on but didn't let go of the crown for a few seconds. "We are."

He didn't even look back as he walked out of the cabin and broke into a run.

RILEY SAT on the couch staring at his suitcase, wondering if he'd just imagined that Colby loved him. Had he also imagined the kiss, long and sweet and nearly perfect? It would have been perfect except that Colby left just as Riley was heating up in all the best ways.

"I'll be back. Soon." Colby had kissed Riley again before leaving.

But now, alone, it seemed impossible Colby would risk losing even a portion of the ranch for Riley. If his heart would stop beating so damn loudly he might be able to think.

It was just like Colby, always putting someone or something ahead of himself, taking on extra responsibility, or trying to make someone else happy. Riley wouldn't let him throw this opportunity away. He couldn't live with himself if Colby had to give up any part of the Z. Riley had already quit. Best to follow through with that and leave Colby free to take whatever path he wanted, without worrying about Riley's feelings.

Riley Emerson, I love you. Well, he'd always have the memory of those words and the way Colby's arms felt around him. The mornings they woke up together and….

He grabbed the suitcase handle and opened the door.

Colby stood on the step. He frowned as he put a hand on Riley's shoulder and slowly backed him into the flat.

"Good thing I've got perfect timing. Stop you from making another big mistake." Colby's frown morphed into a wide grin.

Riley felt heat rising in his cheeks at the mention of the ignominious first meeting.

"My hero, come to rescue me just like a fairy tale? Again."

"Either that, or I'll lock you in the tower so you don't run away. Your choice."

Riley wrapped his arms behind Colby's neck, breathing the smell of the trail, the scent of horses, and Colby's own personal essence.

"Hero. Definitely going with hero." Riley leaned up and kissed Colby.

Without breaking the kiss, Colby reached back and shut the door, then gathered Riley up and pulled him in tightly, and kissed him with all his might.

If ever a kiss was worth a thousand words this was it, but there were just four on Riley's mind when Colby finally pulled back.

"I love you too."

More kissing ensued as Colby maneuvered Riley into the bedroom and they fell, panting, onto the bed, still embracing.

"Care to spend the night, cowboy?"

"First, you're unpacking that bag. I don't want to wake up by myself again." Colby kissed Riley once more, and if Riley had any intention of leaving, he abandoned it. He wanted to get lost in Colby's arms and kisses and… much more.

"Are you sure about this? About me?"

"I've never been so sure of anything in my life. My whole world would be empty without you. Even if you quit your job, please stay here with me, at least for a while. And when you get tired of cows, I hope you'll consider taking me with you."

"You're not supposed to call them cows."

"So you have been paying attention."

"To every word you said. But I'm still a little shaky on that part about you loving me."

"I love you. I love you, I love you."

Chapter Eighteen

ON MONDAY morning, Colby went down to the kitchen with Riley. The rest of the kitchen crew was already there, working on breakfast. They greeted Colby warmly and no one commented on his presence. Riley let out a silent thanks and got to work, a little self-conscious with Colby there.

"Word's going around that Beef is leaving this morning." Leave it to Chuck to bring up the topic. Riley glanced over at Colby who was drinking coffee and trying to steal a piece of crispy bacon from Katrina's workspace.

"That's true," Colby said, quickly stuffing the bacon into his mouth before Katrina tried to steal it back. "I'm about to head over and make sure he leaves. Riley, care to join me?"

"If you can wait until breakfast is served, sure."

"I reckon I can. I don't want to miss my breakfast either." Colby reached out for more bacon, and Katrina threatened him with a wooden spoon till he put it back."

"You gave him till checkout, right?" Riley asked, glad that Colby's presence and their much more obvious relationship hadn't changed anything in the kitchen.

"High noon," Chuck said and whistled a tune from some old Western.

"High noon." Colby nodded.

AFTER BREAKFAST, Colby and Riley headed for the main house. Colby's family greeted Riley like he belonged there. Lynn even handed him a mug of coffee. As Riley took it he noticed it was lopsided, misshapen, like a pottery project gone awry.

"Colby made that mug back in elementary school," Lynn said, winking at Riley.

Colby twisted his mouth into a grimace, but he put an arm around Riley. "I promise never to give you anything that ugly."

"This is a masterpiece in comparison to some of my early pastry projects."

"Even a mangled-looking pastry is gonna taste good. 'Specially those cro-saints," Colby replied and everyone laughed. When the laughter faded away, Colby's expression turned serious again. "Was there any trouble with today's departure?"

"He's out in the driveway, waitin' on his taxi to the airport," Lynn said.

"I'd take him myself just to make sure he goes, if I could stand to spend another minute with him." Colby glanced at Jake, then Riley. "I need to get myself down to the barn. The hands are probably thinking I've quit."

"Marcus has everything under control this morning. But there is a pile of paperwork I'd be happy to hand off to you."

Colby frowned. Rachel came in from the front room. "Taxi's here. Anyone want to bid farewell to Wellington?"

No one responded.

"Let's at least watch him drive away," Jake suggested, and they filed into the front room and out the door. By that time, all that was left was a cloud of dust.

In silence they all watched the dust dissipate. Once it was gone, no one said anything. The initial cheer melted away. Rachel shuffled her feet, and tension appeared around Colby's eyes. Lynn kept tugging at the hem of her apron.

Riley knew that the financial troubles remained, and guilt washed over him. They would have had the investment they needed if he wasn't here.

Just then the taxi reappeared, coming back down the drive toward the house.

"What the devil does he want now?" Jake growled. "I'll handle it."

Riley, Colby, Alicia, and Lynn went back inside. Rachel stayed with her father.

They'd only made it back to the kitchen when Rachel's voice came through. "Riley, Riley! Come outside!"

Riley ran toward the front door with Colby right on his heels.

A taxi had arrived, but it hadn't brought Fitz back. Instead, Stella stood in the driveway, handing the driver some cash.

"Surprise!" Rachel said, squeezing Riley's shoulder. "A good surprise."

"Hey, Riley. I didn't expect the Welcome Wagon." Stella waved, then threw herself into Riley's arms.

"I'm so glad you're here." It had been a year since he'd seen her, and phone conversations were a poor substitute for a visit. He hadn't realized how much he missed her. They hugged for a few moments, and then Riley realized everyone was still standing around watching. Colby's eyes were wide as saucers at first, then went back to normal size.

"This is my sister, Estelle. Stella."

"Hey."

"Good to meet you."

"Welcome."

Lynn even gave her a nice hug.

"I'm a few days early for my reservation, so I hope that couch is still available, Riley."

"You're in luck, Stella," Rachel said. "We've got an unexpected vacancy."

Everyone broke into relieved laughter, except for Stella, who probably thought they'd all gone mad.

"A lot's happened since I talked to you, Stell."

RILEY SAT on the bed in Stella's—formerly Beef's—cabin, and nearly stood back up when he realized it was where Beef had planned to bring Colby. Well, all that was over now. Beef's visit was just a bad taste in everyone's mouth.

"Well, Riles, I can't believe the way things have turned around since the other day when it sounded like the end of the world." Stella had finished unpacking while Riley caught her up on recent events.

"I'm as surprised as you are."

Stella sat next to Riley and put an arm around his shoulders. "I don't think you gave Colby enough credit. For having principles, and for knowing what a catch you are."

Riley planted a kiss on the top of her head. "Colby's the catch. After Denny…"

"Denny's got his head up his ass."

Or someone else's ass, Riley thought.

Stella continued, "You're worth a million Dennys. A bazillion Dennys."

"How many zeroes in that?"

"A zillion." Stella grinned.

"My sister, the math genius."

"You're damn right. That's some of my news. I'm going back to MIT in the fall."

"Really? Back to math?"

She shook her head. "I'm thinking of engineering. Maybe aerospace."

"My sister the rocket scientist." He hugged her until she smacked his head. "What does Lord Voldemort think of that?"

"Dad's outraged. That's how I knew I was making the right decision. 'Engineering's not real science.'"

"Nothing's changed."

She nodded. "Nothing's changed."

"Does he know you're here?"

"Yeah. He didn't say hi. Mum did, though. In her way, and out of Dad's hearing."

"He hasn't had anything to say to me for years." Riley shrugged. He'd gotten over that a long time ago.

Stella got up. "Show me around a little before you have to start working on lunch?"

Riley started the tour in his flat, where he changed into his sturdy boots.

"Where'd you get those? They look authentic."

"Colby gave them to me."

"I like him more every minute. And damn, he's even hunkier than you said. Why didn't you send me any photos?"

"He's not the kind of guy who would like having his picture taken."

"Did you ask?"

Riley shrugged.

"We'll see about that. Now the rest of the tour."

Riley felt an odd sense of pride as he showed Stella around the barn, stopping to point out a few of the horses, then the corrals and paddocks. They came across Colby in the sick paddock with Doc Madison, the vet.

"There was a fire up in one of the pastures the other night," Riley told Stella. "Those cattle were injured." The sense of pride grew as he watched Colby talking to the vet, stroking the frightened animals to calm them during the exam and treatment.

"He's got a way with animals, doesn't he?" Stella asked. "He looks so worried."

"You wouldn't think he could care about every single head of cattle, but he seems to. They only lost two head in the fire and it hit him really hard."

"Was anyone hurt? How much damage is there?"

"I don't know about the damage. Colby hasn't said." Riley's chest hurt when he realized that the fire would put even more strain on the ranch's finances.

Colby touched his hat and nodded as he continued talking with the vet. Then she collected her gear and Colby walked her out of the paddock. He came over to where Riley and Stella leaned against the paddock fence.

"Is Riley giving you the ten-cent tour?"

"Are you kidding? With that view, it's worth at least a dollar." Stella grinned.

"The view's about the only thing that's free around here," Colby said. "You like to ride, Stella?"

"I rode some when I was younger."

"Hope you learned better than Riley."

"Hey!" Riley punched Colby's arm. "I'm not that bad."

"Because I'm a good teacher." Colby's heated gaze implied he wasn't really talking about horseback riding.

Stella gave Riley a piercing look, and Riley felt his neck warming up.

"Well, you should get out on the trails this afternoon. If you need any gear, one of the wranglers will set you up."

"I can't wait."

They left Colby to get back to work and hiked past the guest cabins and lodge.

Stella stopped and did a 360 degree turn, taking in the scenery. She inhaled deeply and let it out. "Wow. You weren't kidding about this place. It's remote."

"It's incredible. I get that gorgeous view every day. You should see the way the sun lights up the mountains at sunrise, especially the snow. Blues and pinks turn into gold." He glanced across the valley and let the beauty sink in again. It didn't seem real, like he was living inside a painting.

"You look amazing, Riles, did I mention that?"

"No."

She brushed his cheek. "You've got some color, and I don't think I've ever seen you this happy. I'm glad. If I hadn't seen it myself, I never would have believed you would like being on a real ranch."

There was a veiled insult and Riley frowned.

"Dude, until now, your main connection with the great outdoors has been Central Park or a ski slope in Gstaad. You'd never have walked past that corral without mentioning the smell, and now…. It's a big change."

She was right. He'd never realized how narrow his world had been, despite his travels and advantages. "At night you can see all the stars. The air is so clear. And if you listen you can hear dozens of different birds."

"Who stole my brother? Joking aside, where are you going at the end of the summer? Back to Paris or New York?"

"I'm going to stay here. If Colby wants me to."

She raised her eyebrows and turned a corner of her mouth down.

"I know it's a big change. But I've changed a lot since I got here. And it's because of Colby. Not because of how I much I care about him. He's opened my eyes up to things I'd never seen before. New experiences. Things I'd like to learn more about." He paused. The skepticism hadn't left her face. "I've traveled and seen a lot of places, and I don't need to go again. Not right away. When I do, I'd like to be able to share them with someone else. For now, Colby's showing me around his world, and there's plenty to explore." He was out of breath and a little dizzy after his speech. Until this moment he didn't realize how much he wanted to stay here.

"You've sold me. I'll see how I feel about ranch living after a week here."

They wandered along the trail another ten minutes before Stella stopped to take some pictures. She made Riley pose with the mountains in the background and took so many shots he felt like a bride on wedding day.

"Colby's family seems to really like you. And apparently you like them too. That's got to be a nice change."

"Tell me about it. I hope it won't wear off once they realize I've just cost them the capital they need to get back on their feet here."

"I take it you haven't mentioned you have a big fat trust fund gathering dust."

Riley shook his head. "I don't even know how I could at this point, without it being insulting. I know they wouldn't take money from me. I feel guilty even taking the wages they pay me."

"Why? You haven't been spending the trust money. You've been living off your earnings for years."

"That's not the point. But I wish there was a way I could help out."

"I can think of two."

"If I invest my money I'm afraid it would change everything between me and Colby and his family. I don't want there to be any sense of obligation. I'm too close to them for it to be a neutral investment."

Stella nodded. "Then you'll have to choose door number two."

Door number two. Riley remembered a story he'd read in middle school, "The Lady or the Tiger." The protagonist had to choose between two doors. Behind one was a beautiful woman he would have to marry, even though he was in love with someone else, and behind the other... well, it wouldn't be pretty. Both doors held an unpleasant result.

Riley's choice felt oddly similar. He might lose his love or alter their relationship if he offered the money. So he opened the door with the tiger and hoped he would survive.

THERE WAS a hayride after dinner so it was late when Riley and Colby finally made their way upstairs to Riley's flat—together.

Once inside, Riley felt an inexplicable flutter in his midsection. Tonight was their first night as a public couple. Would anything be different now that Colby was his official boyfriend?

Nothing was different in the way Colby greeted him with hug and a kiss that got Riley's engine racing. But everything had changed. One set of worries had been replaced with another. In the bedroom Riley started to unbutton his shirt.

"Here, let me do that for you." Colby moved in close and finished the job, then peeled the shirt back so he could kiss Riley's shoulder. Colby's lips sent shudders through Riley's whole body. Colby pulled him in tight. "Riley, what's wrong? You're shaking."

Riley glanced away. "Nothing. I'm fine. That feels good."

"I'll be gentle. I promise." Colby's tone was playful.

"What?"

"You're like a blushing bride tonight, or at least my impression of a blushing bride." He stepped back. "I've seen you naked before. A lot. I like you naked. A lot. A helluva lot."

Riley could see how much by the bulge at Colby's crotch.

"Colby, I love you. So much, I—" The rest of the words disappeared against Colby's lips.

Then Colby stepped back and took his clothes off. He stood in front of Riley. "I won't hurt you. I just hope I'm good enough for you." He paused. "Riley, I love you. And I'm all yours." He held his hands out.

"Then take me to bed, or lose me forever."

Colby scooped Riley up and laid him in bed. Then he demonstrated how well he could follow instructions.

Later, after making slow, sweet, mind-blowing love, they lay together, Colby's head on Riley's chest.

"Riley, your heart's still going a mile a minute. I'd like to take that as a compliment, but I'm worried that something's still wrong. You can talk to me."

This was the moment Riley had been dreading, but he couldn't put it off any longer. "Colby, there's something I haven't told you about me."

"I don't care."

"I do. I have to tell you, but you might not like it."

Colby held up his head and looked into Riley's eyes, but his expression held love and not fear or anger. "If I told you this about me, would it change how you feel about me?"

That was a good question. Riley considered it for a moment. "No. I would want you to tell me, though."

"Is it a matter of life or death?"

"It could be."

"Your life or mine?"

"Neither."

Colby appeared to ponder a moment, then put his head back on Riley's chest. "Save it for tomorrow."

When Riley opened his mouth, Colby pressed a finger to his lips. "Shhh. Tomorrow. But if you have an uncontrollable need to do something with your mouth, I have a few suggestions to keep it occupied."

Chapter Nineteen

COLBY SPENT the following afternoon with Tommo repairing the fences damaged in the fire and pulling up the burned trees that might be a hazard for the stock. The day dragged on slowly, and he couldn't wait to be finished with work and spend time with Riley and with Stella, now that they'd taken their relationship to a more official level.

When he and Tommo got back to the barn, Jake was in the office, banging away on an ancient adding machine and frowning. He had beads of sweat on his forehead.

"What's the problem?" Colby already knew but he asked anyway.

"With the fire, we're running low on fencing supplies. Just trying to figure out how much we can afford to order right now."

"We can use barbed wire in the meantime."

"Neither of us wants to do that."

"Let's see what expenses we *can* cut back on." Colby sat on the edge of the desk so he could see the budget Jake had put together.

The phone rang and Jake answered. He nodded and agreed several times before ending the call.

"That was Rachel. She's calling a family meeting after dinner."

"Did she say why?" Colby's stomach felt even worse than it had when he'd seen the numbers on Jake's note pad.

"Nope. She did sound more chipper than she has been."

Colby looked into Jake's eyes to see if he was hiding anything. He wouldn't put it past Rachel to do something to embarrass him now that everyone knew about him and Riley. Or it could be something to do with Stella's visit. Now he had one more thing to worry about.

He and Jake spent two unpleasant hours making tough choices before Colby left so he could shower before dinner.

WHEN HE got to the dining hall, dinner was in full swing. He headed for the family table. Everyone was there except Rachel, but Stella already seemed right at home. They hadn't gotten food yet, preferring to wait until all the guests had been served. Then they filed through the buffet line, filling their plates.

"If the brisket tastes half as good as it smells, I'd marry Riley," Jake said, savoring the aroma before he stuffed chunks of beef in his mouth. "Mmmmm."

"You're already married, if you remember," Lynn said, jabbing Jake in the ribs. "And Riley's already got a beau."

"Isn't Riley going to join us?" Colby asked.

"I haven't seen him tonight," Lynn said. "He was up at the house, talking in the office with Rachel, but that was hours ago."

"He should take a break to visit with Stella," Jake said.

"I'll get him to come out of the kitchen." Colby took a few more bites of the delicious beef brisket with a spiced-coffee rub. He'd deal with the crispy roasted potatoes, grilled polenta sticks, and buttery green beans when he got back.

But Riley wasn't in the kitchen. He'd asked Willa to take charge of dinner after he'd done most of the prep.

"Stella, do you know where he is?" Colby asked back at the table.

"I don't." She couldn't suppress a smile that forced its way out. That made Colby worry a lot less, at least until the meeting.

COLBY LINGERED when the rest of the family went up to the house, and he dragged his heels heading to the meeting. The dining room was quiet when he arrived, Jake, Lynn, and Alicia were already there, and they all looked up when Colby entered.

"Anyone know what this is about?" Colby asked.

"We're as much in the dark as you are," Lynn said.

A few minutes later, Rachel entered. She had that MBA face on, so this must be serious. Rachel stood at the head of the table. Right behind her came Stella and Riley. Stella had a stack of folders. She put them down in front of Rachel, then sat near Alicia. Riley sat near Rachel, rather than next to Colby, but he flashed a little smile at Colby.

"A lot's happened in the past week" Rachel said. "We know the Wellington thing didn't work out—"

"Hang on a minute," Jake said. "No offense to Riley or Stella, but if this is a financial discussion, maybe it should be family only."

"It's not that kind of financial discussion, Dad. They're the reason we're here right now. But just be patient." She ran her fingers over the folders, then turned her attention back to the family. "I blame myself for not finding out more about Wellington before bringing him out here."

She was looking at Colby when she said that, and he felt a deep sense of shame. Wellington had brought the worst out in him, ready to whore himself out for the ranch. But it didn't assuage the guilt that he'd also been the reason Wellington didn't work out.

"The problem still stands. How can we raise the capital we need?" Rachel glanced over at Riley. "Riley came to me with an idea that solves all the problems. Gets us enough capital while not selling out our principles or having an investor who wants to change everything about our operation."

"Well, don't keep us waiting," Lynn said. "What's this great idea?"

Colby searched Riley's face, but it was blank. Why hadn't Riley talked to him? Colby felt a chill come over him at being left out of things.

Rachel turned to Riley. "Seems that Riley's been holding out on us."

Colby's stomach churned. What was going on here? Riley had wanted to tell him something the night before, and Colby didn't want to know. Was there a connection?

"Riley, why don't you explain?"

Riley stood up and glanced at each person for a moment, his gaze settling on Colby.

"Colby, I didn't want to get your hopes up, or I would have talked to you first. I needed help from Rachel, and then everything happened so fast. I hope you'll forgive me."

Colby inhaled slowly, then nodded. He had to trust Riley.

"What I hadn't mentioned before is that my family has a lot of, uh, capital to invest. I have access to some of it, but my father controls most of it. He's always looking for new investment opportunities, so I asked Stella to write up an official offer like the deal you offered Fitz Wellington. My father looked at the financials and grilled Rachel on the phone for hours." Riley glanced at Rachel with a knowing smile. "He's agreed to invest as a silent partner."

Rachel distributed the folders. "Here's the spreadsheet and forecasts. Take a look."

Colby didn't know what to think. He stared at the blue binder without even opening it up. He had too many emotions fighting inside; his head was ready to explode. Surprise, excitement, worry, relief. He also had a million questions.

"Let me cover the basic points right now. Then we can discuss the details before taking a vote," Rachel said before proceeding to lay out the terms.

Everyone was still shocked and speechless, looking through the folders as she spoke.

"One more thing," Riley said. "The investment isn't tied to me at all. It's completely independent." Riley glanced over at Colby. "So don't worry that he might pull out if I'm... not here." There was a hint of sadness in those last words, an acknowledgement that their relationship might not last. But Colby appreciated the way Riley made sure the ranch would still be okay. Colby might not be so okay without Riley. The chill intensified as he considered not having Riley here with him.

"Any questions?" Rachel asked.

"Where do we sign?" Lynn asked.

"I take it we don't need to vote on this?" Rachel glanced at each person.

"Riley, we can't possibly thank you for arranging this," Lynn said. She got up and hugged him till his eyes nearly popped out.

Colby was still too overwhelmed. Riley came over and sat next to him. "I'm sorry for springing this huge surprise." He reached for Colby's hand and squeezed it, then kissed it.

"Hey, there's dessert. Riley made something special for us, and I found a bottle of champagne left over from New Year's." Rachel said.

"Riley you stay here, we'll get the dessert," Lynn said.

Riley never even looked up. He kept his gaze on Colby.

"I can't imagine how hard it must have been to ask your father."

Riley shrugged. "It felt a little like entering a tiger's cage. But after you slept with me, it was the least I could do." He forced a laugh.

More pressure built in Colby's chest. Riley had tried to make light of what he'd done, but Colby wouldn't. He knew how bad Riley's relationship with his father was. They hadn't spoken in years. That Riley called him to help Colby and the Z meant more than he could put into words.

He didn't. He brought Riley's hand to his lips and kissed it.

"Thank you seems so inadequate."

"You can find plenty of ways to thank me." Riley flashed an impish grin that Colby was getting far too fond of.

They gazed into each other's eyes while Lynn and Alicia bustled around with plates and napkins. Jake lined up champagne flutes at one end of the table and stood with the bottle held up.

"Let's have a toast to our new investor." He popped open the bottle and filled the glasses. Stella handed glasses out and everyone clinked glasses.

The tension in the room finally subsided, but Colby still sat there holding Riley's hand.

"Have some cookies, boys," Lynn said and put a plate down.

Colby looked at the plate. It was filled with peanut butter chocolate kiss cookies.

His chest hurt so much he thought he might cry. That would really be the last straw. He was glad none of the hands could see him right now, holding hands and getting all teary eyed. He had to uphold his image as a tough, no-nonsense, no-frills cowboy.

Riley Emerson knew exactly how to break all his fences.

THEY HAD a joyful family celebration. Their two families were now linked in so many ways. It was scary how much Riley felt for Colby, and the Z. In less than a month, his world had become unrecognizable. And to top it all off, his father almost sounded proud of him on the phone.

Upstairs in Riley's flat, he and Colby snuggled.

"So, you think you might stick around after the summer?"

"Why wouldn't I?"

"It gets mighty cold up here. Can you handle that?"

Riley shook his head. "I prefer to winter in St. Bart's."

"I know ways to keep you warm that Bart hasn't even dreamt of."

Riley chortled as Colby pressed against him from shoulder to toe. "I can't wait for that."

"It is cold. And quiet. Just the family and the hands."

"Rachel pitched the idea of having winter guests to my dad."

"Winter guests?"

"Cross-country skiing, ice fishing, I don't know what else. And lots of fancied-up comfort food. Fitz was right; wealthy people will pay plenty if they think a place is exclusive."

"As long as they stay out of my business, then it sounds fine."

"And me?"

"You are expected to get into my business. On a regular basis."

"I see." Riley traced the line of pale brown hair from Colby's navel towards his cock. He played with the hair until Colby's cock took notice and began to swell.

Colby took Riley's hand away and put it against his chest. "Before you get me too distracted, what were you trying to tell me last night? About the money?"

Riley nodded. "I know the ranch has had a lot of financials setbacks, and I just didn't know how to explain without seeming ungrateful for all the advantages I've had."

"I can understand that. Now I sound terrible for being glad your dad has the money to help us out."

"That's not all of it. I have a lot of my own money. It's a trust fund, and I've never taken any of it out. I wanted to tell you, or to offer to help, but I didn't know how that would affect us." He paused. "There was never a good time. If I said something too early, maybe you'd only see the money, and if I waited too long you'd hate me for not helping. And I also suspected you might not want to take any money from me, because it would just complicate things."

"Yeah, it might have changed things a lot. But if you'd said something sooner, we might not have had the whole Fitz fiasco."

"When he arrived, you and I hadn't really gotten to a place where you would take the money. It was too soon.... But I should have told you about the money instead of letting you sleep with him."

"I won't argue with that. Unless it was some kind of test?"

"No. I was wrong. I'm just lucky that it turned out the way it did."

"You may need to find a way to make it up to me." Colby put Riley's hand back on his cock.

"Actually, I did have an idea. My dad's investment is for the guest ranch. It's going to take some time before that starts generating more profits. Maybe the ranch could use some capital sooner? I would be glad to help out with that." Riley explored Colby's balls with his fingertips, in no hurry to bring him to full hardness yet.

"You mean as an investor? A part owner?"

"No. But maybe I could buy you some cows for your birthday." Riley slid his palm up Colby's shaft, feeling the flesh harden.

"Now that's romantic."

"I can see you think so."

"You know just what a cowboy wants."

"I have learned the way to a cowboy's heart." He wrapped his hand around Colby's perfect erection.

"Through his stomach?" Colby let out a laugh that turned into a sigh as he watched Riley touching him. "You *are* the best cook on the ranch. I've gained weight. None of my jeans fit anymore. Especially at the crotch."

"Well, don't blame that on my cooking." Riley leaned down and planted a soft kiss on Colby's cock, feeling Colby shudder beneath him, then let go. "But that's not what I meant." He got up and went to the foot of the bed. "The way to a cowboy's heart is in his boots." Riley stepped into his shiny black boots, then got back in bed and settled into Colby's lap.

He wrapped his arms around Colby and prepared for the most exciting ride of his life, a future here on the Rocking Z, with his Plaid Cowboy.

Recipes

THERE'S A lot of Western and cowboy lore surrounding the chuck wagon and the cook. Back when cowboys drove cattle hundreds or even thousands of miles to and from good grazing areas or to the sales location, the chuck wagon was an important part of trail life.

The cook had one of the toughest jobs. He had to be up before the cowboys so breakfast could be ready early enough for them to start their day, and he was still cleaning up when they were relaxing or snug in their bedrolls. He'd also have to prepare enough food at breakfast so the cowboys could take something along for their lunch.

But the chuck wagon cook also had the respect of every cowboy, and no one would dare complain if they didn't like the chow. Well, if they did complain, they might not want to do it in front of the cook. With a supply of staples like coffee, flour, beans, molasses, potatoes, salt, dried fruit, and beef, the cook had to come up with enough variety to satisfy hungry cowboys day in and day out.

One thing every chuck wagon cook was sure to have was a dutch oven: a heavy cast-iron pot on legs so it could be set over the coals in the fire. The pots got the name because originally they were obtained by Dutch traders who sold housewares. The dutch oven's lid had a special lip where the cook would place coals. This allowed him to replicate the heat dispersion of a regular oven: from below and above for more even cooking. A good chuck wagon cook could reproduce almost anything made in an oven at home.

Coffee was the key ingredient the cook would carry, but chuck wagon cooks were judged by their sourdough. They'd make biscuits, bread, even desserts with sourdough, and that meant they needed a sourdough starter.

Sourdough Starter

If you thought sourdough starter was hard, toss that idea right out the window. It's easy to start and maintain. Some cooks have kept their starter going for years! A chuck wagon cook might have one he's been using for thirty years. All you need to do is feed it, or use it and then replace what you've used. There's no reason not to give it a try.

1 packet of yeast
4 cups warm water
4 cups flour
2 tablespoons sugar or honey

1. In a large, clean glass jar or bowl, mix the yeast with the water, then stir in flour and honey. Cover the jar with a dishcloth. This lets the starter breathe and absorb any wild yeast, which will give it a more distinctive flavor.
2. Within a day it should start to bubble. That's what you want. Stir it once a day. By the third or fourth day give it a taste. It should have a pleasant sour aroma and have the consistency of pancake batter. Now it's ready to use.
3. To keep your starter going, replace the amount you used with a 1 to 1 ratio of flour to water. So if you use 2 cups for your recipe, put in one cup each of flour and water to keep it going.
4. Store your starter in the refrigerator and give it a stir once a week. If you don't use the starter at least weekly you will need to feed it. Take out 1 cup of starter and replace with 1/2 cup of flour and 1/2 cup of water, stir, and return to the refrigerator. Give that cup of starter to a friend, or bake something!

Sourdough Biscuits

Of course sourdough biscuits were the most-requested item, and the one chuck wagon cooks were judged by (yes, Fitz Wellington was right about one thing!). Out on the range biscuits aren't just for breakfast. As Riley knows, you can and should serve them at every meal.

You can make this recipe in your oven or over a bed of coals on your next camping trip. If you cook outdoors you will need a dutch oven. Indoors, you can also use a casserole dish with a cover.

2 cups sourdough starter

2 cups flour

1 teaspoon salt

1 tablespoon sugar

2 tablespoons bacon grease or melted butter

1. Mix all ingredients except for the bacon grease or butter. Stir to create a soft dough. Roll the dough out into balls roughly the size of golf balls. Roll each ball in the butter or grease, then transfer them to the dutch oven. Pack them in tightly, and they will rise up high. If you don't have a dutch oven, use a casserole dish with a cover.
2. Pack the biscuits in concentric circles or rows, depending on the shape of your dish. Let the dough rise for 10 to 15 minutes.
3. Bake in a 350 degree F oven for 30 minutes or until nicely brown. If you're outdoors, place the dutch oven over hot coals. Make sure to heap up some coals on top, and let it bake for 20 to 30 minutes or until brown on top.

Sourdough Biscuit Variations

You can add in shredded cheese, crumbled bacon, fresh chopped herbs, berries, or a variety of other ingredients to the dough before rolling out the biscuits.

Sourdough Cobbler

Even better than your favorite cobbler recipe when you use sourdough biscuit batter on top. Besides Riley's blueberry version, try the topping on your own favorite fruit cobbler recipe.

Sourdough Blueberry Cobbler

At the Cordon Bleu in Paris, they may not teach all the great traditional American fruit-and-dough desserts. Riley discovered there's a long history of pandowdies, cobblers, grunts, buckles, and slumps. All are variations on fruit and dough. Some have fruit over the dough, while others, like cobblers, have dough scattered over the fruit.

Colby loves this particular one and you will too.

Fruit base

3 pints of blueberries

1/2 cup sugar

2 tablespoons cornstarch

1 teaspoon grated lime or lemon zest

Topping

2 cups sourdough starter

1 cup flour

1-1/2 tablespoons sugar

Pinch of salt

Water

1. Preheat the oven to 375 degrees F.
2. Wash and pat the berries dry. Mix in the sugar, cornstarch, and zest. Spread the fruit mixture in a dutch oven or 11 by 7-inch glass baking dish.
3. Mix starter, flour, sugar, and salt together. Add in enough water to form a soft dough. Pull off pieces 1 to 2 inches in diameter and place on top of the fruit so they are equally distributed.
4. Place a towel over the entire dish for about 15 minutes or until the dough has risen. Depending on the size of your dish, the dough portions may spread into each other or remain separate. Don't worry. There's no wrong way to make a cobbler!
5. Pop the dish into the oven for 30 to 40 minutes or until the biscuits are golden brown.
6. Cool for 15 minutes before eating. It's going to be tough to wait, but the filing will thicken up as the cornstarch cools, otherwise you'll be eating scorching-hot blueberry soup.
7. Serve with whipped cream or french vanilla ice cream. Or both.

Other Sourdough Dishes

You can try substituting your sourdough starter for some or all of the flour called for in a recipe. You may need to adjust the liquid to account for the water in the starter, so use less of the liquid a recipe calls for and add more until you get the right consistency.

You also won't need yeast if you use your sourdough starter because it helps the recipe rise. Like Riley, it may take you some trial and error to get the right proportions. But you will find many sourdough recipes in books and online if you aren't a fan of experimenting. Chances are it will still taste delicious even if it's not perfect.

Sourdough Pancakes

Here's a recipe you won't need to fiddle with, unless you want to dress it up with blueberries, raspberries, chocolate chips, or all three. The best way to incorporate berries is to add a few to each ladleful of batter so you are assured each pancake will have about the same amount of fruit or other add-ins.

Makes 12 pancakes

2 eggs

2 tablespoons sugar

1 teaspoon salt

1 1/2 teaspoons baking soda

1 tablespoon water

2 cups sourdough starter

1. In a large mixing bowl, beat eggs.
2. In a separate bowl, add sugar, salt, baking soda, and water and mix until incorporated. Add to beaten eggs.
3. Add sourdough starter to mixture and beat gently with wooden spoon. Do not beat too long or you'll deflate the starter.
4. Pour 1/4 cup of batter onto a hot griddle for each pancake. Turn when bubbles appear and cook until the bottom is golden.

Blue Cornmeal Bread

After sourdough biscuits, hearty cornbread was a cowboy's second favorite bread. Riley put his own personal touch on this tradition by using blue cornmeal—it's so pretty!—and kernels of corn mixed in. If you can't find blue cornmeal, yellow works just fine.

2 1/4 cups all-purpose flour

1 3/4 cups blue cornmeal* or yellow cornmeal

1/2 cup sugar

3/4 teaspoon baking powder

3/4 teaspoon baking soda

3/4 teaspoon salt

1 1/4 cups whole milk

3/4 cup vegetable oil

3 large eggs

1/2 cup buttermilk

1 1/2 cups frozen corn kernels, thawed, drained

*Blue cornmeal is available at natural foods stores and specialty foods stores.

1. Preheat oven to 350 degrees F.
2. Butter a 13 by 9 by 2-inch glass baking dish. Stir flour, cornmeal, sugar, baking powder, baking soda, and salt in a large bowl to blend.
3. Whisk milk, vegetable oil, eggs, and buttermilk in a medium bowl to blend. Add milk mixture to dry ingredients and whisk until just blended.
4. Fold in corn kernels. Pour batter into buttered dish. Bake until tester inserted into center comes out clean, about 40 minutes. Cut bread into 2-inch squares and serve warm.

Bacon & Cheese Cro-Saints

Marcus would say these are his favorite breakfast item, even if he'd never touch a cro-saint with a ten-foot pole before Riley filled them up with crumbly bacon and cheddar. Old-time chuck wagon cooks might also find these too fancy for the trail, but they'd gobble them up anyway.

A package of puff pastry (usually found in the freezer or refrigerator section of your grocery store) or a tube of ready-to-bake crescent rolls

6 slices of bacon (get good thick bacon at the butcher's counter for the best results)

1 cup shredded sharp cheddar cheese

Note: If you want to make your own puff pastry, check out the step-by-step photos and instructions from Food52.com:

http://food52.com/blog/9742-how-to-make-puff-pastry-step-by-step

1. Preheat oven as directed on the pastry package. Thaw pastry sheets if necessary.
2. Cook bacon about 3 minutes less than usual, until it's not as crispy as you like. It will crisp up more in the oven. Drain bacon and let it cool enough to handle. Crumble bacon.
3. Open up the puff pastry or crescent rolls.
4. Grease a baking pan or use parchment paper.
5. If using puff pastry sheets, cut the sheets into 5-inch squares. Cut each square in half diagonally to form two triangles.
6. If using refrigerator crescent rolls, pull them apart on the parchment paper.
7. You have two choices for how to fill them.
   - Filling in the middle
     - Mix the crumbled bacon and cheese together. Spoon about 1/2 tablespoon onto each puff pastry triangle or about 1 tablespoon onto the crescent roll triangles.
     - Roll the triangles starting from the wide end toward the point. Curve them and transfer to the prepared pan.
   - Evenly distributed filling
     - Sprinkle bacon and cheddar evenly over each triangle, then roll up from widest side toward the point. This way,

bits of cheese and bacon will be wrapped up in each bite, even at the corners.

8. Curve the rolls and transfer to the prepared pan.

9. Bake according to the directions on the pastry package. Check the cro-saints a few minutes early to make sure the bacon hasn't gotten too crispy if using filling method #2. If necessary, move the tray down one rack in the oven to finish baking until the cro-saints are crispy and golden.

Chuck Wagon Beef Stew with a Twist

Riley can't help adding something of his own to every dish he makes. This beef stew is no exception. He took the old Zane recipe and added this twist: sliced lemons!

Beware, this recipe feeds a whole crew of ranch hands (10 servings). You can cut the recipe in half if you've only a got a few cowboys in your crew.

4 pounds lean beef, cubed
4 tablespoons oil
2 cloves garlic, chopped
4 cups hot water
2 large cans crushed tomatoes
2 thin slices lemon
4 medium onions, sliced
2 tablespoons salt
1/2 teaspoon pepper
6 tablespoons sugar
12 carrots, peeled and cut into 1-inch pieces
9 to 10 Yukon potatoes, quartered
Pinch of ground cloves
1/2 teaspoon dried basil leaves
2 cups fresh shelled or frozen peas

1. Heat the oil in the bottom of a dutch oven. Brown the beef in two batches if necessary.
2. Add in the chopped garlic and stir until well distributed.
3. Add water, tomatoes, lemon, onions, salt, pepper, and sugar. Stir until combined.
4. Simmer for 2 hours, stirring occasionally.
5. Add potatoes, garlic, carrots, cloves, and dried basil. Continue to cook until the potatoes are tender.
6. Add the peas and cook until heated through and carrots are tender.
7. If the gravy is too thin, mix 1 tablespoon of water and 1 tablespoon of flour in a small bowl until mixture is the consistency of paste. Add to the stew and stir to thicken.
8. Serve hot with sourdough biscuits.
9. It tastes even better the next day.

Coffee-Spice Rub for Beef

You can rub this mixture on a beef brisket before grilling, on steaks, or even on a tenderloin. Keep leftover rub in an airtight container or spice bottle. If you don't care for an ingredient or can't find it, leave it out. There is enough flavor here without it.

2 tablespoons paprika

2 tablespoons garlic powder

2 tablespoons onion powder

2 tablespoons black pepper

2 tablespoons brown sugar

2 tablespoons ground coffee (not used coffee grounds)

2 tablespoons kosher salt

1 tablespoon white pepper

1 tablespoon chili powder

1 teaspoon cayenne pepper

1. Mix all ingredients thoroughly. Rub into meat before grilling.

Chuck Wagon Peach Cobbler

This one doesn't use sourdough in the topping. Instead, it uses whiskey as the secret ingredient in the filling. You'll have a smile on your face after a portion of this. (Actually, the alcohol cooks off, but the flavor remains).

The dough needs to chill, so get that going before you start on the fruit filling.

Topping

2 cups flour

1 teaspoon sugar

1 teaspoon salt

3/4 cup shortening

1/4 cup water

1 tablespoon cider vinegar

Filling

1 cup butter

6 cups peeled and sliced peaches

1 cup granulated sugar

1 cup brown sugar

1 teaspoon cinnamon

1/2 cup good quality whiskey (you can use tequila or rum, though it won't be as authentic)

2. To make the topping, combine flour, sugar, and salt. Cut in shortening until mixture looks like coarse crumbs.
3. In separate bowl, combine water and vinegar. Add to dry ingredients. Mix until it forms a dough.
4. Refrigerate for 2 hours.
5. To make the filling, melt butter in a dutch oven or large saucepan. Add peaches, sugars, and cinnamon and cook until the mixture boils. Lower heat and simmer for 15 minutes.
6. Add the whiskey and cook for another 15 minutes.
7. If you don't have a dutch oven, transfer the mixture to a glass baking dish.

8. To finish the cobbler, preheat oven to 350 degrees F.

9. Roll the chilled dough out on a floured surface to the size and shape of the dutch oven or casserole dish you are using.

10. Place the dough over the cooked fruit mixture and bake until the dough is golden, about 45 minutes.

11. If cooking outdoors on coals, cover the dutch oven, place it on the coals and heap two to three times that amount of coals on top. Check after about 40 minutes. Cook until the pastry is golden.

About the Author

EM LYNLEY has worked finance, the wine industry, and high-tech, though she'd rather be writing hot man-on-man romance. She spent ten years as an economist and financial analyst, including a year as a White House Staff Economist, but only because all the intern positions were filled. Tired of boring herself and others with dry business reports and articles, her creative muse is back and naughtier than ever. She has lived and worked in London, Tokyo, and Washington, DC, but the San Francisco Bay Area is home for now.

Visit her website at http://www.emlynley.com
her blog at http://emlynley.livejournal.com
her Twitter page at http://twitter.com/emlynley
and her Facebook at http://www.facebook.com/emlynley.

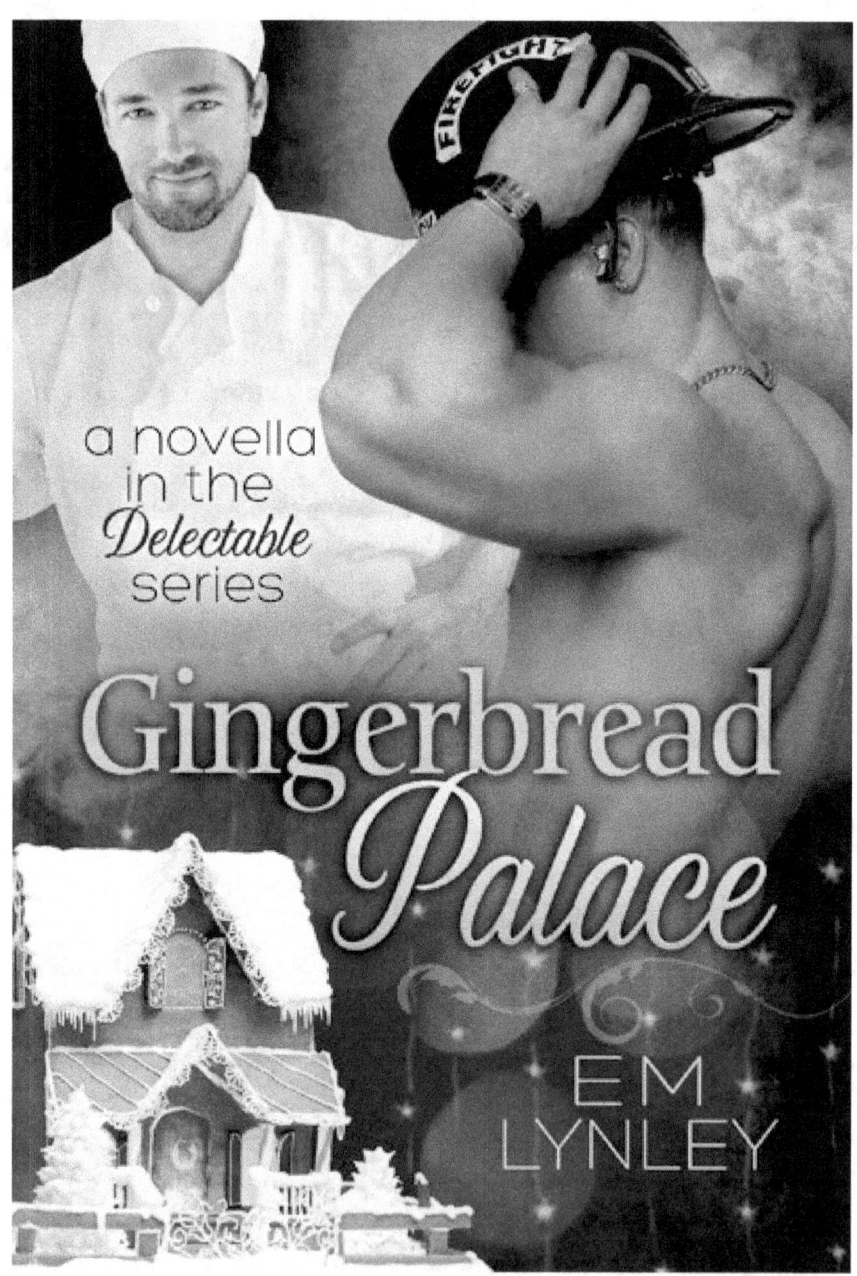

a novella
in the
Delectable
series

Gingerbread
Palace

EM
LYNLEY

http://www.dreamspinnerpress.com

Brand New Flavor

a Delectable novella

EM LYNLEY

http://www.dreamspinnerpress.com

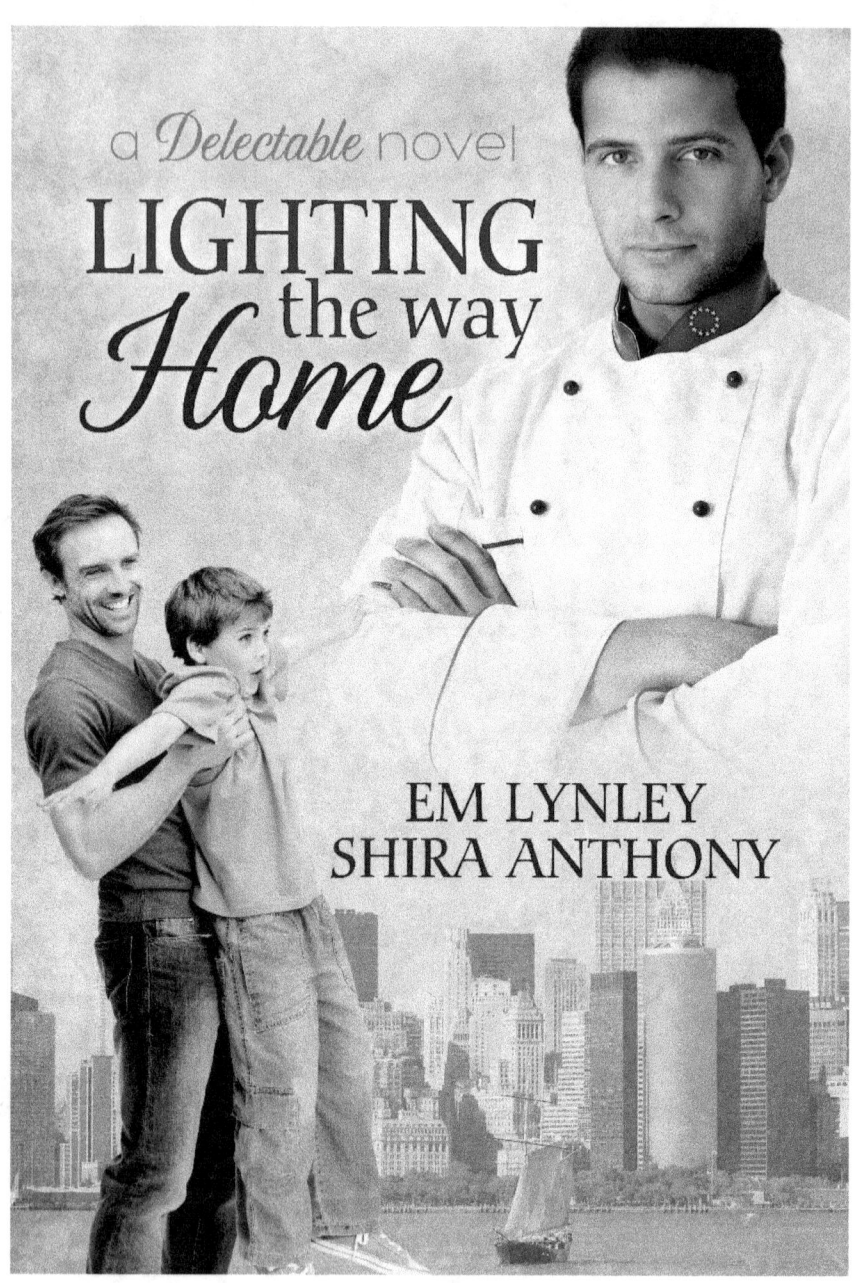

a *Delectable* novel

LIGHTING
the way
Home

EM LYNLEY
SHIRA ANTHONY

http://www.dreamspinnerpress.com

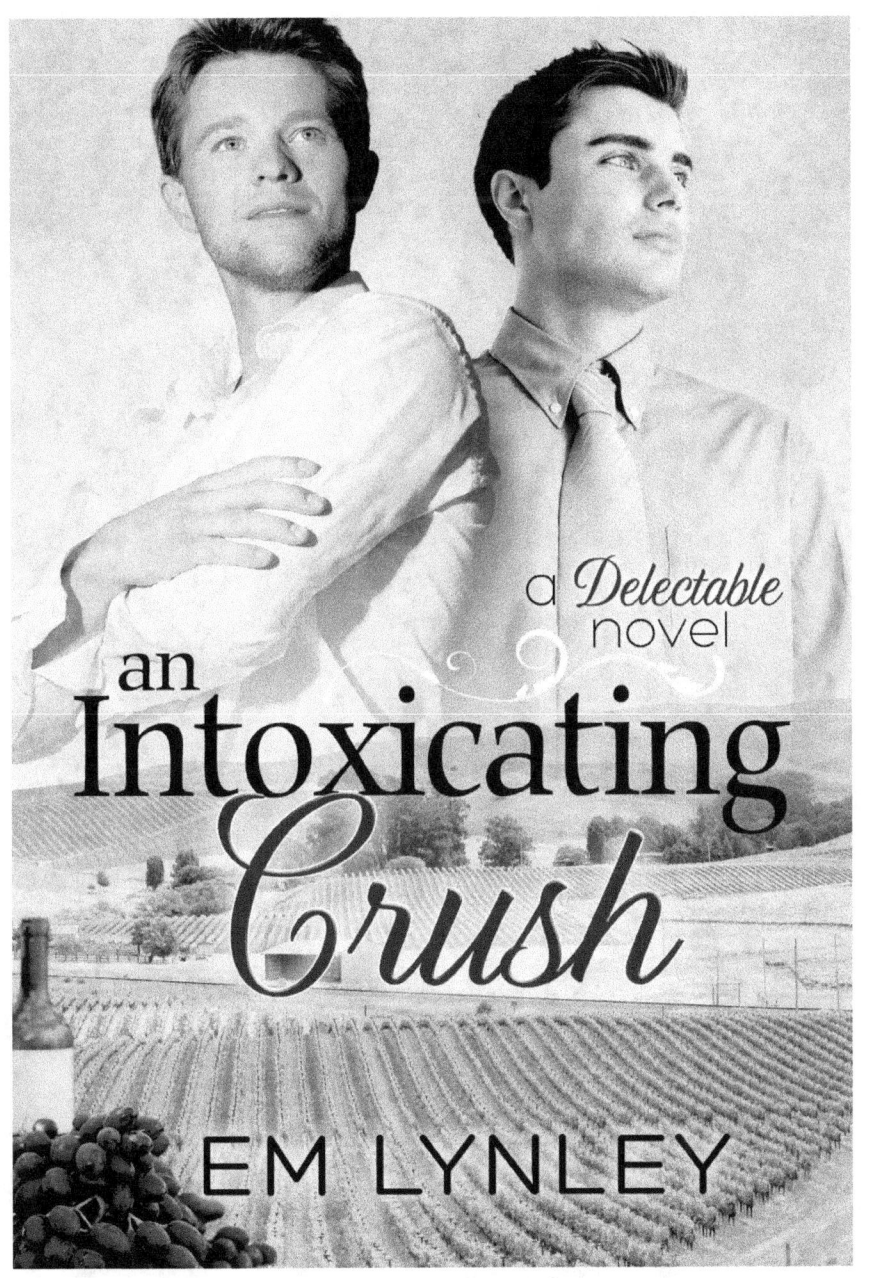

a *Delectable* novel

an
Intoxicating
Crush

EM LYNLEY

http://www.dreamspinnerpress.com

Precious Gems

EM LYNLEY

RARER THAN RUBIES

http://www.dreamspinnerpress.com

Precious Gems

EM LYNLEY

ITALIAN
ICE

A PRECIOUS GEM STORY

http://www.dreamspinnerpress.com

Precious Gems

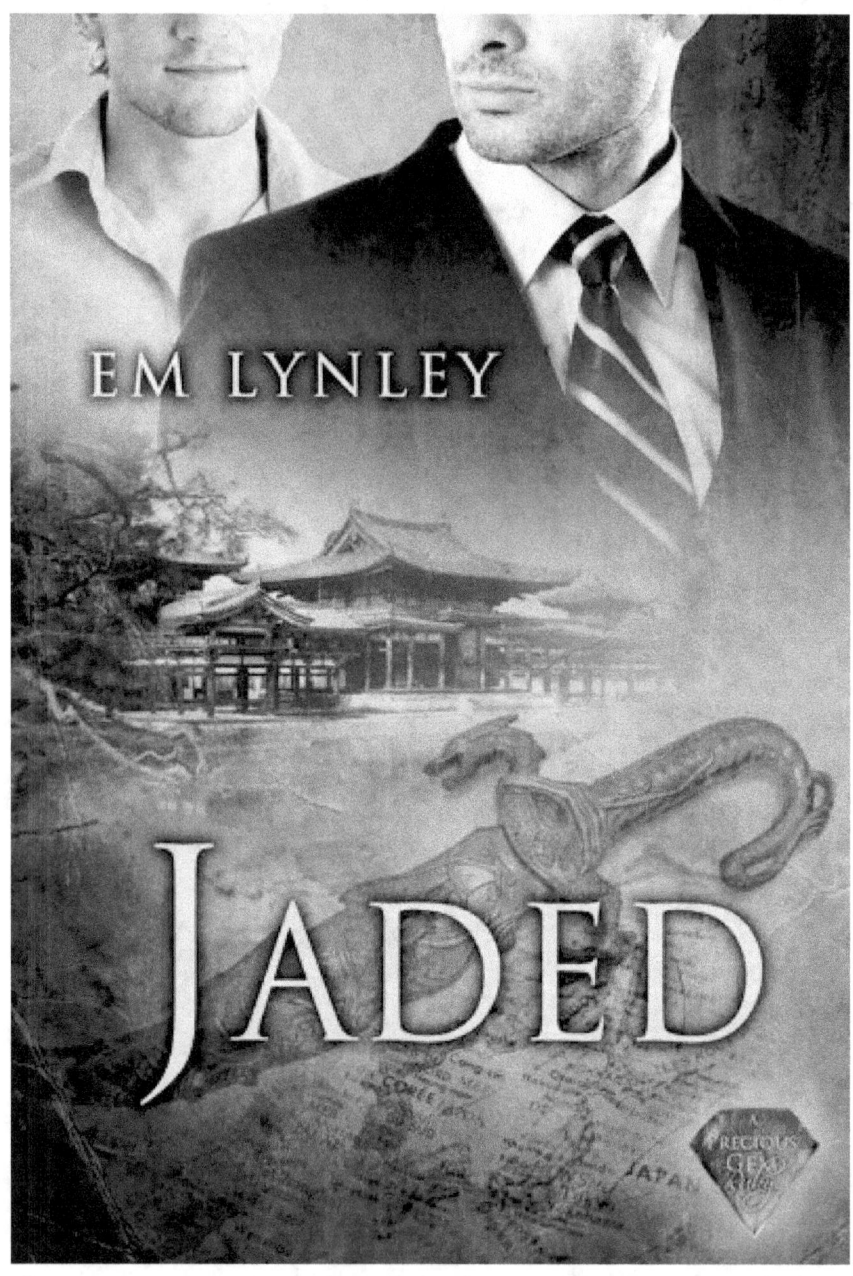

EM LYNLEY

JADED

http://www.dreamspinnerpress.com

BOUND FOR TROUBLE

EM Lynley

"You'll fall for Ryan Griffiths. The more danger
he's in, the hotter BOUND FOR TROUBLE gets."
-Cecilia Tan, author of *Slow Surrender*

http://www.dreamspinnerpress.com

HOSTILE TAKEOVER

EM LYNLEY

http://www.dreamspinnerpress.com

DISGUISES
EM LYNLEY

http://www.dreamspinnerpress.com

OUT
OF THE
GATE

EM LYNLEY

http://www.dreamspinnerpress.com

www.ingramcontent.com/pod-product-compliance
Lightning Source LLC
Chambersburg PA
CBHW070115260626
47160CB00004B/1471